F
Cash

Cash, Dixie.

My heart may be
broken, but my hair
still looks great.

DATE			

My Heart May Be Broken, but My Hair Still Looks Great

Also by Dixie Cash

Since You're Leaving Anyway, Take Out the Trash

WILLIAM MORROW
An Imprint of HarperCollins*Publishers*

My Heart May Be Broken, *but My Hair Still Looks Great*

DIXIE CASH

MY HEART MAY BE BROKEN, BUT MY HAIR STILL LOOKS GREAT. Copyright © 2005 by Dixie Cash. All rights reserved. Printed in the United States of America. No part of this book may be used or reproduced in any manner whatsoever without written permission except in the case of brief quotations embodied in critical articles and reviews. For information address HarperCollins Publishers, 10 East 53rd Street, New York, NY 10022.

HarperCollins books may be purchased for educational, business, or sales promotional use. For information please write: Special Markets Department, HarperCollins Publishers, 10 East 53rd Street, New York, NY 10022.

FIRST EDITION

Designed by Alison Schmidt

Printed on acid-free paper

Library of Congress Cataloging-in-Publication Data

Cash, Dixie
    My heart may be broken, but my hair still looks great / by Dixie Cash.— 1st ed.
      p. cm.
    ISBN-13: 978-0-06-082618-5
    ISBN-10: 0-06-082618-5
    1. Texas—Fiction. I. Title.

PS3603.A864M9 2005
813".6—dc22

                                                      2005041453

---

05 06 07 08 09 WBC/RRD 10 9 8 7 6 5 4 3 2

Acknowledgments

One rarely writes a novel all alone, with no help from anyone, so we would like to acknowledge those who contributed information we couldn't have done without. Thanks to Quint, Richard, Ronald, and O.L., cowboys all, for their willingness to answer "just one more question."

We would be remiss not to acknowledge family and friends who have given their unwavering support—Mom, Diann and Whitt, Janis and Joe, Adrienne and Ceil.

Last, but by no means least, thanks to Annelise Robey, Meg Ruley, and Lucia Macro for having a vision larger than ours.

My Heart May
Be Broken,
but My Hair
Still Looks
Great

prologue

T he cowboy's gaze darted from side to side. He twisted in the seat in his truck cab and looked behind himself. Night's dark curtain hid him, yet he pulled his hat farther down on his forehead. An adrenaline rush went along with the night raids and left a metallic taste in his mouth. He reached for his snuff can instinctively.

He had already scouted the area and knew three horses roamed the pasture in front of him. He was interested in only one, the oldest. Horse owners, he had learned, were less likely to raise a stink if an old horse came up missing. The older animals were more prone to get into trouble or be defenseless in the varied calamities that could take the life of a horse in the unpopulated wilds of West Texas. Every now and then one of them turned out to be a family pet or even a broodmare and he'd had to lie low until the clamor quieted, but things had always calmed down. After all, it was just a horse.

The older ones were easiest to handle, too. Tonight, he had simply thrown a loop over the mare's head, offered some carrots to move her along, and she had followed him with blind trust—up the ramp and right into his trailer.

At first he had taken only one or two horses a year, which hadn't aroused *suspicion. Now, the cash the slaughterhouses paid him for these animals— seven hundred to a thousand dollars a head—had become addictive, and one or two a year wasn't enough. Having extra money in his pocket had become too tempting. He liked dressing in good clothes, liked having appreciative female eyes focused on him, liked going out to dinner in a good steak house.*

Upping his number of night raids had made him more concerned for the legal consequences of horse theft. He had done research and learned that the money he got for these animals made stealing them a Class-A misdemeanor in Texas. Not a felony. Even so, the penalty was confinement in jail for up to twelve months and a fine of as much as $2,500 for each horse.

Going to jail and paying a fine of twice his income were not acceptable options. He still had wild oats to sow. At that thought, he keyed in the phone number of his latest oat, Julie Lynn, and told her he would see her later.

As he pulled away, the younger horses loped to the fence and whinnied, an alarm far-distant ears didn't hear in the wee hours.

one

There's no excuse for a grown woman to be so damned irresponsible. How can you lose an SUV?"

Her father's booming voice set Paige McBride's spinach salad to trembling. She winced. "I haven't lost it, Daddy."

The statement was only a partial fib. She might not know the precise whereabouts of the new Escalade, but she knew who had it. "Judd said he'll bring it back in a few days. He'll take good care of it."

In truth, Judd hadn't *said* anything. In truth, he had left her a note thanking her and promising to return the SUV in about ten days. So ten was a few, wasn't it?

"Judd Stephens is as worthless as tits on a bull. If somebody told him to go to hell he'd have to ask for directions." E. W. McBride, known by all as "Buck," sliced off a bite of medium-rare porterhouse steak and held it poised on the tip of his fork. "It shames me to think my little girl spent a weekend partying and doing God-knows-what. And what's more, with a second-rate bull rider."

Paige winced again at the thought of shaming her daddy, but

why was he so upset? Maybe she and Judd had downed a little too much tequila at the Howling at the Moon bar, but was that a world crisis? It wasn't like Judd was a perfect stranger. She had known him forever, and her daddy knew him, too. They had history.

"You know perfectly well there was no God-knows-what going on between Judd and me, Daddy. Besides, I'm not a little girl."

Paige shifted her left foot with its Ace-bandaged ankle. She had it propped up on a neighboring chair, thankful the Petroleum Club dining room had thickly padded furniture.

Waking yesterday morning with a sore ankle in a La Mansion suite in San Antonio, she had discovered her foot stuck through the side of a Styrofoam cooler. She still didn't know how it got there, but the explanation was bound to be interesting. After finding Judd's note and realizing he really had taken the Escalade, she had no choice but to take the hotel shuttle to the San Antonio airport, then fly to Love Field in Dallas, where she rented a car and drove the thirty-five miles to Fort Worth in rush hour traffic.

After that whole frazzling afternoon, she spent last night un-winding with a pitcher of margaritas, which left her to face today with a headache that matched her ankle ache. She had planned to relax all of today, perhaps tan and get a massage at Panache, the trendy spa a few blocks from her condo. She had *not* planned to have lunch at the Petroleum Club, had *not* planned to tax herself by driving with a wrapped ankle, in heavy traffic to downtown Fort Worth in a Ford Escort. She would have removed the bandage, but a call from Daddy ordering her to appear at twelve-thirty sharp had changed her plans and her thinking. His firm tone had suggested an injured ankle might work in her favor.

And to prove the point, her father craned his neck across the table, looking at her bandage as he chewed. "How's your ankle, sweetheart? Are you in pain?"

His gray eyes were filled with concern. She wished she hadn't disappointed him again. When it came to what he expected of her, she seemed never to do anything right. "No, Daddy. It'll be fine."

Apparently satisfied, he returned to his steak and his lecture. "I mean it, Paige. When Richard Innsbruck called and told me you had to fly back from San Antone and rent a car, I made up my mind. I discussed it with your mother and—"

"Don't call her my mother." Paige speared a spinach leaf, bristling despite the hangover that had her head feeling like a balloon about to be launched. "She may be your *wife,* but she's not my *mother.*" No matter how bad she felt, she could always spout a fair amount of vitriol for her meddling, bossy, social-climbing stepmother.

"I discussed it with *your* mother, the one who gave birth to you, God rest her soul, and we made a decision. The only solution is to cut you loose, girl."

"What's that supposed to mean? I haven't lived under your roof since high school. You might have been paying for my college, but—"

"For your college and every damned other thing in your life, including all your hell-raisin' buddies. Ski trips to Vail, midnight runs to Vegas, shopping jaunts in New York City. My God, Paige, that spring break trip to Cancun cost me ten thousand dollars. You spent four hundred on a haircut. A haircut, forgodsake!"

"But, Daddy, I didn't just have it cut. I had it glitzed and styled by—"

"When I was a boy, my mother cut my hair around a bowl on my head and it turned out just fine." He shook his head. "I'll bet you don't own a pair of shoes I paid less than three hundred dollars for."

Paige tucked her foot in its Lambertson Truex sandal closer to her body, as if a price tag were hanging from the back strap. Damn that Dick Innsbruck. His calling in life seemed to be to report to her daddy every charge she added to her American Express card, no matter how trivial. She had long thought the accountant lived for the thrill of catching her in some misdeed.

She speared another spinach leaf, wishing she had an aspirin. "If Dick-in-the-butt had a life—"

"Watch your mouth." Her daddy pointed the tip of his steak knife at her. "Richard's doing what I told him. A job he gets paid for. A concept you have no grasp of."

Her father leaned forward, thrusting his face closer to hers, willing her to look into his eyes, which she did. Unwillingly.

"Paige, darlin', you don't seem to have a grip on reality. When you didn't go back to school this semester, I thought you had grown up. I thought you were gonna look for a job and take responsibility for your future." He wadded his napkin and dropped it beside his plate, shook his head, and pushed back from the table. "But I blame myself. Margaret Ann's been telling me for years how I've spoiled you."

"She's got a lot of room to talk, with what she spends on—"

Buck's raised palm cut her off, a gesture she had seen silence many. His reputation for a ferocious temperament, among other strong character traits, had made him a Texas legend. But this was the first time his wrath had *ever* been directed at her. And her sitting here with an injury, too. Something crawled up her spine, something creepy and unfamiliar. For lack of another name, she labeled it fear.

Not liking the turn of events one bit, she shifted into defensive mode. With a penitent pout that never failed to win him over to her point of view, she leaned across the table. "Daddy, I'm sorry I've upset you. I only want—"

"Oh, no, you don't. Syrupy words ain't gonna work this time, baby girl. My mind's made up. How much cash you got on you?"

Yikes! Did he expect her to pay for lunch? What was going on? In another universe, worlds must be colliding. Panic darted through her as she reached for the fringed Gucci purse she had bought at Neiman Marcus a couple of weeks ago, suddenly conscious of the six hundred dollars it had cost. She dug out her wallet, flipped it open, and counted.

"Two hundred dollars and some change."

Her father reached back and pulled out his wallet, fanned through a deck of cash, found three crisp bills and handed them to her. "Here's three hundred more. I've instructed Dick to put two thousand dollars in your checking account. That adds up to a monthly income for a lot of girls your age." He put his wallet away. "This is September. Your condo lease is paid up 'til the end of December. By the end of three and a half months, you should be able to pay your own rent."

He braced his forearm on the table. "Sweetheart, you're gonna have to get a job."

"A job!" Paige's eyes bugged. She had been too busy making memories to consider making a living. "I've never had a job. What am I supposed to do?"

"You've got six years of college and that's six years more than I got. Surely to Christ you can do something. When I was your age, I did whatever it took. I worked my ass off, day and night. Went from having nothing to having everything I ever wanted. Paige, you're my only heir and I love you with all my heart, but I'll give the fortune I've made to charity before I'll leave it to a daughter who thinks life's just one big happy hour."

Paige's chin quivered as gathering tears blurred her father's image.

"I know you don't understand it now, darlin', but I'm doing this for your own good." He let out a long sigh, shaking his head again. He picked up his Stetson, rose from his chair, and moved to her side of the table. He ran his rough thumb down her cheek. "I love you too much to ruin you. You're made of high-quality stuff. Time you cowboyed up and showed it."

He walked a couple of steps away before stopping and turning back. "By the way, don't use the plastic. I told Dick to cancel your cards."

BUCK MCBRIDE WATCHED the elevator panel numbers light up in descending order as he rode from the top floor of the Frost National Bank Building down to the lobby. In a life peppered with difficult tasks, none had been harder than the conversation he had just had with his only child, the light of his life, whose mother was the only woman he had ever loved. Would ever love.

Charlotte had left them when Paige was eleven, taken by a sudden fatal illness. Eleven was young for a girl to lose her mother. He had done everything in his power to make it up to his daughter, had denied her nothing. Until today.

Tough love he called kicking her out of the nest. He had to do it, had to make her understand the value of a dollar and the responsibility that accompanied wealth. In December she would turn twenty-five and, unknown to her, take possession of an inheritance established for her by her mother years ago.

As the elevator car neared the garage parking lot, Buck looked heavenward. *I'm doing what I promised you I'd do, Charlotte, honey. I'm getting her ready. Time has gone so fast. I sure wish you were here.*

PAIGE STARED THROUGH the wide Petroleum Club front door where her daddy had exited. Was this the mother of all bad days or what? "Good grief," she mumbled.

Other diners looked at her. She didn't care. People ogled her all the time. They said it was because she was beautiful, but she didn't feel beautiful. What she felt was misunderstood, trapped, and a little pissed off. And her headache would stop a train.

She drained the last drop of golden wine from her glass. *Okay, fine.* She would call his bluff. It couldn't be that hard to get a job. Working might actually be fun—dressing up every day, doing lunch. In a few months she would be wildly successful. Her daddy would call and apologize, and she would laugh in his face. Then she would . . . she would . . .

She would what?

Well . . . well . . . she would show him she was smart like him. She would buy out his companies in a takeover. Hadn't that been how he had acquired his billions? Why, she had contacts all over the Metroplex—college and high school friends who had graduated and had good jobs or owned their own businesses. Tomorrow she would make phone calls. She would be hired by the day after and start work the following Monday. She clubbed the tabletop with a fist, setting china and silverware to tinkling. "Yes!"

Feeling better, Paige made her exit. The Ford Escort rental car waited for her in the parking lot across the street from the bank. Not a vehicle she was accustomed to driving, but the only one available at the time she needed it. Good grief, until she met up with the no-frills compact, she didn't know they made cars without power windows.

SITTING AT A RED LIGHT at an intersection near the Frost Bank Building's outdoor—*and free*—parking lot, Spur Atwater glanced at his wristwatch for the fifth time in five minutes.

Inside that bank at two o'clock the most important appointment of his life awaited him, and with the September temperatures still pushing the mercury up into the nineties and no air-conditioning in his truck, he had sweated through his only dress shirt.

Besides that, he was almost late. The irresponsibility of being late for an appointment didn't dwell in his makeup. He had left his apartment in College Station at eight, giving him more time than he needed to make the four-hour drive to Fort Worth. If he arrived early and had to circle the building or walk the downtown streets for an hour, it would be worth it to present the punctual, no-nonsense borrower he wanted the banker to see.

But, to thwart his plans, just outside the Fort Worth city limits the driver of an eighteen-wheeler had laid his rig on its side and blocked all lanes of traffic for over an hour.

Listening to the labored idle of his fifteen-year-old Chevy's re-built engine, he considered what he was about to do. God, he was about to ask for money. The very thought would have revved up his sweat glands, even if the day wasn't damn hot and humid. He had always prided himself on not asking for favors or help, but on hear-ing of a thriving, state-of-the-art veterinary practice in Salt Lick, Texas, for sale at a bargain price, he had made an exception to the rule. A college buddy had put in a good word for him with a Frost

Bank vice president and now, in less than ten minutes, Spur would be meeting the banker to discuss a loan that could shape his future.

No doubt about it. Spur Atwater had a fire in his belly. His finishing near the top of his class had prompted a dozen established vets and research labs to seek him out for employment, but he wanted to be independent. He wanted to own his own practice. He wanted to do experimental cattle breeding, and he yearned to return to his beloved West Texas.

Being an A&M graduate wouldn't hurt his chances with the banker, especially when said banker was a loyal Aggie alumnus. Texas A&M graduates were a tacit brotherhood, as strong as any fraternity.

Nor would it do any harm that Roy Spur Atwater had been a record-setting quarterback for the Aggies for all of his undergraduate years. Yep, the game of football had paid for the first five years of his education, and feeling obligated to give back, he had played the game well. But he didn't kid himself that he was anything but a novice at the good-ol'-boy networking game. Still, even a rookie recognized an opportunity when it kicked him on the shin. If ever there was a time for a Hail Mary pass, it was now.

As he turned into the bank's parking lot, a long-legged blonde in a teeny-weeny skirt and a bandaged ankle crossed in front of him and crawled into a roller skate of a car, showing plenty of tanned and shapely thigh when her skirt hiked up to paradise. Though he wanted his mind geared for business, his roommate in his boxers reacted in the usual manner, forcing him to readjust his posture and deliver an admonition. "Not now, dammit."

As he crawled toward the blonde's compact, anticipating the emptying slot, he saw that the space was too narrow for his truck. He eased on past. Suddenly her car shot backward. He stomped his accelerator, but too late. The Ford slammed into the side of his truck. His erection shriveled along with his emotional restraint.

The blonde unfolded from the compact and confronted him, fists jammed against her hips. "What is your problem? You're supposed to stop when a car is leaving a parking place. Or were you gawking at the tall buildings in the big city, *Clem?*"

Though Spur felt a little overwhelmed in any city and the gawking insult held more than a grain of truth, it was the last straw. He sprang from his truck cab, his jaw muscles twitching as he eyed the damage to his fender. His faded blue Chevy wasn't much, but he damn sure didn't want to see it any more beat-up than it already was.

"What's *my* problem? *You* plowed into me, Miss America. I know damn well you saw me. Or were you too busy checking your lipstick to look where you were going?" He stuck out a hand. "Just let me have your insurance card. I've got an appointment. I don't have time to fool with this."

"I don't have an insurance card." She began to dig in a leather satchel so huge it looked like she had peeled it off the side of a fullgrown Hereford. "I'll give you the name of one of my father's accountants. He can give you all the information you need."

Shit. A daddy's girl. Rich and spoiled. Spur knew the type, had met a few during his stint at A&M. Most of them wanted him for a charm on their already-full bracelets. He could think of nothing and no one he disliked more.

Well, by God, he was immune to Miss Long-legs, good-looking or not. He climbed back into his truck, fired the engine with a growl, and cranked down the window. He leaned out and pointed toward an empty space at the far, far end of the parking lot. "I'm parking down there. Leave Daddy's accountant's name and phone number under my wiper blade."

"But I have an injury," the blonde whined. "It's hard for me to walk that far."

An Ace bandage garnered no sympathy from him. Almost every joint in his body had been wrapped or taped at different times. "Then pay somebody to do it for you." He moved forward.

"I hope you're late," she shouted.

He chuckled wickedly and deliberately bypassed a just-vacated slot two cars away.

"Asshole," she yelled.

two

Spur slept in until nine, a rare luxury. Yesterday had worn him out. Driving four hours to Fort Worth, then driving four hours *back* to College Station hadn't been so bad. But meeting the banker and asking for money had been one of the most stressful events of his twenty-nine years.

He wasn't due at the cattle auction where he worked as an inspector until after lunch. He lay in bed in his postage stamp–size apartment puzzling over the meeting. Nobody knew any better than he that as a rookie right out of vet school, with little experience and even less credit, plus a portfolio of student loans, he was lucky a banker even gave him an appointment. He had presented a business plan supporting his request for a loan, but to his surprise, the banker only skimmed it. To his further amazement, the banker had seemed almost eager to make the loan. Maybe there was something to this "good-ol'-boy" networking after all.

Networking and politics were unfamiliar and uncomfortable to a guy whose upbringing had been as bleak as Spur's. His father had been an oil field hand, following a job from town to town. At some point, in Odessa, his dad had suffered a severe back injury, and their nomadic existence had come to an end.

In those days, there was no such thing as successfully suing an employer for a work-related injury. Oil field workers took on the hard, dangerous work at their own risk. After his injury, Spur's dad, uneducated and disabled, had found himself unemployable. He sought solace in a whiskey bottle. Spur and his siblings had been fed by various well-meaning ladies from the Baptist Church. For them, delivering foil-wrapped parcels to the Atwaters might have been a charitable act, but to Spur, it was a life-altering mortification.

Being the oldest, he had worked and helped out, but even as a boy, he had seen that education could save him from the quagmire of poverty in which he, his parents, and his five sisters lived. Early on, he had determined *nothing* would prevent his finishing high school. Blessed with intelligence and natural athletic ability, he played football on Odessa's venerated Permian High School team.

After quarterbacking the Panthers to two back-to-back state championships, college became more than a fantasy. He earned a full five-year football scholarship to Texas A&M, the only university in Texas with a veterinary school and a renowned one at that. As a child, he had always loved and been loved by animals.

From the day he set foot on the A&M campus, he had a goal—owning his own veterinary practice, making a decent living, and earning the respect of some community. Nothing had derailed him so far, not a lack of money, time, or sleep. Not a female. And Lord knew, some of them had tried to throw him off track.

Now, the goal was within sight. No more foil-wrapped Christmas dinners from other families' tables. No more one-size-fits-all garments or unisex toys. To add to his delight, he would be returning to his beloved West Texas.

He hauled himself from bed and showered and shaved, dressed in clean jeans and a T-shirt. All that he had removed from his pockets before going to bed last night lay on the dresser. As he opened his wallet to check his cash, he found the banker's assistant's business card. She had jotted her home number on the back of it. "In case you need anything else," she had said when she handed it to him.

He didn't tell her she was wasting her time. He merely touched his hat to her, gave her a smile, and left with a simple "Thank you, ma'am."

Also in his wallet was the note that had been secured under his windshield wiper yesterday. In truth, he was surprised she left it. He knew what he expected to see written in it, so he hadn't bothered reading it yet. The paper was definitely feminine. Curvy edges with pink and white flowers. Embossed in silver were the words "A note from Paige McBride."

He ran his thumb across the raised imprint and thought of the woman. *Paige McBride, rich and spoiled.* He lifted the note to his nose. Mmm. He didn't know one perfume fragrance from another, but this one smelled pretty good.

At last he read what she had written:

Richard Innsbruck, (817) 555-2002.
Personally, I think I improved the looks of your pickup.
Now it has a dent on both sides.   P.M.

He couldn't keep from grinning. She obviously hadn't seen the sticker on his back bumper: HONK IF SOMETHING FALLS OFF.

PAIGE LOOKED at her clock. After ten. She had to get out of bed and face her future. Forcing enthusiasm, she donned jeans and a comfortable shirt, then grabbed the phone, a pen and pad of paper, and her PDA. Networking was the solution to her problem.

Her first phone call was the third to her only longtime friend, Sunny Parker. Where was Sunny and why didn't she call back? Even reaching the crazy redhead's cell phone proved impossible.

Paige and Sunny had met at Hockaday School in Dallas, both of them parked by their rich parents in the elite private high school. They had gravitated to each other like lodestones, the common bond being wealth and loneliness. Nowadays, Sunny lived off a seven-digit income from a trust fund. Her only interests were men, traveling the world with men, and cooking for men. She had attended as many culinary schools as Paige had universities. They no longer socialized together as they once had, but the need for each other's dry shoulders had never gone away entirely.

Paige answered a knock at her door and was met by an Enterprise Leasing Company employee who came to pick up the Ford Escort. As she handed over the keys, the realization that she was now afoot affected her profoundly. She doubted she had ever been without transportation, even as a baby.

As soon as the keys and the car left, she walked to her tiny bar and poured herself a shot of Glenlivet, her drink of choice when life got serious. Beer and margaritas were froufrou drinks, strictly for fun. Single malt Scotch was "oh-shit-we're-all-going-to-die" time.

By two in the afternoon Paige was on her third Glenlivet.

The results of twelve phone calls was shocking if not downright scary. Four of her friends had recently been laid off and had hit her up for a loan. Three more thought her situation hilarious and comforted her with assurances that Buck would get over it and bring her back into the fold. One was currently employed by one of her father's companies. Two voice mails. One number no longer in service, and another individual couldn't remember her. Maybe changing colleges every two years had been a bad idea. Maybe she should have spent less time having fun and more making real friends.

Oh, well. This was only the first day of this insanity. Too soon to let despair raise its ugly head. Daddy was only punishing her. Surely, he *would* get over it. Uncurling from her easy chair she headed for the kitchen to freshen her drink.

Twenty-five hundred dollars. How long could someone live on twenty-five hundred dollars?

The chirping of her phone interrupted her contemplation, and she noted with relief the name on caller ID: Judd Stephens. She had called him several times in the past two days but hadn't yet connected. Giving him the benefit of the doubt, she rationalized he was busy chasing his dream of finishing high enough in bull-riding competitions to be eligible for the National Finals Rodeo in Las Vegas at the end of the year.

She pressed the button and wasted no time on a greeting. "Judd, where are you? You left me alone in San Antonio? Why did you take my SUV?"

"Hold up there, sweetness. The whole thing was your idea. I didn't want to, but you insisted."

Paige frowned and bit down on her lower lip. *Oh, dear.* She didn't remember doing that, but she had a history of doing generous-but-dumb favors for "friends," more often than not to her own detriment. She didn't doubt that at some point in their hard-partying weekend she had lent Judd the new shiny black Escalade her daddy had bought her.

Instead of arguing the point, she related the story of her luncheon with Daddy. Only this time, to ensure a sympathetic response, she embellished just short of saying he had held her at gunpoint.

"What do you want me to do about it?" Judd asked. "Find you a job?"

"Well that remark was less than supportive. What you can do is bring my rig back here. Without wheels, I can't even look."

"Sorry to be the one to break it to you, angel, but it's gonna take more than wheels to get you employed. What can you do besides go shopping, dress up, and look pretty?"

Paige didn't know if the blunt spoken truth or his lack of compassion hurt the most. Tears stung her eyes, and she took a deep breath to steady her voice. "Like I've already said, Judd. I need my rig back. Can you be here with it tomorrow?"

"Tomorrow! Shit, Paige, I'm damn near in Canada. I've already—"

"Judd! You didn't tell me you were taking my Escalade to a foreign country!"

"I'm not in a foreign country. I'm in Idaho. I'm headed for Worley. I've already paid my entry fees. You said you'd get a rental."

"I did, but they picked it up this afternoon. It was, uh, well it was . . . um, a little bit wrecked."

"You wrecked a rental car?"

"I backed into a guy. Daddy upset me so much I wasn't thinking. Even if the car people would let me have another one, Daddy's canceled my American Express card."

"Hell, Paige, this is a real inconvenience for me—"

"An inconvenience for *you*? Dammit, Judd—"

"Good God, Paige. I'm out here trying to make something outta my life—"

"Well, excuse me, Mr. Success. I really must hang up and call those Nobel Prize people and rave about your accomplishments."

"Save the sarcasm for somebody who appreciates it, Paige. You know what this amounts to? You're a spoiled little rich girl who's made Daddy mad. My God, it's over two thousand miles from here to Fort Worth. If I turned around right now, by the time I get there, you'll have batted those big blues at Buck and be back in his good graces. And I'll miss my chance to qualify."

"Hunh. What are you up to now, four or five seconds on the back of a bull?"

"I'll tell you one thing. Talking to me like that ain't gonna get you this Cadillac back any sooner."

"How about me talking to the cops instead? Reporting it stolen in . . . let me see, did you say Idaho? Do you think that'll get it back sooner or am I being sarcastic again?"

Silence. "I can be there by, uh . . . Tuesday or Wednesday, if I don't make the finals. If I do, then sometime Thursday. How's that?" His tone switched to pleading. "*Please,* baby, let me make my ride. I've already paid my money."

Paige crossed her eyes and stared across the room. *Rats.* "Okay, Judd. Thursday at the latest. And don't dare call me and tell me you can't get here."

"Don't worry your empty little head, darlin'. Calling you is something I don't plan on doing ever again."

She opened her mouth to fire back but heard only a dial tone. Well, fine. That was the end of her friendship with Judd Stephens.

She must have the world's longest list of irresponsible friends.

Why did she make such lousy choices? Had growing up without a mom affected her relationships with men in particular and people in general? She had always wondered.

Mulling over the question, Paige replaced the phone on its charging station and went to the vanity area of her huge bedroom. Inside her closet that was large enough to be a bedroom she searched three walls of double-decked clothes racks for an outfit suitable to wear for a job interview. Fringe and conchos probably weren't a good idea. Nor were tight jeans and cowboy boots.

Her mind continued to dwell on the conversation she'd just had with Judd. It wasn't that she went for bad boys—good-looking, devil-may-care jerks with harems of females chasing them and off-the-wall lifestyles. All women, she assumed, went for bad boys, but for some reason, she hooked up with the ones who treated her badly . . . like Judd.

She pulled a tailored white blouse off a hanger and held it in front of her, checking in the full-length mirror how it looked with the tan she spent hours maintaining. Her forearms caught her attention. Lord, her skin looked *sooo* dry.

She hung the blouse back on its rack and reached for a jar of enriched skin cream she had bought at Panache. The jar being close to empty, she made a mental note to pick up a replacement. At least the spa was within walking distance.

The spa! Of course! Every time she went there it seemed their receptionist had just quit. How hard could it be to sit at a pretty desk all day and talk to their clientele?

She rubbed the last dollop of the silky cream onto her arms, satisfied that her employment challenge was met. After all, she was a good Panache customer. Why wouldn't they hire her?

Before leaving the bathroom, she studied her hair. Good Lord, her hairdo was all wrong for job searching. A messy profusion of blond highlighted layers and curls hanging below her shoulder blades would not do. She gathered the untamed layers into an up-do and studied the results. Yep, much more appropriate for interviewing.

Maybe getting a job wasn't such a bad idea. Maybe this was what she needed, a chance to do something on her own. She didn't know if she was capable of supporting herself, but she knew this much. Her daddy had hurt her feelings and made her mad. She would die alone and be buried in a pauper's grave before she would return to the control he and her stepmother wielded over her life. It was one thing to be enrolled against her will in a private high school she hated when she was a teenager, but in three months, she would be twenty-five years old.

Yes indeedy, she recognized a chance to escape when she saw one.

She only wished that a week earlier, when she had chosen *not* to spend $475 on the denim Dolce & Gabbana bustier she had spotted in Neiman Marcus, she had known Daddy was going to cut her off. There were lessons to be learned in life, and she had just discovered an important one: don't put off buying 'til tomorrow what you could be wearing today.

PAIGE CAME AWAY from an unsuccessful meeting with the spa manager stunned more than disappointed. Her expensive spa where she spent a ton of money on tanning, massages, facials, pedicures—you name it—paid starvation wages. In addition, they expected a receptionist to work horrible hours—nine to six, with only a half hour for lunch, five days a week and one Saturday a month. Were they kidding? Why, it was slavery.

When she told the interviewer she had a very fashionable wardrobe that would make a great impression on the spa's customers, the woman informed her the receptionist wore a black nylon smock, and a wardrobe was at the bottom of their list of requirements. Lesson learned. Paige wouldn't make *that* mistake again.

She had a headache, left over from drinking too much Scotch yesterday. She wouldn't do that again, either. She put on her swimsuit and headed for the pool. Twenty-five laps would make her feel better.

The next day's search for work began with a negative. Every ad in the *Star Telegram* classifieds called for a résumé. Paige spent the rest of the day trying various formats, but in the end gave up. She had no employment history to put on a résumé. For education, she could show six years of attendance at good universities—SMU, Texas Tech, and TCU—but no degree. She could barely type, and the only computer knowledge she had acquired was logging on to the Internet to check her e-mail.

The following day, not forgetting that her wardrobe was unimportant, Paige dressed down in a white turtleneck sweater and a simple straight black skirt that struck her midcalf—how could someone get any plainer than that?—and pushed her hair back with a headband into a severe do. She added tall black boots and studied her image. She looked positively drab, so to her earlobes, she added the large diamond studs Daddy had given her for Christmas last year.

She set out on foot, her destination the real estate sales office in a strip center at the end of her block. When she entered, she was surprised by the decor. Compared to the spa, the place was as plain as her attire, but she could adapt. After all, how many hours a day would she spend here?

The office manager, whose nameplate said MS. DENNISON, told her they could use a receptionist. The job started at twenty. Paige did a quick calculation in her head: twenty dollars per hour added up to around forty thousand per year. She certainly couldn't live on less.

"Oh, that's wonderful." Paige had heard from her friends who held down jobs that starting pay was negotiable, so she added, "But do you think you could bump that up to forty-five thousand? A girl does have expenses, you know."

Ms. Dennison's face took on a flat expression. "Dear, we're discussing an annual wage of twenty thousand dollars, which may be more than you're worth. You're an attractive young woman whose appearance would be an asset to our front office, but you have no experience and no skills that I can discern."

Why, the nerve! Who did Ms. Dennison think she had sitting across from her, a potted plant? Stung, Paige rose from her chair, smoothed her lap wrinkles, and summoned a saccharine smile. "I may not know how to type, but that's no reason for *you* to be so rude."

As she made her exit, she thought of the countless number of women who *had* to accept such insulting pay and the attitude that went with it. By walking out on Ms. Dennison, she had struck a blow for *them*.

Feeling heroic, she returned to her condo, where she mixed a pitcher of margaritas, donned her bikini, shoved on her new Sama sunglasses, and marched to the pool. Before long, one of her neighbors and her adorable four-year-old joined her. When Paige told of her job-hunting experiences, the neighbor said the law firm where her husband worked was interviewing for a clerk.

A lawyer's office. Why, absolutely. Why hadn't she thought of it before? That would be a much more prestigious job than receptionist in a spa or a real estate sales office.

Paige awoke the next day to a depressing Sunday and another headache. Yesterday afternoon, the neighbor and her daughter had left the pool and been replaced with a divorced stockbroker from the other end of the complex and one of his friends. When the pitcher of margaritas ran dry, the stockbroker had gone back to his unit and returned with a fifth of Crown Royal. The three of them had partied until well after dark.

With no transportation, she was homebound. All she could do was either watch TV or hang out at the pool again. She was channel surfing when Sunny returned her call. Her friend had just returned from some kind of cooking classes in New Orleans. Paige was in tears by the time she finished telling Sunny her troubles.

"Oh, I know just what this calls for," Sunny said.

"My liquor cabinet's almost bare. I don't want anything to drink anyway."

"Not liquor. Honestly, Paige. What this calls for is chocolate. I'll come over and make you a lava cake. What do I need to bring?"

Paige sniffled. "Everything but an oven."

Sunny came. And left late in the afternoon. They had finished off the tequila. The lava cake had turned out more like chocolate pudding than cake, and they had discovered that deep rich chocolate and tart margaritas did not enhance each other. Sunny's disapproval of the combination of tastes had driven her to declare she needed to take more cooking classes.

Judd appeared in the Escalade on Sunday evening. A cervical collar ringed his neck and a heavy plaster cast cocked his arm at a forty-five-degree angle. He had to turn his entire body to hand her the SUV's keys at her front door. She couldn't find it in her heart to be mad at him.

"Oh, my gosh, Judd. Are you in pain?"

His handsome face took on a scowl. "I'm on drugs. I shouldn't be driving."

Paige sneaked a glance at the dusty Escalade parked in her driveway. It appeared to be all intact and undamaged. She breathed a silent sigh of relief and swung her gaze back to Judd's injuries. "You must have drawn a good bull. Did you qualify?"

A murderous glare shot from his blue eyes. "All I qualified for was disability."

"Do you need a ride somewhere?"

"I've already got a ride."

As he limped away, Paige saw a shiny yellow Corvette parked at the curb. The driver was a glamorous-looking blonde she didn't recognize. Judd must have qualified at *something*.

Which was more than she had done in the past few days.

three

Morning brought new resolve. Paige searched her closet for a respectable suit and decided on a beige two-piece Donna Karan she had never worn. The skirt hit just above the knee, and she pondered if its hemline was a tad too short for a job interview.

She found a peach-colored blouse that accentuated her tan and . . . well, her cleavage, too, but the cleavage wasn't as important as the tan. A bunch of stodgy lawyers probably wouldn't notice what she was wearing anyway.

Last, she added a pair of three-inch honey-colored lizard pumps and checked the mirror again. Her five-feet-ten-inch frame seemed to be all legs. Up until two or three years ago she had thought her long limbs gangly, but she had finally filled out. Oh, well, why debate with herself? The suit was a tailored outfit, wasn't it?

The law firm, located downtown in one of the Bass Towers near the courthouse, was quiet, cool, and formal and done in blue tones. Good. Blue was one of her good colors.

As she passed the receptionist and several women and men she assumed were lawyers, she wished she had left the three-inch heels at home. She was a head taller than everyone she saw.

She had always thought of lawyers as being exceptionally smart. A lawyer was one of the few people to whom Daddy ever listened. When she was shown into the senior partner's office, his lack of mental acuity shocked her. Why, the man forgot the job requirements, and he sweated so much he grabbed a legal document and began mopping his balding head.

Oh, dear. She wasn't sure how she felt about a man who perspired so profusely.

Then it occurred to her he could be having a heart attack. He had to be at least fifty. "Oh, Mr. Blodgett, are you okay? I know CPR—"

"Miss McBride," he blurted, springing to his feet, "this just isn't going to work out. You see, I'm a happily married man."

What did *that* have to do with anything?

Men were so strange, she thought as the assistant escorted her to the front door.

Experience required.
Only Experienced Need Apply.

How was she supposed to get experience if no one would give her a chance? She scanned the classifieds again and zeroed in on an ad:

No experience necessary. Immediate opening. Executive position for the right person willing to work hard. Top pay in short time.

Could this be real? Something so promising and so in tune with her needs had to have a downside.

On the other hand, maybe her luck had taken a turn for the better. Maybe she'd had such bad experiences with those other interviews just so she could find *this* job.

Paige dialed the number and within a matter of minutes had an appointment for tomorrow morning.

The interview with Joe Gist started off so well Paige speculated she could call Daddy this very afternoon and tell him he didn't have to worry about her ever again. She was on her way. *Grab the Windex! Glass ceiling, here I come!*

Polite and professional—but rather short and wearing brown shoes and white socks with a shiny blue suit—Mr. Gist told her she could set her own hours. "But of course," he added, "the more you work, the more you can make."

He gave her a grin that reminded her of a snake. And he looked her up and down like he might jump over the desk and land on her lap. "I'd say you're built, er, tailor-made for this job, Miss McBride. Why, the day might even come when you'd like to go out in the field where you could make some real money. I see you raking in six digits in no time."

"Oh, I'm so thrilled, Mr. Gist. But you haven't told me what I'm supposed to do."

"We do a type of telemarketing here," he said.

His involved explanation left her blinking and dumbfounded for a few seconds. Finally, she found words. "You—you mean you want me to call up strangers and sell them rubbers?"

"Condoms, Miss McBride. Condoms. You have to understand it's a public service. Many men are too intimidated to purchase condoms in a bricks and mortar store. You'll be promoting safe sex. Do you know how many unfortunate people contract STDs each year, or, God forbid, AIDS?"

Paige felt as if her entire body had been given a big shot of Novocain. She shook her head.

"Unwanted pregnancies," Mr. Gist continued. "Have you seen the number of babies born to women who don't want them? Babies left unloved, uncared for, that become abused children?"

Oh, dear. Paige couldn't bear the thought of unloved babies or abused children. She felt herself relenting. "Wow. Gosh, when you put it that way—"

"Oh, splendid." He opened his desk drawer and took out a sheaf of papers. "Now. We have canned presentations you can memorize in no time. Here's an example." He pushed several pages across the desk on which she saw written dialogue.

She scanned it. "Oh, my." Her head began to slowly shake as she read. "Oh, my, no. I don't think I can call up men and discuss the size of—"

"Now, now." Mr. Gist's palm came up. "Don't be discouraged. It's nothing more than research. The right fit is important to making a happy customer."

She read on, then stopped at the end of the last page and stared at him. "Excuse me, but after they agree to buy one, you want me to ask if they'd like help putting it on?"

Mr. Gist's eyes popped wide and both palms flew up. "Oh, don't worry. We don't expect *you* to do it. We have people on staff to—"

"People on staff?" Paige felt her eyes bug as wide as Mr. Gist's. "You want me to be a pimp!"

"Miss McBride, please. No. No, absolutely not. Think of yourself as a, uh . . . a love facilitator." He made a sweeping motion with his arm as if he were skywriting.

Paige yanked up her purse and sprang to her feet. "Sir, I have to go now."

She backed toward the door, feeling behind herself for the knob. He skirted the end of the desk, shoving a business card at her. "Here, take a card. So you can call me. Tell your friends about us."

Her hand closed on the doorknob, but she released it and stared down at her palm. "Yuck!"

As her high heels clacked lickety-split up the hall, she heard him call out, "We offer an excellent dental plan."

OUTSIDE, PAIGE CLIMBED into the Escalade, sank into its buttery leather upholstery, and drew a shaky breath. She had always thought of herself as worldly, but the meeting she had just left set that notion back a step or two.

The grip of determination to succeed was beginning to slip.

She turned the ignition, prepared to back out of the parking lot, when the low fuel light caught her eye. God, it seemed like she had just filled the gas tank. She wished now, when it had been her free choice, she had gone for the VW instead of this gas-guzzling SUV.

She pulled into the next service station. She hung the nozzle in the gas tank and returned to her purse on the passenger seat for the forty-five dollars the gas would cost. She had twenty-five dollars in her wallet. She counted the money a second time before darting to stop the gasoline flow at twelve dollars.

How was it possible she had no more than twenty-five dollars?

Only three weeks had passed since Daddy had delivered his ultimatum and told her he had put twenty-five hundred dollars in her bank account.

Sure, she had purchased a few things—new earrings to match her beige suit, a new purse with matching wallet, her favorite perfume, but it *had* included a free body lotion. That wasn't frivolous. That was smart shopping.

She had replaced several empty bottles in her bar. She had eaten out in a couple of her favorite restaurants. She had to eat, didn't she? Daddy surely didn't expect her to go without food.

Thinking of eating out reminded her she was hungry. The portable sign at the McDonald's next door caught her eye. CHECK OUT OUR $1 MENU ITEMS.

With thirteen dollars in her hand Paige started the engine and made the short trip across the parking lot. She hadn't eaten at a Mickey D's in a long time, but she knew the food was hot and cheap.

Balancing her order on a plastic tray, she found a seat near the cashier. The front of the large dining room seemed to be the safest place because the remainder of the room had been overtaken by birthday revelers. A stream of water ran from the direction of the bathrooms. The pimply-faced teenager behind the counter told her the group celebrating an honoree's fifth birthday had stuffed the toilets with gift wrap. A food fight was in progress, and all of the younger children were wailing.

As she ate, a sign written in chalk below the Employee of the Month picture beckoned to her. NOW HIRING. ASK FOR MANAGER. A lightbulb clicked on inside her head. Maybe fate had pulled her to this spot. Whatever. All she knew for sure was that she was now down to less than ten dollars.

"May I speak to the manager, please?" she asked the harried teenager.

"Is something wrong?" His shoulders sagged with dejection. "Aw, man, if I screwed up your order . . . One more complaint and I'm fixin' to get canned."

"My order was fine. I uh . . . I want to talk to him about something else."

"Is it the noise? I'm sorry. The parents are supposed to keep these little monsters under control."

"I want to talk to him about the job you're advertising."

"What job?" The young man's brow tented over troubled eyes.

Paige pointed to the sign.

"Oh, that. It stays up all the time. We're always looking for somebody. Hold on. I'll get Melvin."

When Melvin rounded the end of the counter, the little that remained of Paige's ego left like air from a punctured balloon. He looked to be not much older than the birthday celebrants. He was five three and maybe weighed a hundred pounds. Above his left shirt pocket, his name was embroidered.

He had to be eighteen, Paige theorized, staring down at ketchup and mustard splotches on his shirt. A pocket protector filled with pens hung on his chest like war medals, and he held a clipboard close to his body. Paige recognized him as the Employee of the Month and glanced again at his picture grinning proudly from inside the black plastic frame.

He pushed his thick glasses back to their place on his nose and looked her up and down. "We don't hire corporate level from this location. You'll have to go to Dallas."

"I'm not looking for a corporate job," Paige said. "I want to apply for the job you have here."

"You're kidding, right? Is this a sorority prank? They do stuff like that to us all the time."

Paige lifted her chin, making her tower over him that much more. "I'm serious. I've never had a job. I don't have any skills, but I'll try my very best. That's all I can say."

A pregnant pause followed. He appeared to be considering the situation. Suddenly he extended his hand and beamed the smile that had surely earned him the monthly employee recognition. "Welcome to McDonald's!"

He gave her a stack of papers to fill out, a set of uniforms, and a brief speech on keeping the uniforms clean and pressed. Paige lifted the garments one by one. Polyester. Pressed? Who did Melvin think he was kidding? As if polyester wasn't bad enough, he handed her a hairnet.

PAIGE SHOWED UP the next day on time, in spite of spending half an hour in front of her vanity mirror wrestling with the hairnet. The skimpy elastic strings barely contained her mane of curls. Flattened on top, her trendy Shelton's hairstyle angled down to a bob about her shoulders. She looked like a mushroom. A mushroom in polyester. If anyone she knew came into McDonald's, she intended to stick her head in the deep fryer.

Melvin assigned her to the grill. Within minutes her acrylic nails had begun to melt, and for the sake of safety and fire prevention, he moved her to the cash register, contorted nails and all.

The cash register was perfect, given Paige's lack of experience. The name of each item served was written on each individual key, and to remove any doubt, a picture of the item was also displayed. The amount of change due a customer was practically shoved into his hand by a change-making machine. Melvin stood by at a discreet distance in case she got in over her head.

Everything went well until the appearance of her fourth customer of the day. Paige heard her coming before she reached the counter. *Scuff-pop, scuff-pop.* The sound was unmistakable. Flip–flops.

Also unmistakable was the three hundred pounds or more the young wearer of the shoes carried on her vertically challenged frame. Yet her makeup application was excellent, and her features were striking. A slimmer version of the woman would have turned heads anywhere.

When she ordered three Big Macs, a super-size order of fries, and an extra-large chocolate milk shake, Paige couldn't resist the urge to advise. "Wouldn't you prefer a salad? Or how about a Fruit and Yogurt Parfait? Those are really delicious, and they're probably low-cal."

The woman jammed chubby fists against her hips. " 'Scuse me? I tol' you what I want."

"I know. But a salad would be so much better for you."

All at once it became Angry Customer Bobble Head Day at McDonald's. The young woman raised a palm. "Oh no you di'n't. You di'n't call me fat?"

Paige couldn't recall uttering the word *fat.* Even if she had, anyone could see her suggestion had the young lady's best interest at heart. "No, heaven's no. I'm not saying you're fat. I just think you could be a little . . . thinner."

"I'll tell you one thing, Barbie Doll. I'm *thin* enough to climb across this counter and make a salad outta your pretty little face. How about that, Barbie? Wanna follow that with some fruit and yogurt?"

Barbie? Paige rolled her eyes. Not the first time someone had compared her to the plastic diva. "Well. There is absolutely no reason for you to get so belligerent and—"

"Did you say belligerent? Honey, I'm past belligerent. Ronald McDonald'll be bringing me breakfast in bed after my lawyer kicks his ass."

Melvin rushed in, pale and shaken, and delivered the angry customer's order. "Here ya go, ma'am. Just as you ordered. I threw in two apple pies for you. Let me know if you'd like some ice cream on top. No charge, of course."

The woman eyed the assortment of food heaped on the tray. "Well, tha's more like it." She shot Paige one more deadly glare and waddled off with her prize.

Paige wanted to cry. Melvin stared up at her, his no-color accusing eyes magnified by the thick lenses of his glasses. "Paige, you're fired."

THE PHONE WAS screeching hysterically when Paige walked into her apartment. Paige wanted to join it, but she picked up and answered with a lifeless voice.

"Paige, honey? Sweetie, are you sick? You sound terrible."

"Oh, hi, Daddy. No, I'm just . . . I'm—" She broke into sobs.

"Paige, what's wrong. Honey, you're scarin' me. I'm fixin' to come over there."

"No, don't." She sniffled and wiped her nose on a sheet of paper towel. "I'm okay. I don't need you to come over."

"Well, what's wrong? It's not like you to be so emotional. Is it Judd? If I have to come over there and straighten—"

"No, no, it isn't Judd. I'm just a little low."

"Darlin', I've talked to Enron executives who didn't sound as despondent as you do. Tell your ol' daddy what's wrong."

"I got fired," she cried. "From McDonald's."

"McDonald & Dietrich? Why, those sonsabitches. They know better than to fuck with me and mine. Tell Daddy what happened."

Paige frowned and sobbed. "Not the law firm. McDonald's. The hamburger place. You know, fast food, drive-thru service?"

A pause. Paige assumed her daddy was recovering from shock.

"Why don't you fill me in on what's been going on with your job search," he said at last. "Start from the beginning. Don't leave anything out."

Paige told him about the past few weeks, ending with the fact that she had no money left. "Daddy, I've really been trying. I know I've got to do this on my own, but I've hit bottom. Would you help me just this once? I don't want you to support me, but you know so many people. If you could just make a phone call or two, I promise to do the rest."

"What kind of work do you *want* to do?"

All she had ever really *wanted* to do was work with horses as her mother had done, work that had earned Charlotte McBride respect that had endured beyond her death. Daddy's refusal to understand, her stepmother's nagging about time spent in the barn with animals, and their trying to force private schools and higher education down her throat had been a source of frustration to Paige for years.

She sniffed. "I want to be like my mom. I want to work with horses. I want Margaret Ann to leave me alone and stay out of my life. . . . But I'll do anything *you* say, Daddy. I'll try hard wherever I go."

"Okay, baby. It's killing me seeing you miserable. Maybe we can figure this out together, just you and me. Let me make a phone call tonight. I'll call you back."

Paige sniffled and blew her nose on a new sheet of paper towel. "Thanks, Daddy."

four

Honey, I've got some good news about a job."

In a sleepy daze, Paige fumbled with the receiver. Though she had slept through a whole night for the first time in she couldn't remember when, the moment she recognized the voice, she became wide awake. "Really? Oh, thank you so much, Daddy."

His chuckle sent a little flurry of uneasiness through her. "Now don't be too quick to thank me. You don't know what the job is yet."

"I don't care what it is. I won't let you down. I promise. Who did you call? Tell me everything."

"Whoa, sweet pea, slow down. You remember Harley Carruthers? Lives in West Texas, little place called Salt Lick? You went there with me once when you were just a kid."

Ohmygod, this was good news beyond belief. The Carruthers Oil & Gas Company was an empire. Paige felt her pulse rate surge.

"Of course I remember Harley. I always wondered what happened to him after his wife was murdered."

The titillating story of Pearl Ann Carruthers's murder had held captive the attention of Texans for months. Many believed the deceased woman had met her just reward.

"Harley's doin' great. Remarried. Still dividing his time between Salt Lick and Midland." Her daddy paused and took a deep breath before continuing. "I told him about you. Gave him a little history."

Paige bit down on her lower lip. Terrific. Now another person knew she was a complete screwup. "You didn't tell him I got fired from McDonald's, did you? I don't want him thinking I can't even hold down a job most teenagers can do."

"I didn't go into that much detail. I just told him you needed a leg up on this job huntin' thing."

"Thanks. That's perfect."

"He thinks he's got something."

"Oh, that's so wonderful. You're the best. Where's the office? Downtown Dallas?" Visions of shopping for career clothes danced in her head. "Ooohh, I can hardly wait. Or is it Fort Worth?"

Silence.

"Daddy?"

"You'll have to relocate, sweetheart. Move out to the Midland area."

Yikes! Midland? "But I don't want to move."

"I didn't think you would, but sweetheart, he's closed his offices in Dallas and relocated all operations to Midland. You know, darlin', Southwest Airlines has daily flights going out of Love Field. Takes less than an hour. Hell, you can be stuck that long in traffic between malls."

Paige couldn't keep the corners of her mouth from turning down into a pout. She loved her condo, loved its location near Hulen Mall for casual shopping, loved being near downtown Fort Worth for entertainment. Why, she was no more than an hour's drive from The Galleria in Dallas. "I can't remember the last time I was in that part of Texas, but I don't think I liked it."

"Since you've got time on your hands, why don't you drive out that way and visit Harley. Meet his new wife. Might lift your spirits."

Paige chewed on one contorted fingernail. She hadn't dared spend the money to have her nails redone after they nearly melted at McDonald's. "I can't."

"Why not? Don't tell me Judd's still got that SUV. Paige, I swear—"

"He brought it back. I don't have the money for a trip out of town."

"I'll cut you a deal. I'll pay for the trip. I'll call it an investment in your future."

Temptation nudged her. *C'mon,* it said, *what could it hurt to talk to Harley? He might have an offer you can't refuse.*

But in Midland?

"Okay," she said, unable to disguise a grudging tone. "It's a deal . . . I think."

"Great, punkin. I knew you'd see it your ol' daddy's way. I've already told him you'd be at his ranch Monday afternoon. Five o'clock. Don't be late, now."

Her father hung up before she could ask why she was to meet Harley at his home rather than his office. She stared at the phone for several beats. So confident she would drop everything and drive four hundred miles to West Texas, her daddy had made an appointment without consulting her. She didn't mind that he knew her so well, but she hated being a foregone conclusion.

❅ ❅ ❅

PAIGE LEFT EARLY Monday morning, intending to take her time and enjoy the drive west. She would get into Midland mid-afternoon, check into a hotel, change clothes, then drive the additional sixty miles to Salt Lick.

Having learned her lesson about dressing for a successful interview, she picked her wardrobe with great care. Harley hadn't seen her since she was a teenager in jeans and a bill cap, when she had accompanied her daddy to the Carruthers ranch on a cattle-buying trip.

Settled into her room at the Hilton in downtown Midland, Paige busied herself redoing her makeup. Then she pulled her long blond hair back and clasped it at her neck with a gold clip. The Albert Nipon godet suit in cherry red—she had bought it before her shopping expeditions had been squelched by poverty—hung in the closet. She slipped on the form-fitting skirt and admired the cute little flounces at the hem. The long sleeves would be perfect for the fall temperature. She buttoned the fitted jacket and straightened the collar. With her ears showing, the diamond studs from her daddy were perfect to complete the image of an upwardly mobile, career-minded young woman. Red leather Pradas and matching handbag lay on the bed.

Taking one last look in the mirror she gave herself a thumbs-up. *"Magnifique,"* she pronounced, which just happened to be the only word she had retained from six semesters studying the ridiculous French language.

Driving through Midland, the city seemed different from when she had last seen it. She remembered it being larger. Busier. The collapse of the oil economy had left a scar that showed more visibly in wide-open West Texas than in the crowded Fort Worth–Dallas

Metroplex. Midland still had its share of millionaires, Daddy had told her, but they weren't as rich as they had once been.

Along the stretch of highway between Midland and Odessa it was impossible to discern where one city ended and the other began. The highway from Odessa to Salt Lick, on the other hand, provided a marked contrast. The long road stretched in front of her like a silver ribbon. She had it all to herself, the vast landscape on either side flat and uncluttered by anything but a few mesquite trees, cactus, and tumbleweeds. And pumpjacks, as still as if they had been frozen midpump. Visible but static testimony to the vast lake of oil that lay beneath the West Texas sands and the engine that had once driven the area economy.

I'd hate to find myself stranded out here, Paige thought. Seconds later, the SUV began to pull to the right and she heard a sickening *whomp-whomp-whomp*. She came to a stop on the shoulder, slid out, and confirmed what she feared. Her right front tire was as flat as her surroundings.

She muttered a string of cuss words she usually didn't use, but a flat tire in the middle of nowhere was enough to make the pope cuss. What in the hell was she going to do? She had changed a flat tire before, but not in a three-hundred-dollar suit. And not on her way to a job interview that could change her life.

Think, Paige, think.

AAA! Auto Club!

Things were looking up. Her daddy had handed her the membership card and a speech about how if she ever got into trouble on the road to call them. She had stuck the card in her wallet and never thought of it again. Until now.

She returned to the cab, found the card, and plucked her cell phone from her purse. She just hoped someone wouldn't dally reaching her. Sitting alone on an isolated highway was not her idea of a good time.

Keying in AAA's emergency number, she noticed no high-pitched beeps accompanying her entry. Without looking, she knew. She hadn't charged the phone in several days. It was as dead as her career at McDonald's. Now it was nothing but a useless piece of plastic.

Daddy's words echoed in her head. *Don't be late, now.*

Late? She would be lucky if she got there at all.

If only she hadn't left her luggage at the hotel. If she had her suitcase, she could put on more appropriate clothing and change the tire. But that thinking made sense only now. To have loaded her SUV with her suitcases, when she was planning on returning to the hotel after meeting with Harley, wouldn't have been logical.

She had returned to the driver's seat, dejected and fighting back tears, when she heard the distant highway noise of a vehicle approaching from behind her. She glanced into her rearview mirror. Sure enough, an old pickup with a lone occupant was nearing. Desperate times called for a desperate prayer. *Lord, don't let this be a rapist. And if it is, please let him change my tire first.*

She leapt from her seat and took a stance in the middle of the highway, waving her arms over her head.

OF ALL THE THINGS Spur Atwater could think of that he didn't need at this moment, number one on the list was a damsel in distress. Leaving a woman, especially a drop-dead, good-looking blonde on the side of the road, was something he would never consider doing.

But if he ever would consider it, today would be that day. He had an appointment to meet Dr. Miller at the veterinary clinic in Salt

Lick for a walk-through. Spur had no intention of arriving late and making a bad impression.

Coming to a stop beside the leggy blonde in the red dress, he leaned across the seat and cranked down the passenger window. "Give you a lift?"

A long level look came at him from sky blue eyes, and something told him he had seen those eyes before.

"Thanks," she said, "but that isn't necessary. I'm in Triple A. If I can just borrow your cell, I'll call them." She held up a hot pink cell phone. "Mine's dead."

"Uh, sorry. Don't have a cell phone. I'm on my way to Salt Lick. If it'll help you out, I'm glad to give you a ride."

Her eyes traveled over his old truck. He thought she was thinking about taking him up on his offer when suddenly she assumed a coquettish look. "You don't remember me, do you?"

God, how he hated that helpless southern belle routine in women. Why couldn't they be direct? Peering over the top of his sunglasses, Spur looked closer at her face. *Shit! Daddy's girl.* What in the hell was she doing in the middle of the West Texas desert?

"I know you," he said, giving her the squint-eye. "The lady with the accountant . . . Or that is, daddy's accountant. Aren't you kinda far from the nearest mall?"

"That's none of your business. I need someone to help me. If you aren't willing, just drive on." She turned her head and stuck her nose in the air.

Spur looked around. Given the emptiness he saw in any direction, he was surprised by her attitude. He had half expected her to break into tears, at which point he would have had to put his truck in reverse and run over her. "I've offered you a ride to town, ma'am. I don't know what else I can do."

"I can't go to town and leave my SUV here. I can't risk it getting stolen or vandalized. Daddy'll—"

"Ma'am," Spur cut in. Daddy again. He didn't want to hear it. "I doubt if vandalism or theft will be a problem. This isn't the big city."

"I'm still not leaving it. Besides, I have to be on the other side of Salt Lick at the Carruthers ranch in less than an hour. If your business is in town, taking me to the Flying C would be out of your way. I don't want to trouble you, but can't you just change the tire?"

Ah, well, that explained some of it. This fancy-dressed socialite was attending a function at the millionaire's home. No surprise that she took no notice that Spur was dressed up himself—a starched white dress shirt, his only one, and starched jeans. And even if she *had* noticed, she wouldn't care. "You think changing a tire's no trouble?"

"Well, not for someone like you."

He tucked back his chin and stared at her. "Someone like me?"

"I meant someone big. And strong. You look like you could— Dammit, are you going to help me or not? I'm happy to pay you if that's what you're worried about."

It was so typical of the rich to whip out the ol' wallet and buy a solution to every problem. Leaving Miss America stranded on the side of the road would serve her right. But it wasn't in him to be that mean.

Throwing open his door, he stepped out of his truck and strode toward her, loosening his cuffs as he walked. Setting his jaw and locking his gaze on her face, he pulled his shirttail from his waistband, unbuttoned his shirt and whipped it off.

Her eyes grew round as saucers. She backed away, yanked off one of her high-heeled shoes, raised it over her head, and hopped into a half-squat like a Sumo wrestler. Her skirt rode up her thighs, clear to her panty line.

"Don't take another step," she warned. "I know martial arts."

Jee-zus Christ. A bona fide nut if he had ever met one. Spur leveled a withering gaze at her as he walked past, extending his shirt in her direction. "Hold this for me, *grasshopper,* while I get this tire changed. And don't let it get wrinkled and dirty."

He marched to the rear end of the—what was it, a Cadillac? "Gimme your keys," he said.

She went to the cab, returned with the keys, and placed them in his hand. "I'm sorry. It's just that I thought—"

"I know what you thought. It doesn't matter. Look, Scarlett, you're not the only one who's got to be somewhere, so just step out of my way and let me get this done."

She watched in silence, thank God, as he dug tools and a spare tire from the back of the Cadillac and set about changing her tire. In less than half an hour, he finished and laid the flat tire and the tire tools inside the back end of the SUV. "That does it. You're all set."

He looked down. Shit. His shined boots and his jeans were covered with white caliche dirt. And black grime. He began to dust the front of the jeans with his dirty palms, making the situation worse. Mumbling and cussing, he yanked his clean handkerchief from his back pocket and began to wipe his hands. "You shouldn't drive on that phony tire any longer than you have to. And you shouldn't drive fast."

She approached with his shirt. When he reached for it, their fingers touched for a second. She jerked her hand back and stared at him as he shrugged into the shirt. He stared back as he buttoned it. He turned then and headed for his truck, undoing his belt and fly and tucking in his shirttail as he went.

"Thank you so much," she said behind him. "I really appreciate it. Maybe we'll—"

He shut her off by climbing into his truck and slamming his dented door. Pulling away, he threw one last look in his rearview mirror. She was still standing in the middle of the highway on those mile-long legs. A part of him felt uncomfortable leaving her out there all alone. He couldn't keep from thinking about one of his sisters being left in the same predicament. He would drive slow, he decided, and watch out for her.

Paige McBride. Her name was engraved on a pink piece of notepaper stuffed in his wallet. She was the last person he expected to ever run into again. She was the last person he should feel drawn to. Wasn't she the epitome of everything that disgusted him in women? Wasn't she way out of his league?

Of course, she was.

He had bigger fish to fry anyway. A dream was within his grasp. Getting tangled up with a ditzy blonde and screwing up everything just wasn't going to happen.

He watched in his rearview mirror as she pulled onto the highway and drove behind him.

five

Drying her hands on a paper towel, Debbie Sue Overstreet walked outside the Styling Station. Her best friend and business partner, Edwina Perkins-Martin, was yelling directions up to her husband, Vic Martin, who worked at mounting an additional sign alongside the Styling Station billboard atop the building. When Vic started this project, the biggest problem, as Debbie Sue could have told anybody, was his dogged determination to do it his way, thereby ignoring Edwina's instructions.

Edwina, who had given up Marlboro Lights a few months back, shoved a stick of gum into her mouth and called out, "Vic, honey, please remember how much I love you when I say this, but if I had a gun right now, I'd shoot you off that roof. Why are you so stubborn? I keep telling you what you need to do and you just go right on like I don't have good sense and do it a different way."

Vic Martin and Edwina had been married a year, after living together several years prior to the wedding. Vic was a retired navy SEAL, now given to the independent solitude of driving big rigs across the country. He would take guff from only one living person, and that was the skinny, long-legged brunette now handing him just that. He gave her a devilish grin. "It's my stubbornness that's kept us together so long, Mama Doll."

Debbie Sue squinted up at Vic and the sign. "How's it going?"

Vic's attention swung to Debbie Sue. "Hey, cowgirl, how's this look?"

DOMESTIC EQUALIZERS the sign read. Debbie Sue still had a hard time believing that the beauty salon she had owned and operated for the past five years was now a private investigation agency as well as a salon. "Super," she answered.

Vic stepped down the ladder and came to stand beside them. Edwina used her hand to block the sunlight as she peered upward. "Well, I'll be damned. It does look great. I take it all back, sugarfoot." She raised on her tiptoes to plant a kiss on Vic's cheek. "You're the best."

Besides being the best, he was the only man Debbie Sue had ever seen with whom Edwina could wear her high-heeled platform shoes and still have to tiptoe to kiss him.

Debbie Sue stared at the new sign, still in awe over what it represented. And all that had transpired in the short year since Alex Martinez had been arrested for Pearl Ann Carruthers's murder.

She had collected a fifty-thousand-dollar reward for solving the murder and facilitating his arrest. She tried to split it with Edwina, as had been their original agreement, but her partner in crime solving had refused to take half.

"We put a lot of the pieces together," Edwina told her at the time, "but our jigsaw turned out to be the wrong puzzle. It was you alone, girlfriend, who figured out the killer's identity. It was *you* who risked your life to catch the bastard."

Though Debbie Sue had remarried her former husband Buddy, who now had a job as a Texas DPS trooper and a regular paycheck, Debbie Sue still sought additional income.

Building on the publicity generated from solving Pearl Ann's murder, she dragged Edwina kicking and screaming into the private detective business. With Debbie Sue's daring and keen eye, Edwina's experience with three cheating, no-good ex-husbands, and opportunity to pick Vic's brain—after all, he was an expert in surveillance and covert techniques—the success of the business was guaranteed.

Edwina had extracted a promise that they would never get involved in anything life threatening. Debbie Sue agreed because Buddy wouldn't stand for the mother of his future children to do something dumb and dangerous.

Buddy had been the sheriff of Salt Lick back when Pearl Ann's murder occurred. Now, working toward his lifelong goal of becoming a Texas Ranger, he was not happy about the Domestic Equalizers and watched both equalizers with as close an eye as his DPS trooper job allowed.

Debbie Sue had never thought the detective gig would catch on, really. She was stunned to find the Domestic Equalizers' phone never stopped ringing. Both men and women sought them out to spy on philandering love interests.

"This calls for a drink," Edwina announced, giving a thumbs-up to the job Vic had done with the sign. "And a toast. I'll make the margaritas." She headed for the storeroom in the back of the Styling Station.

THE REMAINING DRIVE into Salt Lick proved uneventful for Spur. He twisted the radio knob until he came to a clear signal, a country music station. He appreciated the music and the chatter filling the truck cab's emptiness.

As he entered the town, he remembered he had been to Salt Lick as a kid of no more than thirteen. To his astonishment, except for a single hanging traffic light, little had changed. Small businesses still lined the two-lane main street. A metal awning bleached white by the sun still shadowed the store windows. Some new paint might have been added in places to the storefronts.

Spur had lived in several towns like Salt Lick. Small, dusty communities had once thrived in an oil and agriculture economy all over West Texas. Many had declined to almost ghost towns, but Salt Lick appeared to be different. It showed no boarded-up store windows, no run-down, abandoned buildings on the main street. A giant footprint of a Wal-Mart Super Center had yet to be stamped in the sand. The quaint mom-and-pop stores still ruled. That obvious fact, as much as anything, made the place appear to be frozen in time.

Yep, the decision to buy the veterinary practice and move here had been the right one.

Dr. Miller had given up his career for a woman. His assistant of the past fifteen years, Virginia Pratt, was relocating to Nashville, following her own career as a country music composer. Dr. Miller aimed to go with her. Amazing. Where did love of that depth and dimension come from?

"Not me, buddy," Spur mumbled. *No how, no way.*

Ahead loomed a squatty, pumice-stone square building on the corner of Main and Spanish Trail. A sign hung on a post out front. SHERIFF'S OFFICE. A tall, thin cowboy was throwing a lariat loop at a fire hydrant huddled on the corner of the sidewalk.

As Spur stopped to watch, the black Cadillac sped past him. "Thank God," he mumbled, continuing to watch the cowboy, whose rope slipped and knocked his hat to the ground. When the guy bent to pick it up, leaning too far, he lost his balance and fell forward, ensnaring his boots in the slack loop. He hit the ground, throwing his arms up and out in front of himself to cushion his fall and in the process, pulled the rope into a tight noose around his ankles. Within a matter of seconds he had hog-tied himself, and his hat lay crushed between him and the sidewalk.

Instead of being a testimony to the spirit of the West, the episode was a caricature of the lack thereof.

Sighing and shaking his head, Spur rolled down his window, set to ask if the guy needed help, when a frantic, plump woman waddled from the sheriff's office doorway.

"Sheriff, are you all right? Are you hurt?"

Sheriff? Spur grinned.

Yep, this was a place he could grow fond of.

REACHING SALT LICK, Paige was dismayed at how dilapidated and dingy the town looked. She had been here years ago accompanying Daddy on a cattle-buying trip to the Carruthers ranch. Back then, the town hadn't seemed so dinky and dirty. Of course her impression had been prejudiced by her opinion of the Flying C Ranch, which was larger than the McBride spread just outside the city limits of Fort Worth.

What appeared to be the only traffic light in town turned red, allowing a John Deere tractor to cross in front of her. The driver looked to be twelve. He nodded as he passed, his demeanor atypical for an adolescent boy. Paige had forgotten that kids in this part of the country, out of necessity, drove at young ages. Why not? What was there to run over?

Her gaze swerved to what, at first glance, appeared to be a service station on the corner—except that a tall, skinny brunette was busy draping belted trench coats on the two antique gasoline pumps in front. The upturned collars, the fedoras perched on the rounded tops and slender pedestal bottoms made perfect mannequins. What was *that* about?

The sign atop the building read THE STYLING STATION & DOMESTIC EQUALIZERS.

The woman dressing up the gas pumps looked familiar. Then, Paige recognized her. Edwina Perkins. Her picture had appeared in an article in *Texas Monthly.* She was one of the two Salt Lick hairdressers who had solved one of the most infamous murders in the history of West Texas.

Paige made a note of the salon's location. She prayed they did nails, dared not hope they also did massages.

As she left Salt Lick, motoring toward the Flying C, thoughts of the rugged cowboy who had fixed her flat and hefted the tire and tools around as if they were toys refused to leave her mind. Crossing paths with him again was so strange. He must live in this part of Texas. Otherwise, what would he be doing here? Why would anybody—besides her desperate self—be roaming this desolate part of the world if he didn't live here?

No wonder she continued to think of him. How could any normal woman not have stared at those muscular arms as he worked? Who could forget such a finely sculpted chest and abdomen? He had a six-pack all right and it wasn't the drinking kind.

Only two types of activity would develop a body into such good shape—hours in a gym or manual labor. In this part of Texas, the bodybuilding regimen had to be manual labor—working in the oil fields or cowboying for some ranch. *Phooey!* She knew, and had spent too much time, with both types.

She had been in a near swoon by the time he finished changing her tire, but he had given the dirt on his hands—and her—the brush-off. Why, he hadn't even talked to her. No conversation. Period. He grabbed his shirt and drove away as if she were some object in the road that had to be moved before he could move on.

All at once she realized her speed had reduced to a crawl. God, what was wrong with her? Instead of the cowboy's good looks, she should be considering his rudeness. A combination of sex appeal and bad-boy behavior had lured her to men like him in the past. Thank God, he didn't seem the least bit interested in her. That had to be a good thing. With a new life to plan, she didn't need any distractions.

Twenty minutes beyond downtown Salt Lick, Paige crossed the cattle guard entrance to the Flying C Ranch and roared up the caliche driveway. At the adobe-style main house a petite blonde woman crouched on her hands and knees digging among profuse blooms in one of the flower beds.

The woman got to her feet and came forward with a big smile. She had a red bandanna on her head, denim coveralls rolled to the knees, and an undeniable tummy bulge.

"Hi, you must be Paige? I'm Carol Jean Carruthers. Come on in and let me fix you some iced tea."

Was this the new—and improved—Mrs. Carruthers? It was common gossip that the only digging the former Mrs. had done was for gold. Except for beauty, Harley Carruthers's current wife appeared to be the polar opposite of his previous one. Paige slid out of the Escalade. They walked toward the house and Mrs. Carruthers looped her arm inside Paige's as if they had known each other forever.

"I'm sorry you caught me digging in the dirt," the new Mrs. Carruthers said, opening the front door and gesturing Paige inside. They stepped into a large, cool foyer with a red tile floor and golden walls on which hung the several Charles Russell originals that Paige remembered seeing before.

The Carrutherses' main house befitted a ranch located in the outreaches of West Texas—rugged leather furnishings, woven Santa Fe rugs, original western art hanging on the walls. It was everything a real ranch house should be, unlike the baroque antiques and frilly, silly decor her stepmother had filled Daddy's house with. From the day Margaret Ann moved in, Paige had felt like an interloper in that house and hoped she never had to live there again.

"I wanted to take advantage of this beautiful weather we're having," Mrs. Carruthers said. "I was hoping to make the place more, um, homey." She led Paige to a rustic red suede sofa in the giant living room. "Don't you think flowers are a wonderful way to be greeted?"

"Yes, ma'am," Paige said shyly.

"Ma'am? Oh heavens, don't call me that." A bubbly laugh erupted from the second Mrs. Carruthers. "Call me C.J. or Carol Jean. I answer to both. So tell me, how are things in Fort Worth? My girlfriends and I used to party in the Stockyards sometimes. We had so much fun. But that was a long time ago. I love your dress. You look like Career Girl Barbie. Has anyone ever told you, you look just like a life-size Barbie doll?"

Hoping the woman didn't mean to be hurtful by making the comparison, Paige smiled tightly. "Did you mention iced tea before? I would really love something to drink. I had some car trouble on the road—"

"Oh, no! You didn't!" Carol Jean's brow tented. "Are you okay? You should have called us. Were you out there long? Did anyone help you?"

Paige explained about the cowboy lending his assistance, including a detailed physical description. "Does that sound like someone who lives around here?"

Carol Jean tilted her head back and laughed. "That sounds like most of the men in these parts. 'Scuse me, I'll get you that tea."

Paige watched as her new friend left the room. She wanted to ask if a baby was on the way, but felt the question to be too forward. Harley entered with a huge grin on his face and Paige rose from the sofa to meet him. He briskly crossed the room, but instead of shaking Paige's extended right hand, he wrapped her in a big bear hug that threatened to smother her.

He set her away and looked her up and down. "Paige McBride, you're all grown up. I knew you'd be a beautiful woman one day and just look at you. Yep, a real beauty. You look just like—"

"I know. Barbie."

"Well, no, I was going to say you look just like your mother. I had a big crush on her when I was a kid. All of us knuckleheads did. She was an extraordinary woman. I've never seen anyone, man or woman, any better with horses. And she always smelled like an angel would if you ever met one."

Paige felt the sudden smarting of tears. The visual image of her mother had dimmed with time, but one thing she still remembered clearly was indeed her mother had smelled heavenly. "Thank you so much, Harley. That's nice of you to say. Congratulations on your marriage. I know it's been a year, but this is the first time I've seen you."

Carol Jean returned with a tray of tall drinks. Harley was quick to meet her and take the tray. "I guess you met *my* angel," he said, turning his head Paige's way.

"Isn't he just awful?" Carol Jean said. "Here I am, pregnant and big as a heifer, with dirt all over me, and he calls me an angel." She gave an affectionate push against his shoulder.

"When is the baby due?" Paige asked her.

"Four months."

"We can hardly wait," Harley added.

Carol Jean turned to her husband. "Look, sweetie, I'm going to leave you two to conduct your business. If you need anything, just holler. I'll be out in the kitchen." She turned back to Paige with a dimpled smile. "Find me before you leave. I want to show you the nursery."

Harley looked down at his wife with obvious pride. "She designed it herself."

After Carol Jean left the room, Harley took a seat on one end of the sofa and motioned for Paige to sit on the other. "Buck said you've had some problems finding a job in the Metroplex."

Funny how polite and tactful those words sounded. Much less stinging than *so you've been tossed out on your ass in everything you've tried.* "I've run into some bad luck, that's for sure. I appreciate you talking to me. I don't have a lot of office skills, but I'm a hard worker and I'm willing to start at any level."

Harley's expression turned quizzical. "Buck didn't tell you what I've got in mind for you?"

Fearing she was the butt of a joke, Paige smiled weakly. "He just said you thought you had something for me. Not much else. Just that."

"You know the caliber of horses I have here at Flying C. Cutting horses were an indulgence of Pearl Ann's, but one that's proving to be lucrative."

Boy, did Paige ever know the Flying C horses, some of the finest on hooves. She had seen Pearl Ann Carruthers sitting astride the magnificent Flying C mounts in cutting shows.

The joke in the horse society was that Pearl Ann might own good horses that were expert at cutting a calf from the herd and holding it at bay, but her real talent lay in cutting a cowboy from his human herd and cornering him in the nearest dark place. The cowboy might sport a flashy new belt buckle for his efforts in the arena, but everyone knew it was shined by Pearl Ann Carruthers. "I sure do. I still go to the shows in Fort Worth."

"You don't ride anymore?"

Paige sighed. "No. It was just too hard while I was in college. The last show I went to, Lester Clinton was your trainer. Did he stay on with you after . . . well, after—"

"Oh, yes. Lester's still with me."

Paige couldn't read Harley's expression, but she knew by the way he diverted his gaze to the liquid in his glass that she had touched a nerve. Lester Clinton, Pearl Ann's brother, had a reputation in Fort Worth almost as notorious as his sister's.

"That's the reason I wanted to talk to you, Paige. Lester needs an assistant. Someone who knows a cutting horse from a plow horse. I've been promising him I'd hire help. He's come up with a few of his buddies as candidates, but I told him I would be the one to choose. This is a serious business for me. I don't intend to provide housing and beer for his partying friends. He makes frequent trips out of here lately. He says they're business trips, but for all I know, he's looking for work somewhere else. I need someone I can depend on."

"Oh." Paige could feel her pulse quicken. She didn't know what to say. Harley seemed to be headed in a direction she hadn't planned on going or seen coming. She was here to discuss an office job and had prepared herself to accept any work he offered in that venue. Helping with his horses was something out of one of her daydreams and a little scary.

"I understand," Harley went on, "that you were a business major at SMU—"

Oh, drat! Six years had passed since Daddy and her stepmother had badgered her into enrolling in the prestigious SMU business school. "Well, yes, but—well, it was a long time ago."

"I want you to not only help with the daily maintenance of the horses, I want you to take an active role in the business end of the operation as well. You know the people, you know the shows, and you know the horses. You can watch the fees and expenses go out and the income come in. Pearl Ann always insisted that Lester have free rein. I went along, but I've been feeling I'm out of touch with that part of the business. When your dad called me, I saw an opportunity for both of us. Being Charlotte McBride's daughter, you bring a high degree of credibility to my horse operation. Respectability, too. At the same time, you can learn hands on how to breed and train a good cutting horse."

Credibility. Respectability. She had never heard more golden words. So it must be true that Daddy hadn't told about her melting her nail tips on the grill at McDonald's.

"Well, gosh. I'm flattered. But what about Lester. Won't he be upset?"

"If it was anyone but you, I'd say yes. But Lester has never been one to miss an opportunity with a beautiful woman."

"Oh," Paige said again, shrinking deeper into her seat. Just what did Harley expect her to do?

As if he had read her thoughts Harley continued. "All I'm asking you to do is provide some assistance to Lester. If I hired a capable man to help him, Lester would think him too much a threat, but he's chauvinistic enough to see a woman as less than his equal.

"A long time ago, I promised my former wife I'd look after her brother if anything ever happened to her. While she was alive she and I went out of our way to break every vow we made to each other, but now that she's . . . well, passed on, I'd like to try and keep just one. Besides, Lester's been here at the ranch since he was a kid."

Paige watched as Harley ran his finger around the glass rim. Something troubled him.

"Lester thinks he's the last link to the memory of his sister," Harley said, "and that I'd be happier to have him gone. That's not true, of course. My only aim is to upgrade my operation. The Flying C's reputation at horse shows has been tarnished, if you know what I mean. I'd like to restore some grandeur."

Paige was taken aback that he would regard her as someone capable of upgrading *anything*. Maybe she wasn't the screwup she had always felt she was. Harley evidently saw her as a responsible adult.

Whoa! The very thought almost gave her a chill.

This was the absolute last thing she had expected. On the one hand, here was her dream on a platter. The National Cutting Horse Association recognized Flying C horses as some of the best. The very notion of being near a potential champion was intoxicating.

The added task of a little bookkeeping wasn't daunting. She had never failed math. But just to be cautious and wise, she said, "Harley, could I please sleep on this overnight and get an answer back to you tomorrow?"

"By all means. Come out for lunch. I'll show you around the barns and we'll talk about it then."

six

T he cowboy pocketed the receipts the evening supervisor handed him in
exchange for the phony bills of sale for three horses. He bought the
blank bills of sale by the pad at an office supply store and kept them in his
truck's jockey box. No one at TAR had ever questioned their authenticity or
even really looked at them, for that matter.

When he first started bringing horses here he had been so careful to write
the fake name and address of the seller on the correct line. He had done his
homework and made the sales amount appear to be legitimate. The employees who received the horses cared so little about documents, he no longer worried about legitimacy. Now he just scrawled something on a blank bill of sale
and handed it to them. In exchange, he got an official-looking unofficial re-
ceipt verifying that he had made a delivery and was paid an agreed-on
amount.

Today he collected twenty-one hundred dollars. Not as much as he had
hoped to get, not as much as he had been paid in the past, but the three
horses he had delivered today were especially old and underfed. He had done
them a favor.

The foreman, dressed in a white lab coat, stood nearby, watching him shove the ramp back inside his trailer and secure the door latch. The foreman looked right and left and approached him. "Say, you're a pretty good supplier. I'm not allowed to make this offer to just anyone—we have to be on the watch for ASPCA spies—but would you like to take a tour of the facility?"

The cowboy stopped and glanced in the direction of the voice. "No, thanks. I know what goes on in there. I don't have to see it."

The man's shoulders squared, his chin lifted. "Sir, our operation's as humane as any you'll find."

The cowboy raised his palms and turned his head slightly. "Mister, I'm not passing judgment on what you do. As for myself, well, I'm just helping out Mother Nature a little. I've seen what happens to these old nags out in the pasture. Coyotes and ever' other kind of damn varmint you can think of picks 'em off. It's not a pretty sight. This is the best way out for 'em."

"Is that the speech you use to persuade owners to sell to you?"

"Naw, that's just the one I tell myself so I can keep on doing this. I gotta right to a life as much as an old horse does."

seven

In the Styling Station/Domestic Equalizers establishment, Debbie Sue lounged in her hydraulic styling chair. The steady flow of customers had dwindled to the last one, who now sat under the dryer.

Edwina hung up the phone. "That's the second call I've had today. Someone asking if we can track down missing horses. What do you suppose that's all about?"

Debbie Sue laughed. "You kill me, Ed. I'm taking a wild guess here, but I'd venture to say someone's horse is missing."

"No shit, Sherlock. You're a regular Nancy Drew, ain't ya?"

Debbie Sue giggled. She enjoyed nothing more than getting Edwina's goat. Their sarcastic jabs were the result of a long friendship. There was nothing one would fail to do for the other, and they both knew it. "Maybe their fences were bad. Maybe their critter just walked off. Did you ask them about their fences?"

"Now, why would I do that? What do I know about fences? All

they wanted to know was if we tracked down missing horses. And I said, 'only if you want us to spy on somebody who's riding one.' End of story."

"Still, Ed, don't you think it's kind of odd that we'd get two of those calls in one day? Did you ask the age of the horse?"

Edwina stared back with a blank look. "You don't seem to be hearing me. Don't make me hurt you."

"I read an article about a big problem with horse theft in Texas. Mostly older horses." Debbie Sue couldn't keep from thinking of her own older horse, her beloved Rocket Man. "I'd hate to see that starting up around here. If there's another call, let me talk or take their number and I'll call them back."

Edwina unwrapped a Tootsie Pop using her talonlike fingernails. Today her nails were painted a vivid color she called "Janet Jackson's Nipple Ring Red." "Why would somebody bother stealing an old horse?" She tucked the red sucker into her jaw.

"For slaughter, Ed. The great state of Texas is one of the few states left where it's still legal to butcher horses. The slaughterhouses say it's done humanely, but I've read eyewitness accounts." Debbie Sue shook her head. "Trust me, there's nothing humane about it. I'd give you the details, but I can't stand to repeat them."

Edwina's brow knitted into a frown as she popped the lollipop from her mouth. "Slaughter for what? Are we talking the glue factory?"

"Sometimes it's for dog food, but the real money comes from the foreign meat market. Horse meat has always been desirable in some parts of Europe. And now, with the mad cow disease scare over there, the price of horse meat has more than doubled. A well-cared-for older horse can sell for seven hundred dollars or more."

"Why, that's not much," Edwina said, "especially when you think about what Harley Carruthers's horses are worth. He must have more than a million dollars on the hoof."

"The slaughterhouse people don't care whether the horses are performance horses or someone's old plug. They pay the same. They just care about the meat."

"Wow. This is hard to believe." Edwina shook her head. "Where are these slaughterhouses?"

"East of here. Not that far. Not far enough."

"That's disgusting. That's the worst thing I've heard this week."

A visual of Rocket Man being murdered mushroomed in Debbie Sue's mind and tears flew to her eyes. "It's heartbreaking. To think that someone's horse would undergo that kind of terror—"

"Now, don't bubble up. Hon, I know how much you love that horse of yours. It reminds me of when I was a kid and I had a dog I was crazy about. He disappeared and my mom told me he took a job out of the country, but I knew he was dead."

"Why in the world would she tell you something like that?"

"'Cause kids believe anything. She told us the same thing about our relatives. If somebody suddenly didn't show up at Christmas, she'd say, 'Oh, he's taken a job out of town.' When we got older, we learned that meant he was in jail. The more serious the crime, the farther the job. We finally caught on that if a relative had gone to work in another *country*, well, he was most likely on death row."

Debbie Sue stared at Edwina for several beats. Her friend's off-the-wall comments never ceased to amaze her.

Edwina squinted from behind the lenses of her rhinestone-studded cat's-eye glasses. "You learned all that stuff about horse stealing in just one magazine article? You know, if I'm gonna be a crime fighter, I've got to start reading. I usually just thumb through a magazine, looking at the pictures. I never read the articles, unless, of course, it's something about improving your love life or Russell Crowe."

"Hell, Ed, what could possibly improve your love life?" Debbie Sue swallowed the tears that had almost escaped when she thought of losing Rocket Man. "You and Vic have been on a honeymoon for over six years. I hope you don't tell me things are getting stale. You two are my only bright hope for long-term relationships."

Edwina licked her lollipop and grinned. "Vic and I are still like two horny teenagers. There's only one thing missing."

"What's that?"

"Russell Crowe!" Edwina cackled.

Debbie joined in, hiding her anxiety to get home and check on Rocket Man. She intended to talk to Buddy about moving her beloved horse to the pen closer to the house at night, just until the missing horses turned up. Better safe than sorry.

"SURE, I UNDERSTAND your concerns."

Paige was standing beneath a scorching sun on the driveway in front of the Carruthers home, listening to Harley speak. Though the temperature was hot, she felt fall in the air.

She had just told Harley her uncertainty about taking on the job he had laid out for her last night. When she left him and Carol Jean, telling him she wanted to sleep on the job offer, she had been dead serious. What he expected was the last thing *she* had expected, and she honestly did want to think about it.

In doing that, she had tossed and turned all night. Had Daddy known all along the kind of job Harley had for her? A part of her wanted to call him and discuss it; another part wanted to make her own decision like any other adult.

"Here's something to consider," Harley was saying. "Buck told me how much you want to work with horses. This is an opportunity for you to stay on here and do that."

Well, that comment answered her question. Her daddy had known Harley would hire her to help with his horses. "I don't know, Harley. I do love horses. I've always wished I could be like my mother. It's just a lot to think about right now."

Damn, she hated being wishy-washy.

"While you're thinking, want to take a look at my champions?"

"Sure," Paige said. What could be wrong with just looking?

Harley motioned her to follow him. A limestone slab pathway led to the huge barn adjacent to an arena. A few steps later, Harley stopped and said, "Wait while I tell Carol we're going to the barn."

He had scarcely walked away when Paige heard a whinny and a commotion from a circular paddock to her right. She walked a few more feet and spotted a pretty-boy cowboy she recognized as Lester. Cursing at a young horse, he gripped its bridle and planted a kick to the animal's side. The horse screamed, so frightened the whites of its eyes showed.

Without stopping to think, Paige started toward the horse. "Lester," she called out, holding back the rage she felt and hoping to thwart another kick to the poor horse. She forced a smile and kept her voice even. "Hi, Lester. Remember me? Paige McBride from Fort Worth?"

The cowboy turned and gave her a blank look, but at least he stopped abusing the horse.

"I was just talking to Harley," she went on. "I'm going to be your new assistant."

The words that had just spilled from her mouth left her dumbfounded. Something about the terror in the horse's eyes must have moved her mouth to engage before her brain. Before Lester could utter a response, Harley proclaimed from behind her, "Why that's terrific, Paige." He turned to Lester. "Meet your new assistant."

Yikes! Now a retraction was almost out of the question.

In a flash, Lester's expression went from *be*-mused to *a*-mused. It happened so quickly most people would have missed it, but since most people never took her seriously, Paige was accustomed to the look. Well, no matter. Even if the world thought her a dumb bunny, if there was an area in which she felt she could hold her own, it was in caring for animals, especially horses.

Lester led the horse over to the fence and looped the reins over the rails before climbing over. He gave her a head-to-toe, his evaluation so thorough she half expected him to open her mouth and check her teeth.

He laughed a lascivious heh-heh-heh. "Leave it to ol' Harley here to hire the prettiest little gal I've ever seen."

His eyes moved over her one more time before he offered his hand. When Paige shook hands, he enclosed her hand in his and pulled it to his chest. Paige bit back an urge to tell him his attempt at charm was wasted. She had heard enough about him to be apprehensive, and now she had witnessed him doing something that repulsed her.

She made an effort to remove her hand, but he held on tight.

"You say your name's Paige?"

"Yes. I'm from—"

"Fort Worth." He finished her sentence and leered at her with a phony grin.

She pried her hand from his. Now she knew how the calves felt in cutting events when they were separated from their herd and left alone to outmaneuver the horse.

"I remember seeing you at the last cutting in Fort Worth," Lester said, "when Chiquita Pistol won the Triple Crown. I had an entry that should have taken her, but I had some bad luck with the calves."

Leave it to a half-assed cowboy to blame the cow, the horse, or bad luck instead of admitting his own shortcomings. "Chiquita Pistol's a champion all right. Good breeding shows up in animals. . . . And human beings, for that matter."

Lester leaned in. "Sometimes you can't look at breeding alone. Training and discipline can make a difference. Unruly horses have to be handled with a firm hand. I've yet to meet my match with a strong-spirited filly."

Paige narrowed her eyes and turned to face him, primed to bless him with her true thoughts when Harley stepped in. "Paige, we've got living quarters here at the ranch. You're welcome to stay in one of the bunkhouses, but I doubt it's what you're used to. Carol suggested you might prefer to live in town. If that's what you want, she knows some folks who have rentals. Would you like to talk to her about it?"

Deciding she would have her turn with Lester eventually, Paige dropped the miniconfrontation. "That sounds great, Harley."

"Come on up to the house, then. Carol's almost got lunch ready."

As Paige walked away, she looked over her shoulder at Harley's horse handler. "I look forward to working with you, Lester. I'm sure there's a lot you can teach me."

Lester showered her with a movie-actor smile and swept his hat from his head. "I'm looking forward to us getting closer, Miz McBride. This'll be a learning experience for both of us."

Paige shuddered and hurried to catch up with Harley.

Lunch turned out to be one of the most pleasant she had enjoyed in a long time. Carol Jean was entertaining in a down-home way and hospitable. The meal of salad, chicken enchiladas, and black-eyed-pea salsa was delicious. Harley remarked repeatedly that she had no kitchen help.

He looked at his wife with unabashed affection. They frequently touched hands across the table, and each time Carol Jean left to return to the kitchen for something, he rose from his chair. Paige was envious. She had never experienced so loving a relationship with the opposite sex.

Eventually the topic came to the housing situation and Paige was thrilled when Carol Jean said her best friend Debbie Sue Overstreet had a small house for rent in Salt Lick.

"It's just darling," Carol Jean said. "Debbie Sue and Buddy lived there before they got a divorce. Two bedrooms. One bath. After Buddy moved out, Debbie Sue fixed it up so cute. It has a big backyard and a nice covered patio. Lord, I can't even remember all the margaritas I've drunk on that patio with her and Edwina."

Paige's memory harkened back. "I've read about them in *Texas Monthly,* but the article didn't mention that Debbie Sue and her husband were divorced."

Carol Jean seemed momentarily lost in thought, then her face brightened. "Oh, they're not divorced."

"But you just said—"

"This is their second marriage."

"Oh, I thought you said they got a divorce."

"They did get a divorce, but now they're married."

Paige, growing more confused, said, "Well the important thing is they've got a house to rent, right?"

"Right. Debbie Sue's mother's gone to Nashville to write music, and Debbie Sue and Buddy moved into her house. It's bigger and it's on twenty-five acres. Debbie Sue can be near her horse. Rocket Man's one of the family. If she and Buddy ever have kids, Rocket Man will probably be jealous. Before you leave I'll write down her phone number and you can give her a call."

After the meal Paige volunteered to help clean the kitchen. Harley removed himself to the den area so the two women could girl-talk. Paige was enjoying herself, forging a friendship with Carol Jean. She couldn't remember the last time she had spent with a female when she wasn't picking up the tab. Other than Sunny, who was out of town more than half the time, Paige had never had a true girlfriend.

They finished up in the kitchen and joined Harley in the den. He stood when they entered. "Okay, you," he said to Carol Jean. "Time you got off your feet." He tugged her toward the sofa. "Here, you sit down. I've got your lotion. I'll give you a foot rub."

"Is this not the sweetest man ever?" Carol Jean said. "Let me write down something for Paige, then I'm ready."

Fifteen minutes later Paige departed the Flying C with her future landlord's phone number in her fist. She considered calling from her cell phone but decided to wait until the next day. She was anxious to get back to her hotel room and talk to her daddy. She had so much to tell him and there was much for him to tell her. Like, for instance, if he knew the full truth about the job at the Flying C, why he had neglected to tell her.

Going to the ranch and seeing Harley again had helped her make a decision. Meeting Carol Jean had been terrific, but the clincher had been seeing the rough way Lester treated the horses for which he was supposed to care.

Driving through town she spotted a battered pickup that looked all too familiar parked in front of Hogg's Drive-in. For one impetuous moment she considered turning back and going into the hamburger joint. She had run into the pickup's gorgeous, mysterious owner twice now and both encounters had been disasters. Dare she chance a third meeting?

Something told her to drive on. Could it be common sense? Had the short stay in this small town already started a process practically foreign to her before now? Whatever it was, she liked it. She liked the feel of her newfound independence. She liked the idea of making her own money.

Money? She hadn't even asked Harley about the pay. *Well, drat.* She would mark the oversight up to inexperience as a job hunter, but, in truth, it was pure excitement and adrenaline that had clouded her thinking.

Before she knew it she was back in Midland. The time it took to drive from Salt Lick had passed faster than the drive to it. Paige attempted several times to reach Daddy, but she was unable to get a signal. Apparently the wide open spaces of West Texas were beyond Ma Bell's roaming capabilities.

Oh, well, it was probably best she didn't talk to Daddy just yet. She didn't want to let him know she had forgotten to ask about her salary. Yep, before she called him to give him a report or before she called Debbie Sue to rent her house, she would find out the amount of her salary. Wow. Two practical judgment calls within the same day. A pattern could be forming.

She stopped under the canopied entrance to the hotel, giddy

with excitement, flashed the valet a killer smile as she alit from the Escalade, and tipped him generously. Back in her room, with some hesitation, she dialed Harley's number. She felt sure he and Carol Jean had settled in like two lovebirds as soon as she drove off and she hated bothering them. On the third ring Harley answered with a simple "Harley Carruthers" in his "who the hell is this" voice.

"Harley," Paige gushed, "I'm so sorry to bother you, but before I call about renting a house from someone, I thought I'd better find out how much you plan on paying me. I'm sure I was supposed to negotiate before saying yes to your job offer, but I'm a little green at this. Kind of coming in the back door so to speak."

"No problem, Paige. I'm sorry I didn't tell you. I was so happy to hear you say you'd come to work, I forgot to bring it up. Twenty-eight thousand a year. That may not sound like much, but living in Salt Lick is really inexpensive compared to life in the Metroplex. That includes medical and dental of course."

Paige had her PDA in hand and entered the numbers. It came to about twenty-three hundred a month. Hmmm. She had no idea if that was a good salary for her new job. What she did know was that it was a hell of a lot more than the zero dollars she had been offered before now. "That's great, Harley. I'm going to head back to Fort Worth tomorrow morning. Provided I have a place to move into, I'll be back in a few days."

"No problem. I'm sure you and Debbie Sue can work something out. Tell your dad hello for me and I'll see you next week."

The next number she keyed in was Debbie Sue's. A deep male voice answered, "Overstreet."

The voice carried an authoritative, commanding tone. Instantly, Paige determined that Buddy Overstreet was the last person she wanted to hear say "Could I see some ID?" "Uh, sir? Could I please speak to Mrs. Overstreet?" To her ear her own voice sounded child-like and shaky.

When Debbie Sue came on, Paige introduced herself and explained she was interested in the rental house.

"Welcome to Salt Lick," Debbie Sue said. "Where are you and your husband moving from?"

"Oh, I'm not married. It's just me. I'm moving from Fort Worth."

"Really?" Paige heard surprise in the question. "Not a lot of single women move to Salt Lick from Fort Worth. In fact, not a lot of single people move here from anywhere, but this week's been an exception. An unmarried guy came by the shop this afternoon asking about the house."

"Oh, phooey. I'm too late?"

"No. He decided the rent was a little steep. I'm asking four hundred a month, but the utilities are included and it's partially furnished. You'll have to bring your own couch and a chair for the living room. Would you like to see it?"

Paige was bowled over by the amount. The condo in Fort Worth had cost six times that. The utilities alone had run four hundred. "I'll take it. I don't need to see it. Carol Jean Carruthers told me it was darling."

"You know C.J.?"

Paige had learned early in life the benefits to be derived from name-dropping. "I just met her. I had lunch with her and Harley earlier. I'm going to be working at the Flying C, helping the horse handler."

"Wow. Harley wouldn't hire just anyone. You must know a lot

about horses. I'm surprised Lester Clinton's standing still for Harley to bring in a woman. He likes women all right, but for different reasons."

"Let's just say Lester isn't too thrilled, but I'm not going to lose sleep over it."

Debbie Sue let out a wicked laugh. "Paige, you sound like my kind of person. The house is yours."

eight

The small house the Overstreets had for rent would have been perfect for Spur, but, as usual, he couldn't afford it.

Spur Atwater had spent his life putting his desires behind his checkbook, had started with nothing and still had most of it left. But thanks to the best education to be had in Texas, maybe his luck was turning. For now, he would live in an RV parked behind the veterinary clinic. Adequate. That was the word he used after looking at the RV, which was offered by Dr. Miller. *Adequate* was not a word that easily formed on the lips of an overachiever. The word was simply not . . . adequate.

He and Dr. Miller had hit it off right away. The departing vet would miss his life in Salt Lick but made it clear he had no qualms about Spur being able to handle the practice that had taken years to build. Miller spoke of his new life with excitement. He obviously adored Virginia Pratt. Youthful and attractive, she had a down-to-earth attitude and a wicked sense of humor.

From what Spur could see, Virginia's daughter, Debbie Sue Overstreet, had the same qualities. She and her husband, Buddy, had already invited him to supper.

They had warned that life for a single person in Salt Lick wasn't electrifying. Buddy remarked that a fellow might have to travel to Midland or Odessa to meet women to date. Spur couldn't help but notice Debbie Sue gave her husband a murderous glare.

The point was moot. Spur hadn't come here to meet women. He had planned his life like a carefully drawn offensive play. He knew exactly what needed to happen and when. Entanglement with a female wasn't yet in the playbook. Not that he was opposed to a session of casual sex now and then. His roommate in his boxers made it all too clear, and often, that he was being neglected.

ON SATURDAY, PAIGE returned to Salt Lick, her Escalade packed with clothes, shoes, and the kind of accessories that were, in all likelihood, seldom seen in her new location. She had more than enough of what was required for her new job—Wranglers, T-shirts, barn jackets, and boots. In her purse, she had a check for the rent already written. Her daddy had made another investment in her future.

Switching from being a rich student filling empty days with guerrilla shopping sprees and extravagant trips to neat places to horse caretaker in remote West Texas still felt like an out-of-body experience.

Before leaving Fort Worth, she had gone to dinner at the house shared by her daddy and her stepmother, Margaret Ann. When Paige described Salt Lick and outlined her future job, her stepmother's jaw nearly dropped into the salad. More than the social climber could stand, the thought of a woman getting dirt under her fingernails taking care of animals was, in her words, just so unrefined. All the anguish Paige had suffered up to this point had been worth it just to see her stepmother sputter.

It was late in the afternoon when Paige pulled into the parking lot reserved for the Styling Station's customers. She had looked forward to this moment and making a good first impression. But not with her material possessions, because from what she had read of Debbie Sue and Edwina, possessions or status would mean little. All Paige wanted was for them to accept her as a good person, not a rich bimbo propped up by her daddy's wallet.

Sleigh bells whacked the wooden front door and jangled as she entered the Styling Station. From the appearance of the exterior— aged red rock and a rusted tin roof—Paige hadn't known what to expect inside, but to her surprise, the place was bright and airy with a retro look and very clean.

Two elderly women were seated under the only two hair dryers. One was engrossed in a copy of *Truck Stop Confessions*. She didn't look up. The other woman, asleep, was in danger of sliding right off the chair to the floor. With bright auburn hair rolled on green curlers, she looked like a discarded Christmas ornament.

Before Paige could react the woman she recognized from *Texas Monthly* as being Edwina Perkins emerged from behind a drawn curtain, a lollipop stick extending from the corner of her mouth. "Be with you in just a sec, hon."

She walked to the dryer, removed the sucker from her mouth, leaned in, and yelled to be heard above the dryer's roar. "Maudeen? . . . Maudeen, honey, wake up. You're about to slide off the chair."

The old woman roused, mumbling, "Is it better with my teeth in or out?"

"You've got about ten more minutes," Edwina said. "Try to stay awake, hon."

The elderly woman gave a thumbs-up and her eyes fluttered closed again.

Paige watched with concern. "Are you sure she's okay? What was that about her teeth?"

"Trust me, it's probably best not to know." Holding the lollipop stick between her fingers like a cigarette, the lanky brunette planted the opposite hand on her hip and stared down at the sleeping old lady. "God, I sometimes wonder if these chairs need side rails. She's slid off a dozen times. I swear she's just one shampoo and set away from a broken hip." Edwina looked across her shoulder at Paige. "How can I help you, hon?"

"I'm Paige McBride. I was hoping to catch Debbie Sue here."

"Oh." A pause followed. "Debbie Sue told me about you. You're moving to Salt Lick? Well, welcome. Debbie Sue and her hubby just left to run an errand, but they'll be back in a little bit." Edwina looked her up and down in no subtle way. "Make yourself at home."

Paige knew when she was being sized up. She and the circumstances of her move were bound to have been discussed by Harley's wife. "I suppose you're wondering why someone like me would be moving here?"

"Oh, not really. Everybody has to float his own boat, as my honey, Vic, would say."

The telephone warbled and Edwina excused herself. Her tone of voice changed—all-business, no-nonsense. "Thanks for calling Domestic Equalizers. Don't *run* over him, just *get* over him. How may I help you?" She winked at Paige.

While Edwina scribbled on a notepad, muttering an occasional "Uh-huh" and "I understand completely," Paige made a quick scan of the salon, starting with the rusty red Mexican tiled floor. Light tan paint covered the walls and woven white curtains hung on the windows. The only other colors were the teal dryer units with matching hoods and the teal Formica station's countertops. All in all, the Styling Station had the same trappings as many of the salons in which Paige had been a customer.

Personal items scattered about gave the place a comfortable appeal. Paige was inspecting a picture hanging on the wall of a young barrel racer on a paint horse circling a red-white-and-blue oil drum, when the front door's sleigh bells jangled again. Paige looked toward the door and saw a handsome couple come into the room. The man, wearing a DPS trooper's uniform, could have been a double for a younger Tom Selleck, and the woman was pretty and physically fit, with red-blond hair halfway down her back.

Oh sure, Paige had seen beautiful people before. She had functioned in their company all her life. High maintenance, well dressed, impeccably groomed. This couple was different. Nothing was overdone. They were real. This had to be Buddy and Debbie Sue Overstreet.

Buddy apparently didn't see her. "There's a high-dollar moving van out front filled with clothes," he said to Edwina. "Who's driving it?"

"That would be mine," Paige answered. She stepped toward the couple and extended her right hand. "Hi, I'm Paige McBride. You must be the Overstreets."

Debbie Sue looked surprised and shook her hand. "It's good to finally meet you, Paige." Buddy followed up with a smile and a firm handshake.

"I guess I should have called. It's just that I've had so much to do. I've brought a check for the rent." She picked up her purse and after rummaging inside, came up with a check for first and last months' rent and handed it to Debbie Sue.

"We didn't expect you so soon. Saying good-bye to your friends in Fort Worth must have been easier than you thought it would be."

"There really wasn't anyone but my dad. I was hoping I could move into the house today."

A glance passed between Debbie Sue and Buddy.

"Is there a problem? Oh, I hope it's still available."

"Oh, absolutely," Debbie Sue said. "It's just that, well, we've had some painters in there all day. Their equipment is everywhere. They won't finish 'til tonight. If I'd known you were coming so soon—"

"Please don't apologize. I should have called. I'll go back to Midland and get a room for the night."

"I don't mean to tell you how to conduct your business ma'am," Buddy interjected, pushing the brim of his hat back with two fingers, "but as loaded down as your rig is, it wouldn't be safe parked just anywhere, not even in an attended garage."

This tall, deep-voiced man in a Texas Department of Public Safety uniform, with a gun strapped to his belt, was as intimidating in person as his voice had been on the phone. She nodded obediently. "Yessir. You're right, sir. Of course. I wasn't thinking. Uh, uh . . . I'm not sure what to do."

"Don't fret," Debbie Sue said, "you're spending the night with us. We've got plenty of room and we'll get a chance to get to know each other. Your stuff will be safe, too. Our place is way off the beaten path."

"Oh, I couldn't possibly. I wouldn't want to be an inconvenience." She frowned and bit her lip. "This is all my fault—"

"Don't apologize. You're our guest and that's final." She gave Buddy a kiss on his cheek. "Sweetie Pie, could you go by the house and let those painters know they *have* to finish up tonight for sure?" She turned back to Paige. "Our place is easy to find. It's ten miles out of town. Ed's an artist, so she can draw you a map. Plan on being there for supper around seven. I'm not much of a cook, so all I can guarantee is there'll be plenty of food and it'll be filling."

Lighthearted, map drawn with an eyebrow pencil in hand, Paige returned to her SUV. Everyone she had met was so friendly. A good feeling about her move to this small town washed over her. Maybe taking care of Harley's horses wasn't the same as having a gold-embossed degree hanging on the wall, maybe it wasn't a position with a prestigious law firm, but it was something in which she could take pride and something she would do on her own. She had every intention of continuing the practice of random acts of logic and senseless acts of unselfish self-control.

"Mom," she said, looking up at the sky, "I wish you were here. You'd be so proud of me."

Today was the first time Paige had *ever* uttered those words.

DEBBIE SUE AND EDWINA watched as Paige left the parking lot.

"She's pretty, isn't she?" Edwina unwrapped a chocolate Tootsie Pop. "For somebody superrich, she seems down-to-earth. Did C.J. say why she came to a place like Salt Lick and why she's shoveling horseshit for low wages?"

"Just that her dad and Harley have some kind of connection. And something about her wanting to follow in her mother's footsteps."

"Hm. Wonder what life would be like if your daddy was the richest man in Texas."

"Different from ours, that's for sure. By the way Ed, who was on the phone just now?"

"A call for the equalizers. Javelina Huffman from Ozona. Been married ten years. Eight kids. She's convinced her husband's having an affair."

"What makes her think so?"

"He's started taking baths and brushing his teeth. She says that's foreplay for Joe Eddy, and it ain't her he's playing with." Edwina shoved the lollipop into her mouth.

Debbie Sue shook her head. "You know, some people just don't recognize a good thing when it happens to them. If nothing else, we should find out who the lucky woman is so Javelina can send a thank-you note."

"You got that right. Hey, when you invited Paige to spend the night, did you forget that good-looking new vet is coming to your house tonight for supper?"

Debbie Sue curled her lips into a wicked grin. "Nope, I didn't forget."

Edwina grinned, too. "Are we adding matchmaking to the equalizers' duties?"

"Why, whatever do you mean, Ed?"

nine

By nature Paige maintained an upbeat attitude, and today she had something about which to be truly positive. She had been given a new job doing something she knew she would love and had stumbled onto new friends who seemed to like her for herself instead of her daddy's money.

But as she headed toward the Overstreets' home, humming along with the radio, everything felt almost too grand. Her history pestered her and threatened to undo her positive thinking. She was having difficulty defeating the feeling that something was set to go horribly wrong.

Passing through town it occurred to her she would be showing up empty-handed to a dinner in a private home. She should take a gift. A bottle of wine would be appropriate, but Paige saw no place in town that looked like it sold alcohol. Flowers would be suitable, but she didn't see a floral shop, either. *Drat.*

The quickest and best thing to do was stop and ask someone where she could buy wine or flowers. At the edge of town, she saw a business that appeared to be open, Salt Lick Veterinary Medicine. *Oh, good.* Here was her chance to not only get information, but also to introduce herself to a person with whom she would be working closely—the veterinarian.

Door chimes pinged her arrival, but she found the reception room empty. Instead of a smiling, welcoming face, what she saw was a hand-printed sign. RECEPTIONIST NEEDED. REQUIRED TO LIKE ANIMALS AND PEOPLE. *IN THAT ORDER.*

A male voice called out from the back, "Be with you in just a minute."

While she waited for someone to come into the reception room, she scanned the framed documents on the wall, noting that the vet, Dr. Miller, had graduated from Texas A&M. The graduation year meant he was likely in his late fifties or early sixties.

Moving around the room, she continued her perusal of the walls. As she reached a corner, she stopped in the nick of time. Apparently a large dog had been in the room earlier and left a sizable deposit on the floor. "Yuck!"

Recoiling, she stepped backward and felt the three-inch knife-blade heel of her Manolo Blahnik boot make contact with something soft.

"Sonofabitch," a male voice cried.

She did a one-eighty and found herself face-to-face with the libido-enhancing mystery man. Her breath caught. "Oh, my God! I'm so sorry. Did I hurt you?" Even red faced and in pain he was still sexy enough to warm her panty hose. "I mean . . . uh . . . how *badly* did I hurt you? Why aren't you wearing shoes?" She pointed at a red circle that had formed on the top of his socked foot. "That isn't blood, is it?"

"Naw," he ground out from between clenched teeth, "that's not blood. I drew a big red dot on top of my foot so you'd have a target." He yanked off his sock and examined his foot, his face twisted into a grimace. "If you must know, I took my boots off 'cause I've been tromping in cow shit all day." He straightened, dangling his sock from one hand. "You seem determined to do me bodily harm with those things you call shoes."

Oh, hell. Hadn't she made an impression on him at all? The shoe she had threatened him with out on the highway was a red pump. Tonight, she was wearing black ankle boots. Correcting him probably wasn't the best thing to do at this time, but she couldn't let the misconception stand. "These are different shoes," she said and held up one foot.

"And your point is?" He hobbled over and braced a hand against the wall.

"Well you don't have to be sarcastic. I said I was sorry. If you'd done your job and cleaned up this mess and if you hadn't sneaked up behind me—"

"Paige, the only sneaking I'd do in your presence would be to escape in the opposite direction from where you're headed. I've been in tornadoes less dangerous than you." Testing pressure on his foot, he grimaced again. "If you'll excuse me, I'm going to my trailer to take care of this. Please show yourself out."

Short of setting herself on fire she could think of nothing more she could do to get this guy to pay attention to her. The real frustration lay in the fact that he was the first man she had ever met who kept sneaking back into her thoughts.

She watched him limp away. Well, there was a bright side. He *had* remembered her name.

As she turned to leave another thought came to her. He probably worked here cleaning stalls and cages. Would his injury prevent his doing his job? Would it mean lost wages? Perhaps he needed medical attention.

She had to make amends, had to help this man who had helped her.

Clinging to that noble intention, she followed him out the building's back door. A battered travel trailer huddled a hundred feet away on the far side of a gravel parking lot. With its rounded edges and faded green color, it almost looked worse than the beat-up pickup he drove. He pulled open the door and climbed into the trailer.

Paige lifted her wallet from her purse and counted her cash. One hundred fifteen dollars. She had hoped it would last until payday, but her needs no longer mattered. She tucked fifteen dollars—the gas guzzler she drove demanded as much—back into her purse, then picked her way across the parking lot, a hundred dollars tightly gripped in her hand, the high heels of her four-hundred-dollar boots sinking into the gravel with every step.

When she reached the trailer, on a deep breath she reached up and knocked on the door. "Hellooo? . . . It's Paige McBride."

No response.

"Uh, sir? Could you please tell me your name? . . . You know, we've never been properly introduced."

Another moment of silence. For all she knew he could be loading a gun.

"Spur, dammit! My name's Spur!"

The loud voice carried a distinctly unfriendly tone. Paige winced and frowned. "Uhm . . . Mr. Spur? . . . If you'll open the door, I'd like to talk to you."

She heard rustling. He was *definitely* loading a gun. She stood frozen.

A few thumps that sounded like heavy footsteps and the door flew open, almost striking her square in the face. The man looked down at her, laughing . . . Laughing! . . .

. . . And filling the trailer's doorway. And he was beautiful.

"Look," he said, "I'm sorry I was mean. I promise, sarcasm isn't the only side I have. It's just that my foot hurt so damn bad. I know you didn't step on me on purpose."

Hypnotized by his dark eyes filled with mirth, unable to tear her gaze from his perfect lips, Paige's tongue stuck to the roof of her mouth. Finally she found a smile of her own. "I just wanted to see if you needed help with your fuck—I mean, your foot."

"My what?"

Oh my God! She gasped and slapped her fingers against her mouth. She felt as if she had been thrust into a vacuum, felt the earth turning on its axis. *Please, dear God. Please, tell me I didn't say "help with your fuck."*

Mr. Spur threw back his head and roared with laughter. "Now that, lady," he said when he stopped for a breath, "is an original question."

If it were possible to know how red felt, Paige now knew. She fumbled for words. "I'm—I'm so sorry, Mr. Spur. . . . What—what I mean to say—"

"Thanks for the offer. I think my foot'll be fine."

Driven by her mission, Paige stepped forward. "Just in case you need medical attention I want you to have this." She extended her hand with the money. "It's a hundred dollars. I can get more if you need it."

As quick as a slap, the smile fell from his face "That how you handle all your problems, Miss America? A simple 'I'm sorry' won't suffice? You gotta toss some of daddy's money on top? Smear that green salve on every boo-boo. Thanks, but no thanks." He leaned out and grabbed the door that had swung back against the trailer's side. "Take your money and get away from me. And, by the way, just for the record, my name's *Spur*. Not *Mister* Spur. Who the hell ever heard of anybody with a last name, Spur?"

Crash! The metal RV door slammed, leaving her standing alone. She felt like the sole survivor of a plane crash, surrounded by horrific destruction.

Dejected and confused, she turned to leave but was gripped all at once by a fierce anger. How dare he address her in that tone when she had been trying to help? "Well, oh yeah?" she yelled at the door. "Whoever heard of Spur for a *first* name? I happen to know there's a town named Spur and it was probably named after somebody."

She attempted to take her dignity and march away, but as if the gravel parking lot were quicksand, her heels kept sinking and she found herself hobbling. *"Asshole,"* she mumbled.

"AND NOW, FOLKS, the number one tune on the Cow Country Countdown is a collaboration of Virginia Pratt's pen and Deana Carter's music. Here it is, boys and girls. 'My Heart May Be Broken, but My Hair Still Looks Great.' "

A thrill coursed through Debbie Sue every time she heard it. Deana Carter singing one of her mother's songs. She knew the lyrics by heart. After finishing beauty school and passing the state's test for her license, her mother had written the song for her. She squealed and turned up the volume.

Using the spatula as a microphone, she belted out the tune she and her mother had sung in duet many times. C.J. should be here.

As kids, Debbie Sue and C.J. had put on imaginary Grand Ole Opry shows, with Mom playing the piano and Debbie Sue and C.J. singing her lyrics.

After the song came to a climactic end, Debbie Sue checked the pork chops baking in the oven. She had made great strides the last year in competence in the kitchen. Resuming her role as Buddy's wife, she had vowed to be a more traditional spouse, which included learning to cook without burning the food and doing laundry without shrinking or fading every garment.

In her cooking endeavors she stuck with the tried and true, only occasionally venturing into something as exotic as a recipe with more than four ingredients. Luckily, Buddy's tastes were simple, and he didn't expect much.

Tonight's menu was breaded, oven-fried pork chops Vic had told her how to make. She had no problem with doing mashed potatoes, fried okra, and a green salad on her own. She also had yeast rolls Vic had baked. She debated for a fleeting moment if she would reveal that the homemade bread had been baked by someone other than herself. Nah, she decided at last.

Dessert was a chocolate pan cake made from a store-bought mix. Again, only four ingredients. What would the world do without Betty Crocker? She didn't know if she would ever master a layer cake, but weren't goals what made life worth living?

She heard the slap of the screen door closing and called out, "Sweetie, is that you?"

Buddy stepped into the kitchen with a big grin on his face. "That's a safe question for either me or the mailman, isn't it?"

Debbie Sue grinned. "The mailman would never come around this time of day. He's strictly a morning person."

Buddy enveloped her in his arms. "I'm a morning person, too." He nibbled on her neck. "Or have you already forgotten about *this* morning?"

Her body responded, and if they had the time to spare, the kitchen table would have served. Again. If she and Buddy could spend all their time on sex, they would never have a problem. Rolling her eyes, she pushed him away. "C'mon. Let's not start something we can't finish."

"Oh, I intend to finish." Buddy reached for her again.

Debbie Sue did a quick side step. "I don't want our company to come in and see you standing here with a hard-on."

"Flash, I couldn't agree with you more." He made another attempt to grab her.

"Stop it." She giggled and put distance between them. "We've got time for that after everybody goes home."

Just then the sound of tires crunching gravel announced the arrival of one of their guests.

"See there? Now how would it look if they'd caught us?"

TEETH CHATTERING, Spur stumbled from the undersize tub-shower combo and straddled the commode. The hot water heater must be the size of a five-gallon bucket, because the choices in water temperature were *cold* and *colder*. But he had to endure. He couldn't show up for dinner at his new friends' without a shower and clean hair.

Banging his injured instep on the side of the fiberglass tub, he cussed a blue streak as he grabbed a towel. Whoever designed showers for RVs should be shot. No damn way could a man who was six three take a decent shower in a three-by-four bathroom. Jesus

Christ, he practically had to get on his knees just to put his head under the shower spray.

The furnace blew at full blast, but he continued to shiver, certain the trailer had no insulation. Well, it could be worse. He could be in North Dakota.

He dried quickly and briskly, thinking about a home-cooked meal at a table with real silverware. Being a small-town girl, Debbie Sue Overstreet was probably a good cook. Hogg's Drive-in did serve good cheeseburgers, but how many could a man eat? His tiny microwave was capable of heating only the smallest size of TV dinners, which he ate with plastic utensils.

He tugged on his briefs and added a T-shirt. Fall evenings in the high plains of West Texas were chilly. To wear with one of his two pairs of newer Wranglers, he dragged out a maroon sweatshirt, the only one he owned that didn't have A&M or AGGIES splashed across the front.

Sitting on the side of the bunk-size bed and working his sock on, pain re-reminded him of his injury. Four years of college football, playing against the toughest, biggest defensive players a quarterback ever faced and never a sidelining injury. Mostly bruises and turf burns. Now, one statuesque blonde with big blue eyes and a heart-stopping smile had shattered that record and damn near fractured his instep.

The wound's tenderness told him he wouldn't be wearing cowboy boots tonight. That left only an athletic shoe. He slipped on the shoes, left one unlaced, then grabbed his pickup keys and headed for the door, humming the A&M fight song. Nothing *ever* got the best of a Texas Aggie.

✳ ✳ ✳

STILL SHAKEN FROM her third disastrous encounter with the mystery man, Paige brought the Escalade to a stop in front of a vintage home at the end of a long driveway. Welcoming lights glowed in the windows, and after what had just happened, she needed that.

As she scooted out of the Cadillac, Buddy came out of the house and stood on the front porch that wrapped around the house. "Hey, Paige. Glad you found the place. Have any trouble?" The serious, all-professional manner of earlier in the day had disappeared.

"None at all. Edwina drew me a perfect map."

Debbie Sue walked up. "Hi, Paige. We're so happy to have you." Before Paige could speak Debbie Sue enveloped her in a hug. "I hope you don't mind simple cooking. Even if I'm not the best, my effort's sincere. My mom always said that had to count for something."

"I couldn't agree with your mom more. I never cook myself, but my best friend in Fort Worth has gone to a bunch of culinary schools. Unfortunately, she still can't cook." Debbie Sue laughed, so Paige added, "I do mix a margarita that will make you forget your troubles. Six years in college wasn't a total waste."

"That's good to hear. We'll make good use of that education." Debbie Sue took her by the arm and guided her onto the porch. "Did you bring a suitcase or something?"

"Yes, I'll get it."

"I'll get it," Buddy volunteered.

"Hey, that's nice of you." Paige handed him the keys. "It's on the front seat. An overnight kit and a small valise." She turned to Debbie Sue. "I feel just awful coming to your home without bringing a gift, but I—"

"Good Lord. You don't have to worry with stuff like that around us. We were expecting company anyway, so it's not like—"

"Oh, I hope I'm not imposing—"

"Now, hush. We're glad you came. A new guy about our age moved here last week, and we invited him over, too."

Hating being matched up, Paige stopped in her tracks.

Debbie Sue looked up at her quizzically. "Hey, this isn't a fix-up. It's just a coincidence." She bobbed her eyebrows. "But he *is* single. In Salt Lick, that's more rare than raindrops. He's also good-looking and he's a doctor."

"A single doctor?" Paige said, perking up. "Tell me more."

Debbie Sue opened the front door and urged her inside. "Well, he went to—"

"Did I get the right ones?" Before she could finish her sentence Buddy came up behind them and lifted a suitcase with each hand for Paige's inspection.

"Yes, and thanks. I think I'll freshen up a little. Where do you want me?"

"Right this way, ma'am." Buddy walked up a hallway, and Paige followed.

In the small bedroom, Paige dug clean jeans and a bright blue cashmere sweater from her bag, then sat down on the side of the bed and tugged off her fashion boots. She paused, looking at the boots. They had done some damage today. She was glad to know there was a doctor in town. *The* doctor.

She changed clothes, put on leather mules, then took her makeup to the small bathroom off the hall. There she swept her high cheekbones with a frosty pink blush. Keeping eye makeup to a minimum, a little lip gloss completed her look. Her hair had been cut to support a tossed look, so she bent over and tossed it some more. Last, she sprayed on perfume. With one last look she reached for the doorknob.

ten

Paige entered the living room just in time to see Buddy saying hello to—

Oh, my God! This couldn't be real!

The man standing just inside the small entry glanced her way and froze mid-hello. "Uh . . . I didn't know you had company," he said. "We can do this another time." He started backing out the doorway.

Buddy grabbed his arm. "Wait a minute. Our table seats four, and we've got plenty to eat. Come on in. My wife's expecting you."

The new arrival, halted in his tracks by Buddy's grip, removed his hat and nodded in Paige's direction. His tall frame seemed to fill the space in the room not already filled by Buddy's size.

Paige summoned a wan smile.

"Do you two know each other?" Buddy asked, a puzzled expression on his face.

"Uh, n-no," she stammered. "Not really. When I had trouble on the road last week, a flat, he stopped and helped me."

Paige didn't mention backing into Spur's fender in the Frost National Bank parking lot in Fort Worth *and* crushing his instep with her boot heel earlier in the afternoon.

She couldn't take her eyes off the new guest. Surely this couldn't be the doctor. A maroon sweatshirt hugged his torso. The sleeves, pushed up to his elbows, exposed tanned, sinewy forearms. His Wranglers looked as if they had been sewn onto his long, muscular legs and he was wearing white . . .

. . . White tennis shoes? *Oh, dear.* He probably couldn't get his injured foot into a boot . . .

Debbie Sue walked in, smiling and wiping her hands on her apron. "Spur, good to see you again. Did Buddy introduce you to Paige?" She took Spur's hat and whisked it to a table in the living room.

"They already know each other," Buddy said, still obviously puzzled. "Flat tire, right, Paige?"

Spur's gaze bored into her, and a smirk tilted one side of his mouth. He spoke before she could find a word. "Paige was just outside Salt Lick, weren't you? I believe you were on your way to the Carruthers ranch?"

Paige avoided his eyes by looking past him. "You have a good memory."

"Oh, you'd be amazed at what I retain." His head tilted, recapturing her attention. "First impressions are usually the ones that form the most long-lasting opinions."

She glanced to the side. "Sometimes first impressions are deceiving. I hope you don't judge someone on that alone."

From the corner of her eye, she saw the smirk turn into a grin. "Nope," he said. "In truth, second and even third meetings are probably the more telling."

Buddy and Debbie Sue stood between them, shifting looks like spectators at a Ping-Pong tournament. Debbie Sue interrupted the verbal volley. "Spur, why don't you have that right shoe laced up? Have you hurt yourself?"

Spur looked down at his foot. "A filly stepped on my instep this afternoon. It's gonna be all right. Just a little sore." He raised his eyes to Paige and winked. "I'm the new vet in town." He limped a few steps to her and extended his hand. "Spur. Spur Atwater. Pleased to meet you. Come by the clinic on another day and I'll give you a tour."

Paige feared touching his hand again. She could see herself electrified, her arms and legs askew like a cartoon character. Summoning composure, she accepted his hand, marveling at the size and warmth of it, and gave him her runway smile.

"God, I wish I had a nickel for every time I've been stepped on by a horse," Debbie Sue said. "You're lucky it's not broken. C'mon, y'all, let's eat." She led them into the compact dining area.

The positive interaction with Spur had filled Paige with a sense of relief so powerful she wanted to throw herself at him and hug him.

During the meal, she couldn't keep from stealing glances at him, only to discover he was stealing, too. Debbie Sue and Buddy entertained with stories from their childhoods. They had literally grown up together. Paige was impressed. She had literally grown up alone.

After Debbie Sue explained her and Edwina's misadventures solving the murder of Pearl Ann Carruthers, Paige was prompted to relate how she came to be an employee of the Flying C. She didn't tell them about being cut off financially by her wealthy father. Instead she spoke of a lifelong love of horses and a desire to follow her mother's footsteps. She was so comfortable with these three people she didn't even mind telling the story of her failure at McDonald's. Spur and Buddy guffawed when she stood up and did her impersonation of the angry customer who had gotten her fired.

The phone warbled from the kitchen, and still laughing, Buddy excused himself. They couldn't keep from overhearing his conversation.

"I know, Jerry, but I'm not the sheriff now. You'll have to call Billy Don. . . . I know, Jerry. . . . I understand. . . . I don't think the Rangers will take it up."

"He still gets calls," Debbie Sue said in explanation. "The local folks called him with their problems for too many years. They can't get used to Billy Don."

"I don't wonder," Spur said and chuckled. "I saw the sheriff the first day I got to town. He'd hog-tied himself in front of his office."

"Oh, hell," Debbie replied with a frown, "I'll bet he was practicing his roping on the fire hydrant again. When Buddy was sheriff and Billy Don was the deputy, Buddy threatened to strangle him more than once for doing that. Listen, y'all 'scuse me. I've still got rolls warming in the oven."

Paige found herself alone with Spur, totally unprepared to entertain with a sparkling remark.

Fortunately, he wasn't speechless. "I didn't know you were going to be here this evening, but I'm glad you are."

"Really?" Paige heard the skepticism in her own voice.

"I acted like a jerk earlier and well . . . well, I'm glad for the chance to say I'm sorry. I know it was an accident when you stepped on me."

Paige opened her mouth, but before she could say anything, Debbie Sue returned carrying a basket of fresh rolls. "Like I was saying," she said as she set the basket on the table, "folks just can't get used to Billy Don as the new sheriff. I don't know what will happen if there's a serious crime around here."

"Believe me, Jerry, I understand how you feel," Buddy said in the kitchen, and all eyes turned toward his voice. "It's just not something the DPS will investigate at this point. Give Billy Don a chance to resolve it, and if you're still not satisfied, maybe we can do something else. . . . That's okay, Jerry. You know my number. You know you can call me anytime." Buddy returned to the table and resumed eating.

"Who was that?" Debbie Sue asked him.

"Jerry Gilmore. His daughter's horse has disappeared." Buddy said to Spur, "That's the second call I've gotten in recent weeks about a missing horse."

Debbie Sue's brow knit into a frown. "Jerry Gilmore's daughter's horse is old."

Buddy shrugged and shoved a bite of pork into his mouth.

Paige caught Spur directing another stolen glance in her direction. Since she had been interrupted before she had the chance to say she accepted his apology, she smiled, hoping to convey the message.

"Domestic Equalizers has even gotten a couple of calls about horses gone missing," Debbie Sue said. "That's why we've started putting Rocket Man in the barn closest to the house."

"Oh, my gosh," Paige said. "Do you suppose something bad's going on?"

"I don't know. Ed and I are thinking about looking into—"

Buddy stopped her with an arch look. "Debbie Sue, you know—"

"Now, don't get upset. I said we're only *thinking* about it."

"I'll pay close attention when I get calls from horse owners," Spur put in. "I'll let Billy Don know if I hear anything."

"Well, we won't figure it out at this table tonight," Buddy said with a smile. "So, Spur, I've never had an all-American at my supper table. I've watched a few of your games. Why didn't you go pro? You must have had offers."

Paige looked at Spur with wide-eyed wonder. She knew champion rodeo-ers, sure, but they didn't hold the same status in social circles as an all-American football player. "You were an all-American?"

Even behind his tan, Spur's face flushed, and he seemed tongue-tied.

"Starting quarterback at A&M for four years," Buddy said. "Broke half a dozen records, right?"

"Uh, just four. But it wasn't all me. I had good linemen looking out for me. Top-notch receivers, too. And some of the best running backs in college football. They made me look good."

If it was possible, humility made him even more irresistible. "So why *didn't* you go pro?" Paige asked, picking up on Buddy's question. "Sounds like you could have. The money they pay professional ball players is incredible."

"I never really loved the game. I couldn't see myself continuing to play for years. But football gave me what I wanted—an education, which I'm hoping to turn into a comfortable, stable living doing something I've always wanted to do."

Paige leaned forward, intoxicated by the very notion of someone doing something he had always wanted to do. "You don't think you'd achieve that, making millions in professional football? Those guys are national heroes."

"Or they're late-night comic relief. Making millions might make people treat you like a hero, but when your career falters or ends, you're worse than a nobody. You're a has-been." Spur reached for another roll and buttered it. "Besides, I'm not comfortable in the limelight. I don't like people prying into my life."

"Wow," Debbie Sue said, "that's an unusual attitude toward fame and fortune. Tell us, Spur, what are you hiding?"

Spur lowered his eyes to his food. "Nothing. My mom thought a doctor was the most respected profession a man could have. I promised her that's what I'd do. Only I chose animals instead of people. Animals being sick or hurt are needier than humans."

Paige was touched that someone, a guy, loved animals as much as she did.

"That's admirable of you, Spur," Debbie Sue said. "I'll bet your mom's real proud of you."

"She would be, but she died three years ago."

Paige felt her eyes burn. She was such a sucker for a sad tale. " 'Scuse me."

She scooted from the table, scraping her chair against the hardwood floor, and darted to the bathroom. Once inside, she stepped to the mirror and fanned her hands in front of her eyes, a trick she learned long ago to prevent tears.

What was wrong with her? Everything about Spur Atwater put her senses into the stratosphere. All her senses—sight, touch, hearing, taste, smell—overreacted to him. Maybe she was coming down with something. Maybe she was allergic to him.

"That's impossible," she argued with her reflection.

Tonight was the first time their meeting hadn't been painfully confrontational. For all she knew, he didn't like *any* women. Or he could be engaged. Or gay!

Forget that, no way this guy is gay. Nope. Not possible.

Well, whatever was going on, it was making her crazy.

Then she realized she had been gone from the table overly long. Readjusting her bra and tossing her hair, she left the bathroom and returned to the dining room, showing more swagger than she felt.

She found Debbie Sue clearing the table, with Buddy and Spur nowhere to be seen. Panic seized her. Had Spur left? Did she miss telling him good-bye? Didn't he want to tell *her* good-bye?

"Goodness, was I gone that long?" She tried to sound casual. "Here, let me help you with these dishes." She picked up a couple of plates and followed Debbie Sue into the kitchen.

"Just stack them here on the counter. I'll throw 'em in the dish-washer later. Or maybe I'll just throw 'em out the window." Debbie Sue added on a laugh. "Like that actress on those TV reruns. You know, on *Green Acres*?"

Paige laughed with her, not wanting to say she had no clue to what TV show her hostess referred. She loved Debbie Sue's blunt speech and sense of humor.

Debbie Sue pulled four dessert plates from the cupboard. "We'll have cake and coffee in the living room by the fire. Buddy and Spur went to get more logs. The fire almost went out while we were eating."

Just then Paige heard the voices of the men coming back into the house. Debbie Sue sliced the chocolate cake and served up huge chunks. "Spur," she called out, "how do you take your coffee?"

Mr. All-American appeared in the doorway, leveling a glance at the cake. "Uhm, that depends. Chocolate cake, huh?"

"Yep. With fudge frosting. Made it myself. With only a little help from Betty Crocker."

He grinned. "If it's as good as those rolls you made for supper, I might have two pieces."

Debbie Sue smiled. "Why, thank you, Spur."

"Since we're having chocolate cake, I'll take my coffee black."

Debbie Sue handed him a plate. "Now I'm curious. How would you take it if we didn't have cake?"

"Two teaspoons of sugar. But only two. Since I don't get the exercise I used to, I try to be disciplined when it comes to my diet, though Hogg's may prove to be my downfall."

"Hell," Debbie Sue muttered, planting a fist on her hip and watching Spur carry his cake to the living room. "I like sugar on *top* of my cake. When it comes to food, I don't know the meaning of discipline."

Paige nodded, thinking about the three heaping teaspoons of sugar she had just added to her mug. "I know what you mean."

Debbie Sue took the mugs of coffee to the living room, with Paige following with plates of cake.

Buddy and Debbie Sue sat shoulder to shoulder on the sofa, leaving only a love seat for their guests. Paige sat down gingerly, all too aware of her proximity to Spur. She could feel heat from his thigh as it pressed against hers. She half expected to see a blob of melted chocolate goo on the plate where her slice of cake had been.

"Did you rodeo when you were a kid?" Debbie Sue asked Spur. "I ask because of your name. Sounds like a show name."

"Spur's my given name. I did some cowboying growing up, but I never rodeoed." He took a sip of his coffee and continued. "My dad gave all us kids the name of the town where we lived when we were born. You know how it is being a roughneck in the oil fields. We moved a lot. Since he was an orphan and never knew even his birthplace, much less his parents, he figured, with our names, at least we'd always know that much. My younger sisters are Electra, Loraine, and Idalou. My two older ones are Jayton and Lamesa."

Debbie Sue's fork clattered against her plate. "You've got five sisters?"

Spur grinned. "Yes, ma'am. I used to help my mom take care of the younger ones 'til I left home for college. They're all married now except one." He looked in Paige's direction. "Hey, you remind me of one of them now. You've got some cake icing on your cheek."

"Oh. Where?" Paige twisted her tongue around her mouth, trying to touch her cheek. "Did I get it?"

"Here. Let me." He brushed her cheek with his finger. "There, it's gone."

Her own fingers flew to the spot he had touched and their gazes locked. After a few seconds, he looked down at the chocolate on his fingertip as if he didn't know what to do with it. Finally, he stuck the tip of his finger in his mouth and sucked off the chocolate. The gesture struck her as so intimate, so erotic, she felt her face flush.

"Um, well . . . uh, you were lucky with your name," Buddy said, breaking the moment. He seemed to be stammering. He had seen what just passed between her and Spur.

"Spur's not a bad name," Buddy said. "You could've been living in Cut and Shoot when you were born."

"Or Buffalo Gap," Debbie Sue added with a laugh.

Spur laughed, too, the awkward moment seeming to be gone. "I've always thought it was a good thing Dripping Springs wasn't an oil town. Dripping Springs Atwater would have been tough on announcers and sports writers."

Everyone laughed together. Paige was having such a good time she didn't want it to end. Then the talk turned to her again. "Are you going to be living at the Flying C or will you be staying somewhere in town?" Spur asked her.

"In town. I've rented Debbie Sue and Buddy's house. I'm so

excited. This is my first house. I've always lived in condos or town houses." Paige momentarily forgot her intent not to expose her wealthy upbringing and blathered on. "You know, Debbie Sue, I didn't mention when we talked about the rent, but I just about fainted when you told me how much. I paid six times that in Fort Worth."

"Damn," Debbie Sue said, looking at Buddy. "Maybe we should raise the rent."

Spur set his plate and mug on the end table, his mouth fixed in a grim line. Paige could see a tight muscle working in his jaw. Was he angry at her again? And why? She ran through the earlier conversation, seeking a reason for the abrupt change in his demeanor. What Debbie Sue had said when Paige called her about the house rental came back. *A single man looked at the house, but he couldn't afford the rent.*

She envisioned the trailer where Spur lived.

Oh, hell. She had put her foot in her mouth again.

The evening moved forward, but the atmosphere had changed and never returned to the easy fun and relaxation they had felt earlier.

To her disappointment, Spur soon stood and said, "I'd better go." He carried his plate and mug toward the kitchen. "I've got to make a call at five A.M., at the Roberson place west of town."

Buddy rose, too, and followed him. "Five o'clock's a late start for Dick Roberson. He's a good man. You'll like him."

Spur came back into the living room and picked up his hat. "Debbie Sue, Buddy, the supper was delicious. Man, I can't say enough about those homemade rolls and I've really enjoyed the visit."

Inside Paige panicked. Was he just going to leave without saying another word to her? But then he turned in her direction. "Paige, it was nice to see you again. Good luck on your new job."

That's it? Nice to see you again? Paige couldn't keep her face from scrunching in frustration. Joining Debbie Sue and Buddy, she walked with Spur to the front porch and watched as he climbed into his battered pickup and drove away.

Buddy excused himself and headed to the barn to check on Rocket Man, leaving the two women alone, watching Spur's taillights.

"He seems nice," Debbie Sue said.

"Uh-huh. Nice."

"Got his head on straight. Knows what he wants."

"Yeah. Knows what he wants."

"I bet he had a hard life growing up."

"Uh-huh."

"My mom says adversity builds character."

"Character."

"I'd venture to bet that what he really wants and needs he's not even aware of yet."

Paige came back to life. "Really? What do you think he wants and needs?"

"Come help me load the dishwasher and I'll tell you."

THE LIGHTS in the windows of the Overstreets' house grew smaller in Spur's rearview mirror as he eased away from their comfortable home. To peel out and race down the long driveway was his first impulse, but spraying dust all over the people who had just fed him the first decent meal he had eaten in weeks would have been bad manners.

His thoughts settled on Paige McBride. She looked beautiful and sexy, with those long golden-tanned legs. Nothing out of place. The product of wealth. From all the way across the room her blue eyes had pierced him, and against his better judgment, his heart did a cartwheel and his roommate gave him a nudge.

It wasn't just her appearance that unnerved him. Good-looking women had thrown themselves at him since he was a teenager. No, with Paige, it was more. If she had remained the spoiled, pampered brat from his first impression, he would have no problem putting her out of his mind. Tonight she had been anything but that. She had been down-to-earth, warm, and funny, even self-deprecating at times. Unless what he saw tonight was an aberration, not only had she been born with a silver spoon in her mouth, but she also had been given a heart.

He prioritized and classified living beings into three categories. Animals and people. And women. His usual MO with the latter was to shield himself against any attraction he felt, by bravado or humor and sarcasm. An astute female once called him a porcupine, shooting out his quills when threatened by predators. Whatever. So far it had worked. He had avoided entanglements. Oh, sure, he'd had his share of lusty hookups, usually his roommate's idea.

He had worked all evening at not revealing how Paige's presence affected him. Thankfully, the technique he had carefully crafted to hide his emotions never let him down—not on the football field, not in his dealings with people. Or women. The world was a tough, unstable place, and though he was a planner, a man never knew what tomorrow would bring. The niggling fear had been with him since childhood. To expose his feelings would mean a loss, a loss of what, he wasn't sure, but losing anything was an unacceptable option.

His defense mechanism warned him not to tip his hand where

Paige McBride was concerned, and he wouldn't. Wouldn't make a fool of himself. If the woman he had seen tonight was the exception rather than the rule, she would soon trip up and reveal her true self. Her face was an open book.

She would be a terrible poker player, but he wasn't. He had been schooling his face to hide his feelings for his whole life.

Nope, he wouldn't show his hand. Not yet anyway.

eleven

For Paige, the day started with the delicious aroma of bacon frying, made even more enticing by the fact that someone other than herself was cooking it.

A little note of excitement tripped along inside her. Today was all about moving into and working on her new home. Debbie Sue had given a detailed description of the house, and Paige couldn't wait to see it.

She had tons of things to do, like buying a few groceries, buying curtains. Just transferring everything from her SUV into the house would take a while. Luckily it was only Thursday, and Harley didn't expect her until Monday. Between now and then, she might even squeeze in a pedicure.

Oops. Wrong thought. Pedicures were not in her budget at the present time.

She showered and slipped into her loose-fitting comfy jeans, a pale pink soft sweater, socks, and a pair of Roper clogs. After band-ing her hair into a ponytail, from which unruly curls broke free and framed her face, she applied only scant makeup.

She stayed true to one of her tenets: if you can't win 'em over with your personality, dazzle 'em with your accessories. Therefore, she chose one of her favorite pairs of earrings, a small flower molded of sterling silver with petals of cultured pearl and a pink tourmaline center stone hanging from a fourteen-karat gold hoop. Tiny. Not showy, but gorgeous just the same. Wearing the delicate earrings had always made her feel feminine.

She was ready to face the day.

When she walked into the kitchen, Debbie Sue looked up from scrambling eggs at the stove. "Well, don't you look cute."

"Thanks." Paige set her two suitcases on the floor and positioned her purse on top. She grabbed a slice of bacon from a platter.

"These eggs will be done in just a minute," Debbie Sue said.

"I am so excited to be moving into the house, Debbie Sue. I scarcely slept at all last night."

"Lord, I hate moving with a passion. The only good thing about it is that I throw away a lot of crap I didn't need anyway." Debbie Sue handed a plate to Paige. "Here, hold this."

"This will be the first place that will be all mine, that I picked out without Daddy's and my stepmother's approval. And *I'll* be paying the rent and the bills. With money *I've* earned."

"It doesn't take much to excite you, does it?" Debbie Sue scooped the scrambled eggs onto the plate. "Would you look at that? I didn't even burn them."

"Looks great," Paige said, feeling that she and Debbie Sue had formed a friendship. "If anyone had told me six months ago I'd be doing this, I'd have said they were crazy. This freedom forced on me by Daddy is addictive. I honestly hope I don't ever need to go back to having him take care of my every need."

"Someone taking care of my every need," Debbie Sue said. "What a wonderful thought. I think I'd like that kind of life."

"You would not. You could never be a pampered pet. You're too strong and independent. Besides, I think the life you have with Buddy is pretty wonderful."

"Don't let this strong and independent facade fool you. When Buddy and I were divorced I was a wreck. Now that we're together again, it is pretty wonderful. Sometimes we argue like cats and dogs, but more often than not, we take two steps forward but only one step back. Nope, I've tried it without him and I never want to do it again." Debbie Sue picked up her mug and took a long sip of her coffee.

"Where is Buddy this morning?"

"Oh, he leaves early. His territory goes all the way to Ozona. So, how long do you think it'll be before your dad comes for a visit? I'm betting he'll want to see your new living arrangement."

"I'd love for him to come. I just hope, if he does, he doesn't bring Margaret Ann. She's my stepmother."

"Hmm. Doesn't sound like you like her much."

"That's fair to say. I think the main reason daddy married her was because he wanted someone to help him give me a proper upbringing. He's gone from home more than half the time."

Debbie Sue smiled. "That word *proper* leaves a lot to interpretation."

"Funny, but the very thing Margaret Ann tried so hard to keep me away from is now going to be my livelihood."

Debbie Sue looked surprised. "You mean horses? Why in the world would she want to keep you away from horses?"

"Too dirty. Too unrefined. I've always thought she was afraid me having horses would keep the memory of my mom alive. Margaret Ann's so territorial she's afraid of competition, even from a woman who's dead."

"Has she ever been to a cutting horse event? Some of the most refined women I've ever seen compete in those shows. And *rich*. Did I mention rich? That doesn't even take into consideration the bank accounts of the spectators."

"A cutting horse show would be beneath Margaret Ann."

"Is she a Texan? She sounds a little blue-blooded."

Paige couldn't stop a mischievous grin. "I've never seen her blood, but there's always that hope."

Debbie Sue grinned, too. "Meow."

"What about your mom?" Paige asked. "I understand she's doing great things in Nashville. I love 'I'll Get Over You Tomorrow, Just Come Back to Bed Tonight.'"

"Toby Keith singing it, too. Cool, huh? I tease her about her song titles all the time. I think they come from a part of her life I'd just as soon not know about."

Debbie Sue rose from the table. "Listen, I gotta' scoot. Ed and I've got a busy day. But take your time. Have more coffee."

"Thanks, but I need to go, too. I'll follow you into town."

Paige, still new at forming a real friendship, wasn't sure if she should hug Debbie Sue, shake her hand, or simply exit. Before she could decide, Debbie Sue wrapped her in a big hug. "Glad you were able to spend the night, kiddo. I hope you like the house, and if there's anything, anything at all, you need today, you know where to find me."

Paige returned the hug. "I can't thank you enough, Debbie Sue. Tell Buddy I appreciate the hospitality."

"You can tell him yourself. We'll be seeing each other again." Debbie Sue lifted her keys from a hook near the doorway. "Don't forget what I told you last night about Spur. He's a guy who's gonna need a lot of space. Don't push, but always leave him something to think about."

As Paige followed Debbie Sue into Salt Lick, she considered the advice of a woman who had to be at least five years older and who had landed one of the good guys, not once, but twice. Paige felt sure she hadn't pushed anything when it came to Spur and knew without a doubt she'd left him with things to think about. Unfortunately, they were auto repair, a visit to the doctor, and the image of her being a spoiled, overprivileged brat.

As directed, she turned right at the first paved street. Left two blocks down and the third house on the left was hers. One, two . . . and she was there.

In size, the small house resembled the playhouse she had as a child—larger, but not much. It was immaculate. Off-white clapboard siding and barn red shutters framing the windows gave it a festive look. The front door was the same shade of red as the shutters.

Pulling into the driveway she could barely contain her excitement. In her mind she placed geraniums and begonias in clay pots on the front porch. She took a deep breath as she plugged the key into the lock. The door opened with a little push, and here she was. Home.

Hardwood floors gleamed. She could smell fresh paint. The living room was small and cozy. To her left was a dining area just off the kitchen. New white appliances shone against the black-and-white-tiled kitchen floor. She crossed the living area to a hallway with an arched entrance. Three doors later she found a surprisingly large master bedroom and bath. Cool. There was no other word to describe her surroundings. By the time she finished decorating and adding her personal touches, even Margaret Ann would approve.

A reedy voice calling from the living room startled her. "Hello? . . . Hello?"

Paige walked toward the sound and stopped in the doorway. An elderly woman stood in the middle of the room with a foil-wrapped casserole dish in her hands. No more than five feet tall and ninety pounds dripping wet, she had on an assortment of colorful sweat-shirts and sweaters. Her pants looked like flannel pajama bottoms, and Dallas Cowboy house slippers swallowed her feet.

"May I help you?" Paige asked.

Owl-like glasses perched high on the woman's nose overpow-ered her face and magnified her eyes. She addressed the floor lamp near the windows that looked out on the backyard. "I'm Koweba Sanders. I live across the street. Welcome to the neighborhood. I fig-ured you hadn't had time to do any cooking, so I brought a little something over." She thrust the casserole dish at the floor lamp.

Paige moved in front of the woman and took the dish before it hit the floor. "Oh, how kind. My name's Paige McBride."

"I don't know what kind. I keep these made up in the freezer in case someone dies or gets laid up. You know, Pat, in a town like Salt Lick, funerals and broken hips are just a part of everyday life."

"It's Paige, ma'am."

The visitor frowned in puzzlement. "I don't know if I put sage in it or not. Probably not, but I wouldn't swear to it. I usually only put sage in corn bread dressing."

"This is so nice," Paige replied in defeat.

"Rice? Now, it might have rice. Sometimes I do use rice. Say, you're a picky eater, ain't you, Pat?"

"It's Paige, ma'am. Paige McBride."

"McWright?" Miz Sanders shouted. "Any kin to the McWrights in Stonewall County?"

Paige raised her voice. "No, ma'am, it's McBride. Paige McBride."

"Why, Pat, I've known the McWrights all my life." Miz Sanders smiled, showing bright white dentures.

Paige smiled, moved to the dining area, and set the casserole on the table. She turned one of the chairs toward her visitor. "Would you like to sit down?" She yelled this time, loud enough for every neighbor to hear.

"Nope. Gotta go. Gotta drive to town and pick up my mail. Need to get back before my soaps come on. I watch Bridget and Nick on *The Bold and the Beautiful*. They remind me of my fifth husband."

The thought of Koweba Sanders behind the wheel was unnerving. Following her to the door, Paige yelled, "I'm going to town later. Could I pick up your mail for you? It'd be no trouble."

"No thanks, Pat. Mom lives with me now, and she likes to get out of the house." She leaned forward and whispered, "We don't let her drive anymore, so a ride to town keeps her happy."

Paige was lost for a response. As Miz Sanders shuffled out the front door, Paige made a mental note to be cautious while driving in the neighborhood.

The upside of the visit was she now had lunch. She returned to the casserole on the dining table and noticed a piece of masking tape across the top of the foil. Written in a shaky scrawl was a date: *June 3, 2000.*

Oops. Maybe today was a good day for lunch at Hogg's.

❈ ❈ ❈

SPUR SCRATCHED the stubble on his chin and tried to concentrate on the application in his hand. Hiring a receptionist had not been the piece of cake he had anticipated. Most of the women in Salt Lick who needed or wanted to work drove into Midland or Odessa. He couldn't compete with the salaries and benefits of the neighboring small cities. The leftovers in Salt Lick proved to be slim pickings. His concentration wasn't enhanced by the fact that the overweight young woman sitting across from him periodically blew a huge pink bubble, then slurped it back into her mouth.

"I'm sorry," Spur said, "but could we get rid of that gum for right now?"

"Oh. Yeah. Sorry." The girl swallowed with apparent effort.

Spur stared at her, a little alarmed. "I didn't mean you had to swallow it."

"That's okay. I do it all the time." She began to bounce her knee in a rapid rhythm.

"Uh, okay. Your name's Judy?"

"Yeah. Judi with an *i.*"

"Got it." He nodded in a show of understanding and continued reading the page. "Oh, yes. I can see that here. The *i*'s underlined three times. Thanks. Uh . . . I see you worked at Kmart in customer service? Good. Did you enjoy that job?"

"I hated it." She began to dig at her cuticles.

"Really? What did you hate about it?"

"Working with people. I *hate* working with people. That's one of the reasons I thought I'd do good here."

"But, Judi," Spur started slowly, "you'd have to work with people here. As a receptionist you'd be greeting people all day."

"I thought I'd be working with animals."

"Well, you would. But the animals have owners. The owners

have to be dealt with also. You'd be answering the phone, setting up appointments. You have to greet the owners when they come in and you have to collect the money—"

"Uh-oh," Judi with an *i* said and rose to her feet. "I can't be collecting money. My parole won't let me."

"You're on parole?" Spur asked, his voice losing tenor.

"Yeah. It's a bitch. Knocked me out of a good job at Sonic, too. Don't guess you could come up front and take the money?"

"No, that wouldn't be possible." Spur shook his head emphatically.

"My parole officer comes by and checks on me. Unannounced. If he saw me handling cash he'd have a cat."

"Well, he'd be in the right place," Spur said, standing, too. "Thanks for coming in, Judi. I wish you luck."

Judi pulled several pieces of bubble gum from her jeans pocket and popped one into her mouth. At the door she stopped and turned back, laughing. "Have a cat. Be in the right place. I get it now. That's funny." She walked out still laughing.

Spur rolled her application into a ball and tossed a lofty pass into the arms of the waiting trash can receiver.

In just a few days, he had accumulated a stack of two dozen applications, had interviewed no fewer than ten women. Obviously jobs were few and far between in Salt Lick.

He propped his elbows on the receptionist desk, rubbed his eyes, and sighed. He couldn't afford a staff of employees. He needed one good reliable woman capable of doing a variety of clerical tasks, plus having the stomach and ability to help him with his patients if need be. Where would he find such an employee?

Then he had a lightbulb moment. He knew just the person. He picked up the phone.

twelve

Before Paige was ready, 5:00 A.M. on Monday morning arrived. The past few days had gone by in a blur as she feverishly worked at putting her new little cottage in order. Little cottage. She loved the sound of that.

Her kitchen was stocked with the basics she had brought from her bar and pantry in Fort Worth—a fifth of Jose Cuervo, a bucket of On the Border margarita mix. Brie and cocktail crackers, Milano cookies, and an assortment of organic cereals. She would have to wait for payday to add more.

Her bathroom and bedroom furnishings belied her current financial situation but spoke volumes about her previous one. A dozen thick ringspun Egyptian cotton towels that had cost fifty dollars apiece from Horchow's catalog filled a small linen closet shelf. In the luxury condo Daddy had leased for her in Fort Worth, the cushy towels had seemed at home in the master bath suite. In her Salt Lick rental, they looked as if they could be draperies for the living room.

In the bedroom, an Ann Gish two-thousand-dollar comforter and pillow cover set, in the cooling color combination of aqua and sand, swallowed her bed. Her love for the beautiful colors almost overcame the fact that the comforter, sized to fit a queen-size, was too large for the regular-size bed.

Studying how to remedy the problem of the too-large comforter took her mind off the living room furnishings, which consisted of three webbed aluminum folding chairs. Paige wasn't long on patience when it came to something she wanted. The only waiting period that had existed in her prior life had been the time it took to dig her credit card from her purse. But she was learning. Perhaps the satisfaction of someday buying a sofa with her own hard-earned money would make up for the current spartan living.

She picked up her purse and keys but stopped in the tiny front entry for one last survey of the house. She had done the best she could with what she had. On a sigh, she left.

Despite the early hour a healthy show of activity hummed in Salt Lick. The horseshoe-shaped parking area at Hogg's Drive-in looked like a truck dealer's sales lot. She scanned the vehicles, looking for Spur's battered Chevy.

He had dominated her thoughts since dinner at Debbie Sue and Buddy's house, but even if she saw his truck, she wouldn't go into Hogg's. How pathetic would she be, making her attraction to him so obvious? She had her pride, after all. If he had really been a football star at Texas A&M, a trail of groupies followed him, everything from waitresses to heiresses, and she didn't want to be just another one of the group.

She continued to think of him as she left the city limits, heading for the Flying C. The mental image of being with him in *that* way, rising to heights beyond her experience with men, wouldn't leave her, and she didn't understand those thoughts. She had never been obsessed with sex, and in truth, other than knowing Tab A fit Slot B, she didn't know much about the finer points.

Oh, sure, she'd had her share of making-out sessions, even a couple of disappointing experiences with Judd Stephens that went further than making out. After one particularly embarrassing episode, they both concluded they should be "just friends." A few days later, after two too many margaritas, Paige confided to Sunny that she didn't think she had ever had an orgasm. Sunny assured her that if she didn't think she had, she could bank on it that she hadn't.

So if she was a sexual neophyte, which she was, what was it about Spur Atwater that directed her mind to sex and Spur in the same sentence? His physique? True, it was right out of a bodybuilder's magazine, but then, there was no shortage of great bodies. His ruggedness? Nah. She had grown up with masculine ruggedness. What man could be more rough and tough than her daddy? Pheromones? She had taken chemistry, but couldn't remember studying human pheromones. What she had learned about the alluring, hypnotic reproductive aid provided by nature came from studying a perfume ad in *Cosmopolitan*. The notion of the body releasing sexually arousing odors like a subtle laser had been laughable to her at the time. Now, looking back over the past couple of weeks, she had to acquiesce to the notion that *something* was at work here. *Something* that made her unable to stop her imagination when it came to the new vet.

Arriving at the Flying C halted that degree of deep thinking. She rumbled across the Flying C's cattle guard, reminding herself of the responsible role Harley had given her.

She parked the Escalade alongside other pickups near the main barn's entrance, as captivated today by the Carruthers horse facility as she had been the first time she saw it. Styled like a hacienda, the expansive two-story barn was not only nicer than what most humans called home, but it was also nicer than anything many might ever get the chance to visit.

Entering the front part of the big barn, Paige saw no activity but could smell coffee. On her left was a door with a sign that said OFFICE. She opened the heavy wooden door a crack and saw Lester tilted back in a desk chair, his ankles crossed on the desktop, a phone receiver pressed to his ear.

He motioned for her to come in and covered the mouthpiece with his hand. "Make yourself at home," he mouthed, then turned back to his phone conversation. His intimate tone told Paige he must be talking to a woman.

She took the opportunity to look around. The perfunctory needs of an office were all in place—desk, two chairs, fax machine, a couple of four-drawer steel filing cabinets, a computer and printer.

Two refrigerators, one larger than the other, stood side by side. Hoping to find orange juice, she opened the larger unit's door and found it filled to capacity with cans of Coors beer. *Yep, all you need right at hand.*

Spying the coffeepot, she walked over, lifted a mug from an assortment that was turned upside down on a towel. After checking it for cleanliness, she poured it to the brim with the black brew from the pot. She was looking for a sugar substitute when she heard thumping noises. She glanced across her shoulder toward Lester and saw him tapping his finger on the desktop to get her attention. Pointing to his own cup, he indicated he wanted a refill.

It was an innocent enough gesture, and normally, Paige wouldn't hesitate to oblige. But after hearing Harley say Lester felt superior to women, Paige made a snap decision. Harley had hired her to be

Lester's assistant, not his servant. She smiled brightly, lifted her own cup, and pointed to it. "Thanks," she said in a stage whisper, "I found the cups."

She ducked out of the office and made for the barn area. The company of the horses was preferable to that of the horse's ass on the phone.

As she strolled through the wide dirt aisles, sipping her coffee and taking in her surroundings, the smell of hay, dirt, and manure played with her senses. Funny that so many precious memories were associated with them.

She found the interior of Harley's barn to be as impressive as the exterior. Even a novice could see no expense had been spared. There was a fly-mist system, a horse shower and grooming area with a concrete floor, a huge tack room, medical treatment slot, video surveillance cameras. She couldn't guess what was housed on the second floor.

She strolled to the stalls where on the outside of each a hanging placard bore the occupant's name, some part of which went back to its sire. Paige didn't have to see the registration papers to know she was seeing horses bred from two cutting champions that consistently sired winners, the legendary stallions Travalena and Pepto-boonsmal.

She was awestruck. To the unknowledgeable eye they looked like any other well-kept horses, but these were the equine equivalents of the Michael Jordans, the Joe Montanas, or the Nolan Ryans. As she studied them, they stared back from huge soft brown eyes with bored detachment, as if they didn't care that the blood of champions coursed through their veins.

Through an immense doorway leading out to a sunbaked pasture, she saw a circular ring with a four-horse walker setup and a

circular trench furrowed into the grass around it. Throwing the remainder of her coffee on the ground, she walked toward it. Horse
walkers had always reminded her of merry-go-rounds.

Lester caught up with her and gave her a grin she classified
somewhere between cocky and insulting. "That's a horse walker,"
he said.

Well, as distasteful as she found him, she had to get along with
him, so she smiled. "I know that."

"Ready to get to work?"

"Absolutely. I've been looking forward to it."

"Then let's go on back to the barn and get started." They walked
side by side toward the barn. "You do know, dollbaby, that there's a
lot of hard work to be done? It's not all riding into an arena with all
eyes on you."

Paige bit her tongue and replied sweetly, "I know. I remember."

He looked her up and down and back again. "You mean your
daddy didn't hire someone to do it all for you?"

Paige bit her tongue harder. "You don't know Daddy. He's a
firm believer that hard work never hurt anybody. He believes work
builds character."

Lester sneered. "It also breaks backs. I know about your daddy,
how he became the richest man in Texas the hard way, but I'll bet
his hands ain't been dirty in a while." His face broke into a big grin.
"That's what I'm gonna be one day. A man that don't get his hands
dirty. I don't intend to be another man's lackey all my life. I got
plans."

"The admirable thing about my daddy is he might no longer *need*
to get his hands dirty, but he still does and he doesn't mind it a bit."

They walked into the barn and stopped in front of a stall where
a beautiful bay mare waited for them. Paige was grateful to direct

the conversation to the horses. "Uhm . . . does Harley come out and work with the horses much?"

Lester opened the stall gate, entered, and slid a halter on the bay. "Now there's a man that don't know the first thing about getting his hands dirty. Had everything handed to him his whole life. Rides around in big trucks, big cars, attending big meetings. He's what I call a windshield cowboy."

Lester hooked a lead rope onto the halter and led the bay out of the stall. He placed the lead rope into Paige's hand. She almost shuddered at the thrill of being allowed to ride this magnificent horse.

"My sister's the one that started up this cutting operation," Lester went on. "Harley never gave two hoots in hell about the horses 'til they started making him money." Lester leaned toward her menacingly, tapping a thumb against his chest. " 'Til, *I* started making him money."

Paige suppressed a gasp at what she had just learned. Lester disliked Harley! His facial expression, his words, his body language left no doubt. Did Harley know? Being aware of this new information left her thoughts in a jumble. "Oh. Well, he must think you're doing a good job, then. I, uh, hope to learn about cutting from you. I've seen you ride several times. You always appear so cool and calm. It amazes me you can stay in the saddle under all that pressure." She made a nervous titter. "I'd probably land on my butt the first real cut."

Lester reached out, grasped her shoulders, and turned her in a half circle. "I'd say you got the perfect ass for a cutting saddle."

Wrenching from his grip, Paige spun and faced him. He gave her a leering grin and pushed his hat back with his thumb. "Yessir, a heart-shaped ass is made for riding . . . Or being ridden."

Paige felt her face flame. She was willing to kiss up to him to get her job done, but she had her limits. "Lester. I don't know how I might have given you the wrong impression, but let's clear up one thing early. Our relationship is purely professional. I'll work hard and do everything I can to help you, but I don't sleep around."

Lester threw his head back and laughed. "You think I'm asking you? With me? Honey, you sure think a lot of yourself, don't you?"

Paige gripped the lead rope tighter in her fist. "I assume you want me to exercise this horse this morning. Which one do you want me to ride first?"

Lester continued to grin like a monkey. "Okay, I know when I'm whipped. Let's put this little girl on the walker for some exercise, then we'll do a walk-around. I need to show you where everything is. Does that meet with your approval, Miz McBride?"

"That sounds great," Paige snapped, anger leaving her with an unsettled feeling in her stomach.

Together they led the mare to the walker, then began the tour of the barns. While they walked Lester told her there were ten horses in training. Each had to be fed, watered, exercised, and groomed, preferably daily. The workday would start at 6:00 A.M. and end when everything was done.

It crossed Paige's mind that so many tasks had to have been daunting for one person to do with no help, especially when training was essential for prospects as promising as these horses. It was credible, she supposed, that Lester had been keeping up with these duties alone thus far, but she hadn't forgotten his display of cruelty to a colt.

Having satisfied all of her questions like "Where is this?" and "What are those?" Lester concluded the tour.

"What about the office?" Paige asked, mindful that Harley had mentioned her doing the bookkeeping. "We didn't go over anything in there."

Lester pulled a tin of snoose from his back pocket and shoved a pinch between his cheek and gums. "That's none o' your business. None o' *anybody's* business. I take care of all the paperwork."

"There's paperwork?" Paige said, batting her lashes.

Lester sighed and shook his head as if she were too stupid to live. "Sure is, sweet thing, but I'm guessing you wouldn't know the first thing about paying bills. There's dues and fees, registration papers, farrier bills, feed and supplies bills, vet bills—"

"Vet bills?" Paige's ears perked up.

Lester walked to another stall, opened the gate, and went inside, talking as he slipped a halter on a strawberry roan. "Well, yah Paige, vet bills. I ain't no hands-on healer or no horse whisperer, neither."

"Well, uh, it's just that—well, I heard the vet was leaving town."

Lester led the roan out of the stall. "You can start out riding this baby. You do know how to ride, right?"

The horse came close to Paige and snorted and nuzzled her. A burst of sheer joy rose in her chest. "Yes, Lester. I do know how to ride."

"Yep, ol' Doc Miller's leaving," Lester said, "and it's too damn bad. He's a helluva guy. We'll miss him around here, that's for damn sure."

"Is someone replacing him?"

"You bet there is. Harley saw to that. He put the vet clinic together. Bought a lot of the equipment. Got Doc Miller anything he needed. Harley could've hired a vet to work right here at the ranch, but he thought the town needed a vet's services. Says the Carruthers clan believes in *supporting the community.*"

Lester made a cynical heh-heh-heh. "What Harley believes in is having only the best at his beck and call to take care of *his* animals. Yessir, Salt Lick ain't got no doctor or no hospital, but we got a world-class veterinary clinic. Since his new wife's pregnant, some folks wonder if maybe he'll think about building a hospital."

They reached the tack room and Lester pointed out a saddle she could use. "Some smart-ass football hero out of A&M bought Doc's practice. Being an Aggie himself, Harley checked the dude out a little, made some phone calls to a banker in Fort Worth, and just like magic, the new guy's loan got approved. Those Aggies all stick together, you know."

"Oh," Paige said, thinking about Spur and his pride. "I wonder if the new person knows that?"

Lester looked at her quizzically. "What difference does it make? You got an interest in football players?"

"Uh, no. Of course not. I don't know one football player from another."

thirteen

Paige's first day of gainful employment ended on a whisper almost undetectable by human ears. Actually, it was a half groan, half whimper. She couldn't remember ever being dirtier or more exhausted. Or more content. Since the day her daddy had married Margaret Ann, before Paige became a teenager, the joy of doing almost anything she loved had been denied her. Oh sure, walking into her favorite store in the mall and finding a tremendous sale was a rush, but it paled in comparison to today's feeling of high spirits. She wasn't even upset over several broken nails.

She had discovered early in the day that a couple of the hired hands did many of the dirtiest jobs, like cleaning stalls and pitching hay. That explained how Lester had managed to work without a real assistant for so long.

The chores left were still enough to tax Paige's body. She didn't mind though, recognizing the physical benefit from the bending, pulling, lifting, and pushing. Still, what she wouldn't give to sink into the whirlpool bath at Panache or lie down for a full-body massage.

Driving through town on her way home, she couldn't keep from looking for Spur's battered pickup and hoping for a glimpse of him. Since the dinner at the Overstreets', she had wished a hundred times that he would show up at her door or at the very least, call Debbie Sue and ask for her phone number.

As she passed the Styling Station, seeing Debbie Sue's pickup and Edwina's vintage Mustang surprised her. On impulse she braked and made a sharp turn across the highway into the parking lot, eager to talk to someone about her day. Besides, they might have gossip to share about the hot Dr. Atwater.

Through the window she could see the two women lounging in the hydraulic chairs. Ohmygosh, they had what appeared to be margaritas in their hands. *Hallelujah!*

Paige dismounted and charged in, the sleigh bells hanging on the front doorknob announcing her arrival.

"We're closed." Edwina's eyes didn't open. "Unless you've come to rub my feet, go away."

"You rub mine and I'll rub yours," Paige said, laughing.

"My God," Edwina drawled, sitting upright. "Those are the very words Vic said to me last night." A big grin turned up the corners of the hairdresser's brilliant red lips as her gaze settled on Paige. "Well, honey, just look at you. You look like something the dog drug in 'cause the cat wouldn't."

Paige laughed and glimpsed her image in front of the mirrors. She couldn't remember the last time she had seen herself looking so disheveled. Even diving in Cancun, she managed to keep up her appearance. "Good Lord. I do, don't I? I need a hot bath and clean clothes."

"What you need is a margarita," Debbie Sue said. "There's a pitcher already made in the fridge in the storeroom and a glass on the shelf. There's even a bowl of salt. Help yourself. And while you're at it, bring back the pitcher and top mine off."

In the tiny back room, Paige salted the rim of a glass, poured herself a drink, then returned to the salon area. "Why are y'all open? I thought you'd be closed on Monday." She refilled Debbie Sue's and Edwina's glasses.

"We usually are," Debbie Sue said, "but there's a dance at the Peaceful Oasis tonight. So many of those old ladies needed to get all dolled up, we decided to open. Besides, Ed and I are both batching. Vic's on the road, and Buddy's gone to a school in Odessa."

Paige frowned and sat down in one of the teal seats affixed to a dryer. "What's Peaceful Oasis, a private club?"

"Oh, it's private all right," Edwina said. "Membership requires you to be at least eighty. Honestly, those crazy old women have given me new hope on aging. I've never been around a hornier bunch. They should rename that place—'Not Quite Sex, Not Quite the City.'" The lanky brunette popped a red lollipop into her mouth.

Paige giggled. "You're kidding, right?"

"Nope, she's not kidding," Debbie Sue said. "The bad thing is, there's about five women for every man."

"And that one poor geezer," Edwina added, "is doing all he can, thanks to Viagra. Yep, aging's a bitch. I intend to wear mine completely out before I get that old. Then I won't even want sex or miss it." Edwina lifted her glass and drained it.

"That'll be the day," Debbie Sue put in.

"What can I say, girlfriend. When you're the Bill Gates of sexuality, you gotta flaunt it."

The two women laughed, and Paige joined in, wondering just how many margaritas the two friends had already consumed. She and Sunny rarely discussed sex unless Paige asked her specific questions. Paige found herself enjoying the ease these older women seemed to have with the topic.

"So, tell us how your first day went," Debbie Sue said. "Lester didn't give you too hard a time, did he?"

Edwina pointed at her with her lollipop. "Don't you take any crap off Lester. I've known him since he was a little kid with a dirty face and diaper to match. He always was one to smile and tip his hat while he was reaching into your purse for your wallet. He's that much like his deceased sister."

"Ed, you shouldn't speak ill of the departed," Debbie Sue scolded. "She was a good customer."

"He wasn't so bad," Paige replied, unsure how to respond to such venomous comments, even about Lester.

"Just don't let him win you over with his charm," Edwina said. "He's fathered at least two kids that I know of around here and walked away from both of them. Even bragged about it in the open. He's just flat-out no good." Edwina shoved the red lollipop back into her jaw and frowned. "Hmm. I think I've discovered a new flavor. Cherry Tootsie Pop and margaritas."

The bit of news about Lester, coupled with the horse abuse Paige had witnessed earlier, downgraded Paige's opinion of him further. The thought of how he had looked her up and down gave her the creeps. "How awful," Paige said. "And the poor little kids—"

"Yep. Mandy Holland's dad keeps a loaded shotgun in his truck, just hoping he'll have the chance to empty it at Lester. Child support ain't enough, he says."

"Buddy already kept Butch Peterson from taking care of him with his fists," Debbie Sue added. "Butch told Buddy that if he ever gets the opportunity, even the Texas Rangers can't keep him from settling up with Lester for what he did to his daughter and his granddaughter."

"Hand me that margarita pitcher," Edwina ordered, and Paige stood up and complied. "He's hanging out now with a married woman. She and her husband have already got three kids, but she's so in love with Lester, she'll probably be his next victim. Lester calls her a broodmare, the bastard."

Paige felt her eyes bug. Lester was even worse than she had thought. "Oh, my gosh!" She swallowed a big gulp of her drink.

"Maybe her husband'll do what Mandy Holland's dad hasn't been able to." Edwina rose and clomped to the back room, carrying the empty margarita pitcher. She returned with it refilled and poured glasses full all around. "Personally, I don't know how he can afford his lifestyle. I imagine Harley pays him a decent wage, but ol' Les spends money like water."

"Yep," Debbie Sue agreed. "Buys his clothes at Leddy's in Fort Worth. Flashes jewelry like a pimp. But, hey, let's change the subject. Who cares about Lester?"

"What're we gonna talk about?" Edwina asked. "We've covered the dance at Peaceful Oasis. What else is there? . . . Oh, I know. That new vet. I got a gander at him a couple of days ago in the grocery store. Lord, that man's good-looking. He was with a black-haired woman. They were laughing and carrying on to beat all." Edwina returned to her seat in the hydraulic chair, gesturing toward Paige with her glass. "If I was you, that's the one I'd set my hat for."

Paige felt a sensation she couldn't explain. A sick feeling. So he was involved with someone. That was why she hadn't heard from him or seen him. That explained his aloofness. But then, how could he not be taken? How could she have been so foolish to think this gorgeous man, this catch of all catches, wouldn't already be caught?

The thought of him laughing with someone bothered her the most. He had never laughed with her. She had seen only a rare smile from him, but it was enough to make her long for more. She wanted to throw her glass against the wall, yell "fuck," and leave the salon. But she willed herself to remain seated and expressionless. "Oh, are you talking about Dr. Atwater? I met him the other night at Debbie Sue's. He seems nice enough, but if he's taken—"

"Taken? Who said anything about him being taken?" Edwina slurred. "He was buying groceries, not wedding rings. Lord, hon, no band on his hand means he's fair game."

"Leave her alone, Ed," Debbie Sue admonished. "Don't pay any attention to her, Paige. She once told a guy's girlfriend she had only a week to live, so his girlfriend would let him go out with her. Then she married him."

Paige stared at Edwina and blinked.

"I don't know who Spur was with," Debbie Sue said, "but I saw the way he looked at you the other night over supper. He's interested. Very interested."

"God, I hope you're right," Paige blurted out before she thought. Oops. She had let the cat out of the bag. She waited for an onslaught of questions from the women, but none came. They both just nodded, as if they already knew.

Edwina was right. Spur wasn't married and surely, if he was engaged, it would have come out at Debbie Sue's when he was discussing his future plans. Paige's competitive nature surged. Yep, he was still on the market, and she, being one to never miss an opportunity to go shopping, was going to cruise his aisles every chance she got. If Edwina and Debbie Sue didn't know the woman he was with, that meant she didn't live in Salt Lick. Paige McBride had the home field advantage.

Begging off a third margarita, Paige left the ladies of the Styling Station. Even more enticing than the tequila and good company was a warm sudsy bubble bath followed by slathering lotion all over her sore body. She wanted to call Daddy before going to bed and tell him about her day. She might even try to make contact with Sunny.

As she pulled from her parking spot she lowered the Escalade's windows. The perfect fall evening shouldn't be shut out. The aromas of the evening were delectable—moist soil, hay, and decaying leaves mixed with the smell of burning wood and somebody's supper cooking. This luxury of driving with open windows had been unthinkable in the city, what with the noise and the foul swampy air. But here, the air was clean and dry. There was definitely no swampy air and no swamp. So far, she hadn't seen *any* water except what came from the tap.

Paige closed her eyes and felt an incredible sense of peace, followed by an all-consuming pang of hunger. The lunch she packed for herself that morning—brie and cocktail crackers—had seemed adequate at the time, but she had devoured it hours ago.

The thought of fixing something cold at home sounded yucky. She would make good use of the drive-in window at Hogg's. She'd heard from more than one person that the food was good, hot, and greasy. Just the thought made her mouth water. Spotting the pink and black sign on the right side of the road, she turned in to the busy eatery's drive-through line.

The menu was limited, to be sure. Hamburgers with or without cheese, french fries, onion rings, chocolate or vanilla malts, and a variety of soft drinks. Not exactly a mind-taxing choice, but most definitely a fattening one. Paige knew what she wanted and drove forward only to be stopped by a sawhorse with a makeshift sign attached— SPEAKERS BROKE. COME ON INSIDE. WE DON'T CARE HOW YOU LOOK.

No way was Paige going home without a sack of fat-saturated food. As she circled the café she scanned the parked vehicles for

Spur's pickup but didn't see it. Good. She didn't want him to see her looking like a field hand. She gave the mirror a quick glance, rubbed some dirt off her forehead, and gave up. What the heck? She'd be in and out before anyone saw her.

THE FIRST THING Spur spotted when he pulled into Hogg's parking lot was Paige McBride's black Cadillac. He didn't know how many more encounters with her he could endure without making an ass of himself. He had been trying unsuccessfully to put her out of his mind for days.

One thing he supposed he would have to accept living in a small town was the inevitability that he would run into her or be thrown into her company. He sat in the cab of his idling truck mulling over his options. He could drive back to his trailer and find . . . what? Cereal? He still had a box of Wheaties, but no milk. A sandwich? There was baloney in the fridge, but he had finished off the last of the bread at breakfast. Damn. He had just bought groceries, too, but the trailer's tiny cupboards didn't even allow for necessities, much less surplus. After a quick analysis, he determined dry cereal, baloney, and a pack of Twinkies were not a suitable reward for the day's work he had just finished. He would go in, grab something to go, and get out fast. Besides, maybe she had only parked there and wasn't inside. She didn't really look like the greasy food type.

Resolve in place, he killed the engine and slid out of his truck. Stuffing his keys into his jeans pocket, he nodded hello to a pack of teenagers sitting at the two picnic tables just outside the door. A couple of the boys he recognized. They had come by the clinic asking to see his Southwest Conference Championship rings. News of his football career had spread quickly through Salt Lick, and the fact that he was an Aggie and a college hero made him a celebrity. In that way, Salt Lick was like most West Texas towns.

The teenage girls were less subtle. His being nearly thirty didn't keep them from giving him the once-over, giggling and making attempts to appear alluring. God, women, no matter their ages, confused him.

Everyone assumed he was an expert on women because there had been a few. He had taken advantage of certain opportunities his status had brought him—what man wouldn't? The encounters had been nothing more than hookups, and while physically satisfying, they had left him feeling empty so many times, he now worked to avoid them. Though groupies expected nothing more than a session of raunchy sex with a sports hero, he couldn't keep from thinking how angry he would be if a man treated one of his sisters in such a casual way.

The first thing he spotted when he entered the brightly lit dining room was *Her,* and his step faltered. Her hair hung in a golden cascade of curls down her back, contrasting against a pink sweatshirt. Those long legs filled worn, dirty Wranglers, and her boots had seen better days.

She stood in the order line, weight on one foot, one hip cocked to the side, lazily rocking side to side as she read the menu. Oh, man, she looked as good from the back as she did from the front. Keep your naked, bare-it-all *Playboy* centerfolds. The woman standing in front of him was the real deal and sexy as hell. His roommate thought so anyway. He removed his hat, partly because he was taught to always do so when entering a room, but mainly to hide his alter ego.

A hay straw clung to one of her blond curls. Stepping behind her, but being careful to keep a safe distance, he gently plucked it from the ringlet. "Is this something for your scrapbook, to remind you of your first day on the job?"

Paige turned so quickly she stumbled, and he reached out and caught her elbow. Her eyes were blue as the sky on a clear day and they held a startled expression. "Huh? Oh, no!" She twisted, trying to see her back side. "Do I have hay all over me?"

Spur grinned. "No, just this one little straw."

She had splotches of dirt on her forehead and nose and not much makeup. As far as he was concerned, she could never be more beautiful.

"I must look a fright." She began dusting at her sleeves. "I tried to go through the drive-up window, but it's broken. Please don't look at me. I'm so embarrassed."

"Oh, c'mon, now. You look pretty good to me. But then I've been looking at the south end of heifers most of the day."

She laughed. "Well, thanks a lot. That makes me feel so much better."

Spur laughed, too. Striving for casual, he said, "So, did you get moved in to your new place?"

"Yes. Yes I did. I love it. I don't have any furniture in the living room yet, but I will. Christmas is two months away, and I've already decided where I'm putting the Christmas tree. I have the perfect place for a tree."

"What's with women and Christmas trees? When I was a kid every time we moved to a new place my mom would worry about where to put the Christmas tree."

Paige smiled, her eyes warm. She had the most perfect white teeth he had ever seen. But then she had probably had a whole team of dentists, the best money could buy.

"You orderin', ma'am?" the counter helper asked.

"Uh, yes. I'll have a Chuck Wagon Meal."

"Yes, ma'am. You get a big Coke with that."

"Great." After paying, Paige stepped out of line, went to the cold drink machine, and filled a Styrofoam cup. She took a nearby seat at a small square table. No time like the present, Spur told himself as he paid for his own order. He walked over to her table. "Mind if I sit with you?"

"No, of course not. Please do."

He sat down opposite her and placed his hat on an empty chair seat.

"How's your foot?" she asked, leaning over to look at his boot.

"It's okay. Didn't slow me down a bit. You're getting off work kinda late, aren't you?"

Paige explained that she'd had a margarita with Debbie Sue and Edwina earlier.

"I really like Debbie Sue and Buddy," Spur said. "Nice folks. But I don't know what to make of Edwina."

"I know what you mean. She may be one of those people you have to get to know, but I like her anyway. She doesn't hesitate to say what's on her mind."

"Maybe that's it. I like honesty, but I'm almost afraid of what she's going to say." Spur shifted his large frame in the small chair, bumping Paige's knee.

"'Scuse me," he said, hoping a big grin hid the fact that his pulse surged.

"Oh, that's okay." She moved her knee and laughed. "It's my long legs. Sometimes I don't know where to put them."

He could think of a place but decided it best not to say it. "No, it's my fault. I'm long-legged, too." They laughed together.

"Guess we do make quite a pair of giants," she said. You must be what, six two or three? I'm five ten."

"I'd say you're just about right." He smiled. Shocked at himself for saying such a thing, he felt a flush crawling up his neck. "So," he started, feeling a need for a change of subject, "wonder what single people do in this town for entertainment?" *Shit, could he sound any hokier?*

Before she could answer or he could embarrass himself further, a female voice called over a loudspeaker, "Number tee-un. Number tee-un."

At the same time, a laugh burst out of him and Paige both. "I know this is West Texas where we all talk funny," he said, "but I don't think I ever heard anybody say *ten* with two syllables."

Paige glanced at the slip of paper in her hand. "Oh! That's me." Still smiling, she got up, went to the counter, and picked up the brown paper sack, a grease stain already showing through. She came back to the table. "Well, I guess I'd better go. Got an early day tomorrow."

"Oh, yeah. Sure." Spur stood, not sure what to do or say at this point and suddenly aware of a host of eyes turned on them. "It was good to see you, Paige. You take care, now, you hear?"

As he watched her climb into the Cadillac, Spur thought of a dozen things he should have said. Maybe he should be satisfied with the fact that this encounter had gone better than previous meet-ups. Nothing had been damaged and no one had been injured. Perhaps when he ran into her again, he would have grown a backbone and acquired the ability to coordinate his brain and tongue in her presence.

fourteen

As Paige unlocked the front door and heard the phone, the only two people who had her new number leapt into her thoughts. Daddy and Sunny. Either would be a welcome voice. She crammed the last bite of cheeseburger in her mouth and fumbled with the lock until the door sprang open. She dashed to the bedroom, and on what seemed to be the hundredth ring she snatched the receiver off its cradle.

"Hello, don't hang up."

"Paige? Where you been, punkin? I've been calling for hours. It's after eight o'clock. I was afraid you might've been trampled by one of those horses."

"Daddy! I'm so glad you called. I stopped off to visit friends, then grabbed a bite to eat. You should see me. I'm covered with dirt, sweat, and horse crap and I'm happy about it."

"I can hear that in your voice. Think you're gonna like your new job, do ya?"

Words began to tumble out, like her mouth couldn't move fast enough to tell everything. "I love it, but I may not be able to get out of bed tomorrow. I used a lot of muscle today. Daddy, I'm taking care of ten horses. Lester's got two signed up for the futurity in Fort Worth in December. I'm hoping Harley will let me go. That may be the only chance I get to come back between now and then."

"Why, daughter, I haven't heard you this excited since you called me from New York City when you'd stumbled onto some kind of shoe sale."

Paige laughed. "It was 'Seventh on Sixth,' Daddy. Fashion week. That's a world away from what I've been doing today."

"Well, it's just good to hear you happy. Do you need anything?"

"I'm fine. I don't need a thing."

"You're bound to need something, sweetie. You didn't leave here with a lot of cash. You got groceries? Gasoline? That Caddy running okay?"

"I really am okay, Daddy. My cabinets have food, my tank's got gas, and there's cold beer in the fridge. My bank account's empty, but I'll be fine until payday. We get paid on Fridays. Just four days away."

"I wish you'd let me do something. I feel bad."

"Why, you old softie. You're afraid I'm going to get too independent, aren't you? You actually miss me running up the credit card bill, don't you? I'll bet Dick In-the-Butt has gone into a deep depression."

Her dad's baritone chuckle rumbled like West Texas thunder. "Richard's holding up just fine, but I heard the CFO at Neiman Marcus called an emergency meeting to discuss the sudden drop in revenue."

It was so good to be teasing with her daddy again. Sensing the old rhythm returning in their good-natured jabs at each other thrilled her.

"So give me details about your day. Let me hear all of it, too. Don't give me just the parts you think I'll approve of."

Paige told him everything about her long workday—how she had set things straight between herself and Lester, her new friendship with Debbie Sue and Edwina, stopping at Hogg's, where Elvis had eaten once. The only thing she didn't share was meeting Dr. Atwater. It felt too soon to share those emotions.

"By God, Paige, I'm proud of you, honey." His tone took on a softness. "Your mama would be proud, too. You're still the best thing the two of us ever did."

She forced herself to think of something that would squelch her emotions. "Where's Margaret Ann tonight?"

"Oh, hell, who knows? She's chairman of some damn foolishness. I come in, she's on the phone. I go to bed, she's on the phone. I get up, it's the same damn thing. I could pluck a Mexican out of the Rio Grande and have better conversations than I do with her. Sometimes I wish I'd . . . Oh, hell, never mind."

A knot formed in Paige's throat, and her eyes stung with tears. She would love to wrap her arms around her daddy's neck at this very moment. Her father led a lonely life. She heard it in his voice, even though he talked with his usual brusqueness. Even after all these years, he still loved her mother.

"Daddy, why don't you come visit me for a few days? I know Harley would enjoy seeing you, and I want to show you my little house. I could introduce you to my new friends. They're such terrific people. Please?"

"I'll make it out there soon. Maybe I'll bring you a turkey if you don't think you'll be back to Fort Worth on Thanksgiving. Think between the two of us we could cook that ol' bird?"

Paige laughed. "I know we could. I've got an oven and everything. I could get directions from Sunny . . . I miss you, Daddy."

"I miss you too, sweet pea. Call me in a few days and let me know how things are going."

"Okay. Thanks for calling. I love you."

She heard him mutter he loved her, too, before he hung up.

Funny, in all the years she'd been away from home she had never said she missed him with such heartfelt conviction. She had imagined pulling away would be hard, but she wasn't prepared for the real physical pain in her chest. Leaving his financial support was one thing, leaving the nest was a whole other issue.

Paige stripped her grimy clothes and carried them to the laundry bin at the end of the hallway. A washing machine had not been a high priority on her list of necessities, but it was becoming one.

She gathered an armload of fragrant bath salts, coconut shampoo and conditioner and took them to the bathroom off the master bedroom. She turned the shower on full blast and stepped into the warm spray. Soon the room was foggy as a steam room. The West Texas hard water didn't yield the voluminous lather she was accustomed to, but it was hot and it hit the sore spots, which more than made up for the absence of suds.

After drying herself, applying moisturizing lotion to her body, and drying her hair she was ready for bed. She pulled an oversize Dallas Stars jersey over her head, slipped into a pair of flannel boxers, and grabbed the most recent copy of the NCHA *Cutting Horse Chatter* magazine. She had no more than settled into the comfort of the feather bed when the chimes from the doorbell echoed through the sparsely furnished house.

It was after ten o'clock. Wasn't that a late hour for a small town?

"Debbie Sue? You there, darlin'?" The voice was male. More raps on the door. "C'mon, sugar. It's me. Open up."

Paige threw back the covers, slid from the bed, and tiptoed to the door. When Buddy dropped by earlier in the week and installed a sliding chain lock she had laughed and told him she doubted she would use it. Sure enough, it now hung there unhooked and useless. Picking up the chain she gingerly slid it through the slot and informed the visitor, "Debbie Sue doesn't live here anymore."

"C'mon, darlin', I recognize your voice. You can't still be mad at me. Open up, sugar. I want to tell you something."

The visitor sounded like he might have been drinking, but he didn't sound all-the-way drunk. If he was someone Debbie Sue knew, he must be harmless. Taking a deep breath, Paige cracked the door and peered out. The mystery man had taken a seat on the top step and was turning his cowboy hat among his fingers. His back looked broad and muscular. His clothes were starched and pressed in true cowboy style. Only his profile was visible, but what she saw looked good.

Beyond him, parked at the curb at a skewed angle, was a black Lincoln Navigator. Well, maybe he was drunker than she thought.

At the sound of the door opening he leapt to his feet with a big grin that quickly evaporated. "You're not Debbie Sue," he said.

"Like I told you, she doesn't live here anymore."

"Are you sure? I know that was her voice." Trying to peer through the opening, he called out again, "Debbie Sue!"

"Listen," Paige said more firmly, "she doesn't live here. I moved in about a week ago. Debbie Sue and Buddy live east of town, at her mom's place."

"You're shittin' me. They moved in together?"

"Uh, uh, well, no," Paige stammered. "They're married. Or I guess remarried would be the accurate thing to say."

He stared at her a few beats, as if he didn't believe her. Finally he clapped his hat onto his head. "Damn. My timing with that woman was always off. I knew she was still crazy about Buddy, but I didn't think he felt the same way."

"Can I give her a message? If you give me your name, I'll tell her you came by."

His forlorn expression grew into a cocky smirk. "You don't recognize me?" His eyes roamed up and down the part of her body that showed through the door crack.

The change in his demeanor came so fast Paige was confused. Maybe he was just putting on a good front. "I'm sorry, I don't. Should I?"

He hooked his thumbs through his front belt loops, a grin now cemented on his face. "I'm Quint Matthews."

He said it as if the statement explained itself. "Okay." Paige waited for a more detailed explanation. The name did ring familiar, but she couldn't quite place it. "Sorry, but it doesn't register."

"Quint. Matthews." He repeated the two words, as if she hadn't heard them clearly. "Three-time world champion bull rider, spokesman for Wranglers and the PRCA? Why, darlin', *Texas Monthly* named me the Most Eligible Bachelor in Texas two years ago. Any of that ring a bell?"

Paige recognized a bad boy when she saw one. Despite the good looks and definite charm, she could see why Debbie Sue wisely chose Buddy. "Oh, yeah, Quint Matthews," she said brightly. "I thought you were dead."

"Why would you think I was dead?"

"I remember seeing you ride at the rodeo in Fort Worth once. You took a really nasty spill off Bodacious. He stepped right in the middle of your straw hat when your head was still in it. First time I ever saw a cowboy wearing his hat around his neck. They carried you out of the arena."

"My God. I must have ridden a thousand bulls in my career and the only ride anyone seems to remember is that rank sonofabitch Bodacious."

"At least you're remembered for something," Paige said sincerely.

"Honey, I'm remembered for a lot of things. Just ask Debbie Sue." He reached for the screen door handle.

"I think I'll just stick to telling her you came by. Good night."

Paige started to close the door, but her visitor moved like lightning and stuck his boot between the door and the jamb. "Hey, darlin', how about I come in and we get acquainted? If Debbie Sue's not available, I'd just as soon hear more about *you*."

She looked at the boot and then at him. "Thanks, but you're going to be too busy."

"Think so? What am I gonna be doing, darlin'?"

"Changing your flat tire."

Quint turned to his left and looked at his SUV.

"Good evening, Mr. Matthews," Paige sang. "Your eight seconds is up."

She slammed the door and locked it.

PAIGE SHUT OFF the alarm clock. Her first waking thought was telling Debbie Sue about the late-night visitor. She had assumed, with no supporting facts, that when Debbie Sue and Buddy were separated, Debbie Sue had pined for him until he finally saw the light. From the looks of the sexy, crestfallen cowboy she met last night, *pine* was not the right word.

She threw back the covers, padded to the bathroom, and began her morning ritual. The possibility of running into Spur made her take great pains with her hair and makeup. She didn't intend to risk doing anything that would put him off. After donning a pair of Wranglers, a sweatshirt, and boots, she was out the door.

As she drove through town she eyed her cell phone lying on the passenger's seat. She would love to talk to Sunny, but it was 5:30 A.M. Sunny didn't know a day had two 5:30s, so instead of calling, Paige picked the phone up and dropped it into her purse.

She saw only one store open. The Kwik Stop convenience store. She had already passed it when she remembered she needed to grab something for breakfast and lunch. She made a sharp U-turn and doubled back, only to discover that the tiny store's parking lot was crowded with extended cab pickups and oversize trucks hauling horse trailers. She parked on the side and walked around to the front entrance.

An elderly Mexican man stood at the register, grinning and greeting everyone who entered. Tejano music pounded from a radio on a back shelf. She looked around and saw a block-shaped Mexican woman cooking at a grill located near the front cash register. The aromas of onions and chorizo filled the air, and Paige's hunger pangs revved up.

She turned toward the cold drinks at the back of the store. With muscles stiff and sore, she groaned as she squatted at one of the cold cases and reached for a bottle of orange juice. A couple of breakfast burritos smothered in salsa were all that filled her mind . . . until she heard the voice of Dr. Spur Atwater. He had to have just entered because she hadn't seen him or his old pickup when she came in. She was just about to rise and approach him when she heard him give a breakfast order to the senora.

"Four burritos, please," he said. "Two with eggs, onions, and sausage, and two with eggs and bacon only. No onions on those last two please, ma'am. Just eggs and bacon. I'll also need a large coffee and a Dr Pepper."

A two-person order if she ever heard one. What did *that* mean? Paige peered down a long aisle, looking to see if the other person was with him, but saw no one. Okay, he could be ordering for a male friend. But instinct told her otherwise. Was his girlfriend in his truck or at his trailer waiting in a flimsy nightgown? *Damn.*

Well, she had to avoid him. She couldn't bear to embarrass him or herself.

Still squatting, she duckwalked around the end aisle for a better view of the front of the store. She could see his cute backside, and he appeared to be alone. She moved closer to the large storefront window and peeked out. Sitting in the cab of his pickup was a brunette. Undoubtedly the "sweet young thing" Edwina had described.

More than ever, Paige didn't want to be seen by him, especially after she had been hiding this long. She couldn't just pop up like some jack-in-the-box, could she? But a cramp had seized her right calf, and the pain was approaching the excruciating point. Standing to relieve the agony was not an option, so she grabbed a loaf of bread from a shelf and bit into it, muffling a scream.

The cramp had almost relaxed when she heard the Mexican woman tell Spur he would have to get the soft drink from the back. Sheer panic leaped into Paige. Through the pain she looked for a back exit. She saw only one door and it stood open. She limped through the doorway and discovered she had stepped into the walk-in cooler. The air felt cold on her skin, but at least she was out of sight. She breathed a sigh of relief.

Peering out from the cooler's darkness, she watched as Spur walked within six feet and scanned the soft drink cases. He moved nearer, and she began to panic. Then she realized part of the bank of cold cases was behind the cooler's open door. He opened a cold case door and at the same time pushed the cooler door shut. The heavy outside latch clanged in a sickening, pitch-black finality. Paige's breath caught in her throat. The hum of a compressor suddenly became a maddening roar, and she began to shiver from the cold. *Don't panic. Don't panic.*

She needed a plan in lieu of pounding on the door and screeching. *Calm down, calm down.*

Just wait long enough for Spur to leave the store, then summon someone. Or perhaps the clerks will need something and open the cooler door themselves.

An eternity passed. Her feet began to feel numb. Spur had to be gone. She knocked on the door and called out, but hearing nothing from the outside but the steady beat of the Tejano music, she had a terrifying thought. If she couldn't hear them, could they hear her?

"Hey," she yelled. "Can anybody hear me?" She counted to a hundred and called out again. And again. Nothing.

She heard the muted ring of a phone and remembered she had put her cell phone in her purse. Using the braille method, she fumbled through her bag until she felt the cold plastic phone housing. Yanking it free, she flipped it open and was bathed in green fluorescent light from the tiny screen.

According to the phone's clock, she had been in the freezer about ten minutes, though it felt like an hour had gone by. She dialed information and almost wept with happiness when the monotonous-sounding operator's voice answered.

"What city please?"

"S-s-salt Lick," Paige said, her teeth chattering.

"Utah?"

"Huh? No, I'm in Texas."

"One moment, please."

Another operator came on the line. "This is Tasheka. How may I help you?"

"I need the n-number for the K-kwik Stop c-convenience store." Paige fumbled inside her purse again, found a pen, and poised to write the number on her open palm.

"I'm sorry, ma'am. I don't have a listing for a Kwik Stop in Salt Lake."

"Do you mean Utah? Are you thinking I want a number in Utah?"

"I don't show a listing for a Kwik Stop in Salt Lake City."

"No, ma'am, p-please. It's not Salt Lake. It's Salt *Lick, Texas.*"

"Hold on, please. . . . I don't show a listing in Salt Lick."

"It's th-the one on Ma-main Street," Paige said, feeling she was rapidly running out of time to hold on. "It's the only one in town. It's K-k-*k-w-i-k*-k-k. Would you ch-check again please?"

Silence. "I'm sorry. I don't have a listing for a Kwik, *K-w-i-k* Stop."

"But they ha-have a phone. I'm in the b-b-b-back of the store and I've heard it r-r-r-ring a couple of times."

"Is this a prank call?" Tasheka's tone became threatening. "Because we have ways of tracing you—"

"N-no, wait. Listen. This is not a pr-prank. I'm locked in the cooler. I need to call the m-manager to let me out."

Tasheka's voice jumped a full octave. "I'm transferring you to a nine-one-one operator."

"No, wait—"

Gone! Tasheka's voice was replaced by a burr.

"Nine-one-one. What is your emergency?"

"I do-don't have an emergency. I just want th-the num-m-m-m-ber for the Kwik Stop in Salt Lick."

"Ma'am, you should have called the operator for information. There are penalties for making false reports to a nine-one-one operator."

"No report. I only asked for a ph-phone number and the operator tr-transferred me to you."

"Why would she do that, ma'am?"

"I don't know. I told her I wa-wanted to call Kwik Stop because I'm l-l-locked in the c-cooler."

"You're locked in the cooler?"

"I'm in the c-c-cooler. I want to c-c-call the store clerk—"

"Try to stay calm, ma'am."

"I'm c-c-calm. But I'm cold—"

"How long have you been entombed?"

"I'm not entombed! The door c-closed accidentally and I want to call—"

"Give me your location, please."

"The K-kwik Stop in Salt Lick."

"I can't find a listing for Quick Stop. Can you give me their number?"

Paige could no longer contain her tears. "If I c-could give you their n-number I wouldn't b-be in here."

"Please stay calm, ma'am. And whatever you do, resist the urge to fall asleep. Stay on the line. I'm going to contact your local sheriff."

Sheriff?

Paige could hear rings on the line, and after at least ten, a half-asleep male voice said, "Hullo?"

"This is the nine-one-one operator. Is this Sheriff Roberts?"

"Hullo?"

"Is this Sheriff Roberts?"

"Uh-huh."

"I'm a nine-one-one operator and we have a situation."

"What is it?" A note of fear came into the sheriff's voice. Something crashed, followed by a noise like breaking glass, then cursing.

"Sheriff Roberts? Sheriff Roberts are you still there?"

"Damn. That's gonna leave a scar."

"Sheriff?"

"I'm here. I'm hurt, but I'm okay. What's the problem?"

"I have a caller on the line who's trapped in the cooler of one of your local businesses."

"How the hell did that happen?"

"I don't know, sir. Can you address the situation?"

"Can I what?"

"Can you take care of the situation?"

"Heck, yeah. I can do that."

Silence. "Sir?" the operator said. "Are you ready to take the information?"

"Oh, yeah. Hold on. Let me get a pen."

More fumbling, crashing, and cursing. After too many minutes the sheriff returned. "Okay, shoot."

"The caller is in a business called the Quick Stop. Do you know that location, sir?"

"Oh, you mean Manuel and Rosa's La Tienda. Yeah, I know the place. I'll be there in a minute."

"Can I report to my supervisor the situation is being resolved?"

"Yeah. Tell 'em everything's okeydoke."

In less than five minutes Paige could hear the same male voice that she had heard on the other side of the locked door.

"Manuel, how you doin' this morning? Hey, Miz Rosa, would you fix me up one of those burritos, *por favor*? Put everything on it. Throw some of them taters in there, too. I love them taters mixed up with them jalapeños."

Suddenly the cooler door opened and a lanky young man dressed in jeans and a striped pajama shirt stood there. He had a star on his chest and a thick bandage on his thumb. The Mexican store owner and the woman stood beside him, their eyes filled with concern. A big grin broke out on the sheriff's long face. "Well, beat all. There you are, little lady. You okay?"

Instead of answering, Paige pushed past him into the blessed warmth of the convenience store. "I'm frozen. Do you think you could have let me out before you ordered breakfast?"

"Huh? Oh, yeah, I sure could've. I forgot. Sorry."

Paige just wanted to leave, but she had to know one thing. "How come Kwik Stop doesn't have a listed phone number? I called the operator and she said she didn't show a number."

"Oh, it hasn't been Kwik Stop for years. It's been Manuel and Rosa's La Tienda a long time, but they've never spent the money to change the sign. Everybody knows that."

"Not everyone," Paige snapped.

The Mexican man began jabbering in Spanish, and the woman sank to her knees and crossed herself.

"I'm okay," Paige repeated several times.

Manuel grabbed a giant paper sack from behind the counter and began stuffing it with food and merchandise. When it was full to the top, he pressed the bag into her arms.

Paige, assuming this was an out-of-court settlement, smiled and accepted. After all, she was still hungry.

Even with the turn of events at La Tienda she was only fifteen minutes late reaching the Flying C. Amazing how quickly the day had gone to hell. If she couldn't convince herself that things couldn't get worse, she would have to turn around and go home.

Rumbling over the Flying C cattle guard she saw the vet's white mobile clinic parked at the barn. Spur. God, she hoped he was alone. If not, her detour through Manuel and Rosa's walk-in cooler had been for naught.

She pulled beside the truck and stopped. Glancing in the mirror she smoothed her hair and wet her lips, then fished out a purse-size atomizer and spritzed perfume behind her ears. A girl had to take advantage of every opportune moment.

As she slid the barn door open, she saw Lester and Spur standing near one of the stalls, both laughing. Lester wiped tears from his eyes with his shirtsleeve. Spur had his back to her, but as she approached she heard him say, "I don't know who it was, but I can't figure anyone being dumb enough to get themselves locked in a convenience store cooler."

Damn. She had heard news traveled fast in a small town, but this was ridiculous.

fifteen

G ood morning," Paige said, feigning nonchalance. "What's so funny?"

Spur turned and touched the brim of his hat. A little shiver traveled through her, and it had nothing to do with the earlier episode in the convenience store cooler.

Lester landed his customary leering grin on her. "You're late. I was beginning to think you got cold feet."

Paige's pulse quickened. Hadn't she distinctly heard Spur say he didn't know who had locked herself in the cooler? "Why would you say that? Why would you say I had cold feet?"

"Whoa, there. It's just an expression. What, got PMS or something?" Lester gave Spur a good-ol'-boy wink, but Spur glared at him.

A ribbon of hot indignation crawled up Paige's neck. "That's a disgusting thing to say."

"Hell, Doc," Lester said to Spur, "I can't seem to quit stepping in it. I guess some women are just hard to get along with at certain times of the month."

"I'd say it depends on your approach," Spur said. "I was raised in a houseful of sisters. If I'd said something like that to one of 'em, I'd be afraid to go to sleep at night." Spur smiled in her direction.

"Thank you, Spur," she said, still smarting. He was every bit the hero who rescued the maiden in distress.

"Spur?" Lester said. "What's up with that? This is Dr. Atwater."

Paige ignored him and looked up at Spur. "You're here so early. Is something wrong?" She wanted to also ask, *Did you drop off your girlfriend?* but the phone ringing from the office interrupted. Lester excused himself and jogged to answer it.

"Lester asked me to check on the horses while he's out of town," Spur said, "so while I was out this way, I thought I'd drop in. When he asked me, he didn't mention you, so he must not have known you were going to work here."

"Maybe not," Paige said. "My decision was a bit sudden. I hadn't heard he's going out of town, but then, this is just my second day on the job." She glanced toward the office, watching for Lester's return. "Did he say how long he'll be gone? Or where he's going?"

"He said just a few days. Is there a problem? Since you'll be here, do I still need to come by and check on things?"

"No problem that I know about. I just wondered where he's going. No, there's no need in your coming by unless you want . . . uh . . . I mean, if you feel you should, uh, um, you can come by anytime." She hated herself for stuttering and stammering, but the image of the brunette sitting in his pickup in the early morning hours was still fresh in her mind.

Taking a step toward her, but still watching the office door, Spur removed his hat. "Paige, uh . . . I'm just wondering if you might like to have supper with me some evening?"

Not trusting her ears, Paige stared at him. "Excuse me?"

"I wonder if I could take you to supper sometime. I heard there's some good places to eat in Odessa and Midland. I thought you might like to try something different from the places, or place, in Salt Lick. Just for a change, I mean. But if you don't want to—"

"Oh . . . Gosh. I'd like that. I really would. Thanks." Paige's face didn't have room for the smile that grew from her toes to her mouth. She only hoped her joy didn't show too much.

A sigh escaped from Spur's throat, and his face broke into a huge smile, totally surprising her. He was actually nervous about asking her out.

Suddenly memory pinched her. Okay, he had asked her for a date, but who was the brunette?

The office door opened, and Lester sauntered out. Apparently the phone call had gone well. He was practically gloating.

"Doc, I don't see any reason you need to drop by here while I'm gone, now that we've got Paige here. I decided after yesterday she'll do just fine here all by herself. She's got things well in hand, and there's plenty of help here."

He attempted to grab her shoulder in a one-armed hug, but she sidestepped and he missed. "I'm glad you trust me, Lester. How long are you going to be gone? And when did you say you're leaving?"

"What's the rush, sweet thing? You eager to get rid of me so soon?"

She gave him her best reptilian smile. "Just wondering."

"I shouldn't be gone more than three, four days, tops. I'll leave you a work list. If you need help, one of the hands'll always be around."

"Look's like you've got things to talk about," Spur said. "I'll be running on. Paige, I'll talk to you later."

After Spur disappeared, Lester turned to Paige. "You fibbed to me, darlin'. Said you didn't sleep around."

Paige faced him squarely, planting her fists on her hips. "You are such an ass. I'm not going to dignify your tacky remarks with conversation." She pushed past him and stamped toward the office. "Let's go over your travel schedule, Lester. Maybe you can leave a little earlier than planned."

Lester laughed. "Now that's what I like. Women who play hard to get."

The news that her nemesis was leaving for a few days had caught Paige off guard. She hadn't anticipated having the place all to herself so soon. Suddenly a cup of hot, strong coffee sounded good, along with every food item Manuel had stuffed into the brown paper sack. Lester's leaving was something to celebrate.

DRIVING BACK to town, Spur gripped the steering wheel as if his ol' truck might take on a mind of its own and bolt. He had just gone against his every conviction. He didn't have the time or the money for a woman and all that dating crap, but his sister Electra had been unrelenting in her determination to see him "find someone." She had talked about little else since he told her about Paige. That was where he had messed up. He shouldn't have mentioned Paige to Electra, but after the fender bender in Fort Worth, the coincidence of meeting Paige again in an out-of-the-way place like Salt Lick bore telling.

Electra's reaction had been electric. He remembered her words—*This is serendipity. Kismet. She's your soul mate.*

Women. Electra had the perfect marriage to her childhood sweetheart. She held a firm belief that fate provided a mate for everyone, and building a life as two was far better than going it alone.

Electra would never let him rest. If he ignored her attempts at matchmaking too long, she would enlist the aid of the other four sisters, and he would stand no chance at all. Being the only brother of five sisters had taught him many things about women, one of which was to stop resisting early.

To avoid the embarrassment of planned encounters and awkward moments, it was best he take control. He would take Paige to supper. Afterward, he would tell his sister she was wrong, that he and Paige McBride had nothing in common. No chemistry. Their pairing up was a dismal failure. Not a chance in hell. Nope. There was no such thing as kismet, and serendipity was bullshit.

His strongest misgiving lay in what only he knew—the way he reacted when he saw Paige, heard her voice, or smelled her perfume. His pulse quickened and his palms got sweaty. Of course, that could be because it had been so long since he had been with a woman. The real barometer was the roommate in his shorts. Every time he got close to Paige, his roomie tried to stand at attention.

From blocks away he caught sight of the clinic's sign. SALT LICK VETERINARY CLINIC. He still couldn't believe he owned his own practice. Or was in the process of owning it. The bank loan was big, but the interest rate was low, and with a built-in clientele, he had a chance to make a comfortable living. He would have to work hard, but he was no stranger to that.

As long as he could remember, he had been working. When his dad gave up living and crawled into the warmth and security of a whiskey bottle, Spur had found odd jobs, helping put food on the table for his mother and sisters. There had been times when there wasn't enough to go around and more than once he had gone to bed hungry. In those days, he was thankful he had a bed to go to.

He had wanted to drop out of school and get a full-time job, but his mother wouldn't hear of it. She took in ironing so he could play football, called his athletic ability his "God-given ticket to bigger and better things." If only she had lived long enough to see him now.

Spur parked his old Chevy in the back of the clinic. It was too early to start seeing his four-legged patients, but not too early to start his day.

As he opened the door, the aroma of coffee greeted him. The other odors—medications, cleaning solutions, urine, and feces— were mixed in, but he hardly noticed them. His senses had long ago become accustomed to the pungent smells associated with caring for animals.

He heard the sound of a metal cage door and a sweet female voice. "Good morning, little one. How're you this morning? You're going to be just fine. You're in good hands. Yes, you are. Yes, you are. . . . Settle down now. . . . Okay, give me kisses. . . . Oh, my goodness. You are such a love."

Spur stopped at the end of the row of cages and watched the tall brunette cradling the tiny bichon frise in her right arm. She was everything he could want in an assistant. She handled the front desk and phones with finesse. She wasn't at all put off with working in the back with the animals or with cleaning up after them. She showered them with love and attention, and best yet, she worked for free.

Electra and her husband had a small place between Salt Lick and Odessa. She had offered to help Spur until he could find a suitable permanent receptionist or Ronny went back to working nights. She liked to be home when her husband was there. They had only one vehicle, so Spur drove the distance twice a day to pick her up and take her home. A small price to pay for someone who did as good a job as she did. She refused pay, reminding him of all he had done for her. Of all his sisters, Spur had the most in common with Electra.

" 'Lectra, I swear. You've spoiled her so bad, she won't want to go home with her owners." Spur stroked the tiny dog's head with his finger.

His sister smiled down at the hairy, squirming bundle in her arms. "I can't help it. They're all so sweet. You know me, Spur. If I had my way, I'd have a ranch with nothing but dogs and cats roaming everywhere."

A childhood memory came back. "Boy, do I remember. Every stray in the county somehow followed you home, no matter how hard they fought against it. I can still hear you pleading with Mom, 'Just let me keep him until he gets run over.' "

"Remember that day I brought that dog home on a leash I made from my shoestrings?"

"Yep. You came in the door and announced 'Look what followed me home from school!' To this day, that was the mangiest, scrawniest dog I've ever seen."

They laughed together. "I know. I chased him through a berry patch and lost the only pair of shoes I had. You named him Ol' Stupid."

Spur scruffed her hair. "Yeah, and I took on a paper route to buy you a new pair of shoes."

"But you liked him. He was the best dog. We had him the longest. I loved him so much."

"He lasted the longest because he charmed the neighbors into feeding him. All the others got run over or ran off when they got hungry. Now that I think about it, Ol' Stupid wasn't so stupid after all. At least he always had a full belly."

As she put the bichon back into a cage, she looked up at him, grinning. "Did you do it? Did you ask her out?"

"Yes, 'Lectra. I did it. Now, will you please just let it rest?"

"Okay, okay. Just a couple of questions, though." She latched the cage door and pressed her hands together under her chin. "When are you going out and when do I get to meet her?"

"Well, I didn't actually make a time. I just asked if she'd like to have supper with me some evening."

"What did she say?"

"She said she'd like that."

"And you didn't set a time? Why not?"

Spur felt a need to be defensive creeping up on him. When it came to women, he always seemed to be saying the wrong thing or making the wrong move. "I told her I'd call her."

Electra planted her hands on her slender hips. "Spur Atwater, we're no better off than we were before."

"We? When did this become *we*? I didn't see you anywhere in Carruthers's barn sticking *your* neck out. Or should I say, *our* neck?"

Electra squinted her eyes, lost in thought. "Okay, here's the next step. Today is Tuesday. You need to call her Thursday. In the morning. Ask her out for Saturday night. Take her somewhere nice."

"Hey, now, let's don't get carried away. I'm too broke for nice. I was thinking of barbecue and beer."

"You're kidding," his sister said indignantly. "Spur, honey, the woman you described to me wouldn't be impressed with barbecue and beer."

"I'm not trying to impress her, 'Lectra. She's bound to know I'm not a man of wealth. She's seen where I live. Besides, if I have to work at making an impression, then something's wrong. Me," he said, pointing a thumb at his chest. "She has to like *me*, not the places I can take her or the things I can buy her."

Electra reached up and placed a hand on the back of his neck, pulled him down to her level, and kissed the top of his head. "You're right, bro. I'm sorry for even suggesting it. You're the prize.

You be yourself. If she can't see what a catch you are, then best to learn early."

"Thanks. I appreciate you looking out for me. It's probably a waste of time anyway. Hell, she's driving a rig worth more than I'll make this year. Can we change the subject now?"

"Just one more thing. I hope she likes me enough to ask me to be one of her bridesmaids in y'all's wedding. I've always wanted an expensive designer dress, even if it is a bridesmaid's gown."

"God help me." Spur threw up his arms and walked away.

"You can walk away from me, Spur, but you can't turn your back on fate. Kismet. Damn it all to hell, it's kismet."

AFTER SPUR LEFT, Paige had thrown herself into another day of work. Now, taking a break, she called the Styling Station. Edwina answered. "Hey, baby doll, what's shakin'?"

"Not much," Paige said.

"Did you hear what happened in town this morning? It was awful. Just awful."

"Gosh, I don't guess I did. What happened?"

"Some poor woman got locked in the cooler at Manuel's. They had to call the sheriff to get her out."

"Oh?" Paige said weakly. "I didn't hear."

"They say she was stiff as a board and turning blue. Billy Don wasn't able to revive her, but they saved the baby."

"Baby?"

"Yep. Saddest damn thing I ever heard. No one knows who she was. Nine months pregnant. I don't know what'll become of the baby. Just breaks my heart."

Paige was dumbstruck. She looked down at her stomach. *Nine months pregnant indeed.* "Uh, that's sad, really sad. Uh, would Debbie Sue happen to be around?"

"Hey, Debbie Sue," Edwina yelled. "Pick up the extension. It's Paige."

Debbie Sue's voice came on the line. "Hey, did Ed tell you about the poor woman in the cooler?"

"Uh, yes, she mentioned it."

"That has to be a tall tale started by Roxie Jean Koonce. You probably haven't met her. She's the dispatcher at the sheriff's office. Not a mean bone in her body, but she'll stretch the truth to make Billy Don look good. She's afraid he won't get reelected and she'll be out of a job."

Paige wanted to change the subject before she said the wrong thing and revealed the truth. She lowered her voice. After all, she was talking to a married woman. "Debbie Sue, uh, I called to tell you that someone came to the house late last night. He thought you still lived there."

"A guy? Late at night? I can't imagine who that would be."

"He said his name was Clint. Clint Matthews."

"Say that again," Edwina said.

"He said his name was—"

"Quint. Quint Matthews." Debbie Sue finished the sentence. "So what happened?"

Paige related the conversation with her late-night visitor at the front door.

"How'd he look?" Debbie Sue asked.

"I thought he looked good, kind of sexy. Maybe he was a little sure of himself. Of course, I've never met him up close before. But I've seen him ride once."

"Quint's not only sure of himself, but everyone else around him. But he's fun, I'll give him that. He's a helluva lot of fun."

"How long did y'all see each other? Does Buddy know him?" Paige asked, now intrigued.

"We go a long way back, but hey, I've got a haircut to do. Why don't you come by the shop when you finish and we can talk more?"

Paige disconnected and returned to the horses. Whatever love triangle Debbie Sue was involved in occupied her thoughts throughout the morning.

Snacking on a scrambled egg and sausage burrito, an assortment of chocolate candy, and two Atomic FireBalls enabled her to work straight through without stopping to eat lunch. She felt bad that Manuel had been so shaken when he saw her emerge from the cooler shivering. But she had to admit, accepting his bribe had been the smartest thing she had done today.

By giving up a lunch hour, she found herself at three-thirty with her day's work done. "Hey, Lester. Would it be okay if I head back to town? I need to talk to Debbie Sue before she leaves her shop."

Lester glanced up from a magazine. "You already done?"

"Yeah. Listen, I'm in a hurry. There's something about Debbie Sue's house I need to discuss with her." That wasn't a lie. Quint *had* come by the house. "Are you still planning on leaving town next week or have you decided to leave sooner?"

"Yep, next week. Can't possibly go before then. Got some things to see to first." He lowered the magazine to his lap and assumed a cocky grin. "Want me to stay? I might consider waiting a day or two if I thought it'd be worth my time."

Paige walked away, throwing a barb over her shoulder. "Sorry, Lester, but it's not worth *anyone's* time."

sixteen

Paige was eager to see Debbie Sue and Edwina again. They were so fun. Passing the veterinary clinic she slowed, hoping to catch a glimpse of Spur. A glimpse wouldn't change the course of anything, but she had to look anyway.

His pickup was nowhere to be seen. He could be making a call on a dozen different places, checking everything from birds to bulls, but she couldn't stop thinking he could be with the brunette, probably trying to decide if he was in love with the vixen with dyed hair. He had probably asked her, Paige, out to dinner to test his real feelings. *Well, that's a lousy thing to do.* Annoyance built inside her.

Or maybe the so-called beauty had broken up with him and he was on the rebound, asking other women out to heal his wounded heart. And now, at this very moment, he was kissing and making up with the dark-haired woman, his hands entangled in her overprocessed split ends, telling her he hoped they never quarreled again. They would marry and have children and they would ask Paige to teach them how to ride horseback. Snotty-nosed rug rats. *Hell.*

I hope he calls me tonight, was her final thought as she parked in front of the Styling Station. Whatever reason he might have for *not* calling, her lack of maturity couldn't possibly be one of them.

As she entered the salon, the scent of shampoos, hair sprays, and chemicals tickled her nose. Edwina was teasing and styling a patron's blue hair into a do shaped like a football helmet. Empty margarita glasses sat on the station counter.

Edwina appeared to have an enormous cud of gum, her jaws moving with the speed of an Olympian gum chewer. Every few seconds popping and snapping was interrupted by the emergence from Edwina's mouth of a pink bubble, which she sucked back in, and the process started again. *Pop, snap, blow. Pop, snap, blow.* She was in The Zone.

Edwina tilted her head back in a greeting. "Hey, kiddo, pull up a chair and grab a margarita in back."

Paige smiled, partly because she was glad to see her new friend, but mostly in appreciation for what said friend was wearing. Bright pink shorts. Edwina's long skinny legs ended in the tops of white boots. The rest of the ensemble was a tie-dyed T-shirt topped with a crocheted vest and hoop earrings as big around as beer cans. Priceless. Paige had seen pictures of the fashions from the 1970s, but this was the first time she had viewed it in real life.

Debbie Sue's head poked past the floral curtain that filled the storeroom doorway. "I've already got one for you." She came out and handed Paige a cold, salted drink. "So the great Quint Matthews came by and harassed you, huh?"

"Well, he came by."

"Doesn't surprise me a bit," Edwina said and began spraying a cloud of hair spray. The customer pinched her eyes shut.

"Why?" Paige asked, puzzled.

Debbie Sue rolled her eyes. "Oh, no. You said the wrong thing. Here we go."

"Simple human behavioral response," Edwina said. "Nothing's more alluring to the male of the species than the unconquered female. Men by nature are hunters. They get off on trying to get what they can't have. The conquest."

"Amen," mumbled the customer through a towel she was holding over her closed eyes. "The primal need to dominate women is strong in an alpha man. I'm sure he enjoys the challenge even more, now that women are more empowered than ever."

"Why, that's right, Madge," Edwina said. "You must have read the same book I did. *The Naked Ape.* And Quint Matthews is the ultimate naked ape."

"God bless him," Madge said. "When can I meet him?"

Paige had no reply and could only stare, not believing her good fortune at stumbling into an intellectual discussion of the battle of the sexes. Now she had not only the benefit of Edwina's and Debbie Sue's wisdom, but also that of another woman who looked old enough to be her grandmother.

"Don't pay any attention to Ed," Debbie Sue said. "She's trying to quit smoking. She's taken up reading everything she can get her hands on to take her mind off the nicotine craving. She's become a regular Barnes and Noble."

"Oh," Paige said, blinking.

"And listen, whatever you do, don't bring up the Middle East. A couple of days ago she thought the Middle East was somewhere around Dallas, but now . . . well, just don't bring it up."

Paige was interested in what Edwina had to say. In her current situation, any information from an experienced friend was welcome. "Alpha male? What *is* that?"

Edwina removed the black drape from her customer's shoulders and took on the stance of a professor lecturing a class, her voice changing to a tone of authority. She even halted the gum minicombo. "The term comes from the animal kingdom. The alpha male means the male in charge, the strongest of all males in the group. The alpha male is usually the only one that gets to screw the females. It's his job to keep the females satisfied."

"Don't forget fertilized," Madge said and hooted.

"Except for the fertilized part, that's the perfect description of Quint," Debbie Sue said, "especially the screwing part."

The customer stood and slid her glasses on. "Girls, when can I meet this man?"

All three women laughed.

"Seriously, Debbie Sue, who is this man?" The customer picked up her purse and walked to the payout counter.

"Oh, you've heard me talk about him, Madge. We were both seventeen. Following the high school rodeo circuit the summer before our senior year. Our hormones were raging, and the competition kept our adrenaline rushing. What can I say?"

Paige felt disappointed. "When you were seventeen? Phooey, I thought I was going to hear something more current than that."

Edwina spoke up. "It started when they were seventeen, honey. Then there was Buddy. Then there was no Buddy. Then there was Buddy again. That about sums it up. The last go-round, Quint practically killed himself trying to get Debbie Sue into bed and back into his life."

"You're better off with Buddy," Madge said, digging cash from her purse. "I'd faint if I saw a man more alpha than Buddy."

"I know," Debbie Sue said, taking her money and stuffing it into a drawer at the payout counter.

"Gosh, from the way this Quint guy looked when I told him you and Buddy had remarried, I'd say he's still crazy about you."

"Nah. And I'll prove it. I'll bet he asked you out when he heard I wasn't there, didn't he?"

"Well, no—"

"Okay, let me think. He probably asked for your name and phone number."

"Nope. Wrong again."

"I thought he gave up bullriding," Edwina said. "Because it sounds to me like he's been tossed on his head again."

Paige was enjoying herself and decided to give up the hoax. "Actually—"

"Aha," Edwina said, gloating in triumph. "I knew there was an *actually* in there. I'd have bet my life on it."

Paige grinned, enjoying being a part of the wicked fun. "*Actually,* once I told him you were married, he stopped me from closing the front door and suggested we get to know each other better."

Debbie Sue and Edwina cackled and high-fived. Madge joined in the laugher.

"That's a relief," Debbie Sue said, wiping a tear of mirth from her eye. "I was beginning to think he might have changed."

"Some things never change," Edwina added. "You can put a pair of boots in the oven, but that don't make 'em biscuits."

WEDNESDAY MORNING Paige awoke eager to get to work. She had known plenty of people who talked about going to work with the enthusiasm of a man on his way to the gallows. She was lucky to feel upbeat and excited about taking care of Harley's horses. That was the result of doing something she loved, something about which she was passionate.

She dressed in her work clothes, drove to the Flying C, and started her day exercising the horses. Lester seemed preoccupied and left her alone to do her job, which was fine with her because she had thinking to do.

She had to decide what to wear when she went to supper with Spur. Just the idea of sitting across the table from him, one to one, made her work faster. Goodness, if she was this nervous now, how uptight would she be when the actual date rolled around?

If it rolled around.

The last thought made her rein her mount to a stop. Spur hadn't actually set a date. In fact, the invitation had been vague at best. He could change his mind. The mystery brunette could change his mind.

For the first time in her life she truly cared if someone of the opposite sex invited her out, and here she had blown her opportunity. When he asked if she would like to have supper sometime, she should have said, "How about tonight?" An amateurish mistake. Debbie Sue or Edwina would never have made such an error. Add another task to her to-do list: find a way to cross paths with Spur again. If he didn't break the ice and set a date, then she would. After all, this was the twenty-first century. Women didn't have to wait for a man to ask them out like in the old days.

Noon found Paige sitting in the small office eating a sandwich and flipping through the pages of the most recent issue of *Vogue*. Funny, she had often envied the models on these pages, but today they looked anorexic and sad. Well dressed, but still anorexic and sad.

As she slid open the glued flap of a perfume ad to test the fragrance the phone rang. Lifting the receiver with her free hand she answered, "Flying C Ranch, this is Paige."

"I forgot to tell you, tonight is girls' night out," Debbie Sue said. "Every Wednesday." Paige smiled. She loved the way Debbie Sue just starting talking. No hello, no scripted conversation. Just direct and to the point. "Come on by after work," Debbie Sue continued. "Ed and I are having margaritas. And we've got an interesting evening planned."

"Gosh, thanks. Okay. Can I bring something?"

"Just your ol' sweet self."

"Oh, okay. What happens on girls' night out? And mind you, Debbie Sue, I'm almost afraid to ask you that."

"Oh, hell, nothing. We're old married women. Just come by the shop and we'll have drinks and supper together. Harmless."

Paige doubted that much of what Debbie Sue had thrown herself into in life had been totally harmless, but she agreed and hung up, glad she had something to look forward to at the end of the day.

By late afternoon Paige was so tired she was tempted to call and beg out of stopping by the beauty shop, but, in the end, she decided to make only a short visit.

Before she knew what happened, her intention to stop in, have a margarita, and go home had turned into a shampoo and protein pack, courtesy of Debbie Sue.

"I say it's time to eat," Debbie Sue said when she finished blow-drying Paige's locks. She turned up the radio as Gretchen Wilson broke into "Redneck Woman" and danced around the salon.

"I was planning on having that big chunk of Mississippi mud pie my honey made," Edwina said, working on her nails with an emery board. "After I do your nails."

"Mud pie's for dessert, goofball," Debbie Sue replied, twirling and doing a smooth two-step. "You know I can't keep nails. I might hurt Buddy in a delicate place." The two women cackled, with Debbie Sue never missing a beat to the music. When the song ended, Debbie Sue flopped into one of the hydraulic chairs. "If ever a song was written that's my song, that one's it." She turned to Paige. "Had supper?"

"Well, no, but—"

"Good. I'll go get something."

"Do you need any money?" Paige asked, grabbing for her purse.

Debbie Sue waved her effort off. "Forget it. Your money's no good in here."

As Debbie Sue left, Edwina went to the manicure table. "Come over here, Paige, and let me do your nails. After working in horseshit all day, they probably need it."

"But I can't afford—"

"On the house, sweetie. I'm in the mood to create." She picked up a dish and disappeared behind the floral curtain that hid the storeroom and shampoo room and returned with a dish of soapy water and the margarita pitcher. She topped off their glasses.

Paige took a seat opposite Edwina at the manicure table.

"Here, soak your fingers in this," Edwina told her, setting the dish of soapy water in front of her. The lanky brunette laid out brushes, bottles, and jars. "And tell me the story of your life."

Paige laughed. She loved her two new friends.

"Your folks showed up to see you yet?" Edwina asked.

"I don't have folks. It's just my dad. My mom died when I was little."

"Awww. Your dad didn't remarry?"

"Oh, he remarried. The oldest debutante in Texas. She spent her whole life preparing to catch the right husband, who turned out to be my dad. She's been determined I'd do the same."

Normally, Paige found it difficult to discuss her stepmother with anyone but Sunny. Somehow, with Edwina, it seemed easy and right. She went on to explain that from the age of thirteen she had been preparing, on her stepmother's instructions, for the role of "perfect"—perfect hair, perfect face, perfect lady. Also being the perfect spouse alongside the perfect husband. "Margaret Ann never let me forget that charm was the key to everything, even if it made your face crack."

"Hmmm," Edwina said as she skillfully applied acrylic to one of Paige's nails. "My mom had a speech for us girls when we were growing up, too. It went something like this. Come home knocked up and you're on your own."

Edwina seemed to have a steady supply of one-liners. "But you didn't take her seriously."

"Had to." Edwina blew a bubble and popped it. "I was two months late when she said it."

Paige laughed. "You and Debbie Sue are just plain crazy."

Debbie Sue returned with a six-pack of Dr Pepper and a bag of chicken strips, buttered Texas toast, fries, and a side of cream gravy. She spread the fare on her station counter, and the aroma filled the air. Only then did Edwina toss away her bubble gum. The three of them dug in.

"Uh-oh," Paige said, looking over the abundance of fried food. "It's a good thing I work off calories during the day."

Edwina picked up a breaded chicken strip and dipped it into the cream gravy. "Calories have never been a problem for me."

"Your metabolism is like your mouth," Debbie Sue quipped. "It never stops running." She swung a look to Paige. "You don't need to worry about a diet. You look like some model from Victoria's Secret."

"Well, at least you didn't say Barbie." Paige helped herself to a chicken strip and dunked it into the gravy. Even with all the calories, it beat what she had at home—Mrs. Sanders's five-year-old casserole and an assortment of happy-hour food. "I feel terrible keeping y'all in here so late."

"You haven't kept us," Edwina said. "We're working right now. We're surveilling."

A little dart of excitement rushed through Paige's blood. "Really? Where?"

"See that dark blue Ford Explorer parked at the curb across the street? The jerk who drives it, his wife hired us to watch him. He parked there three hours ago. A Toyota picked him up. We've got time-stamped pictures of him crawling into it. When he gets back we'll take some more. We'll show them to his wife, and she can decide how exciting things are going to get."

"Really? Oh, my God! This is so thrilling. What should I do? How should I act? I feel like I'm in a spy movie." She strode to the window, crouched, and cupped hands beside her eyes, peering out.

"Sugar," Edwina said, "the first rule is to act naturally. Using your hands for binoculars is a dead giveaway."

"It isn't all that exciting," Debbie Sue put in, popping the tops of three cans of Dr Pepper. "We get a lot of information just working here in the beauty shop. Sometimes I wonder if slopping shampoo on the female skull releases an enzyme in a woman's brain because it definitely affects her mouth. If we listen real good and ask the right questions, we can find out more than we ever wanted to know right here."

"All I can say," Edwina said, dipping a french fry into ketchup, "is it was damn sure convenient of Mr. Ford Explorer to hook up with his new bed partner right across the street from us. I kinda like sitting here having supper while I'm spying. Being a PI is the best job I've ever had. The most fun, too." Edwina stuffed the french fry into her mouth.

"But what if he doesn't come back for hours?" Paige asked. "Or days?"

"Sweetie, in Salt Lick, if some gal's husband is gone for days for a good reason, everybody in town knows when he left, where he went, and when he'll be back. If he's fooling around and disappears for days, the news gets around faster than a priest in a troop of Boy Scouts. So we only concern ourselves with the ones who disappear for hours."

"No kidding?" Paige said, wide-eyed. "Y'all are such a trip. I've spent the last six years of my life going to school. Surrounded by people that had a string of alphabet letters behind their names, and none of them are as smart or wise as you two."

"See there, Debbie Sue," Edwina said. "I was right. Schoolings fine for some people, but most of us just gotta rely on the good sense we're born with." She turned her attention back to Paige. "Trouble is most people don't have the smarts to figure out you have to open the window before you throw out the contents of a bedpan."

Paige laughed at another Edwinaism. "But what if he's gone really late? You don't have to sit here the entire time do you?"

"If he doesn't come back before we decide to go home," Debbie Sue added, "we use a tried-and-true method for determining how long a cheater's gone. We keep a box of watches in the back room, all wound up, all set to the right time. None of those digital things. We put one under his back tire. When he leaves he'll run over it, then tomorrow morning we'll pick up the crushed watch with the time frozen."

"No kidding?" Paige said again. "That really works?"

"It worked for me in two of my divorces," Edwina said. "That little trick is one of my contributions to the technical skill of our operation."

Paige couldn't be more excited talking to the CIA. "Y'all are just too cool. Do you ever get into trouble? Isn't this business dangerous?"

"Depends on your technique," Debbie Sue said. "We aren't confrontational, and we're never conspicuous. If it looks like there could be trouble, we back out. Buddy's a real cop. He'd divorce me for the second time if I got into a scrape."

"Tonight's not a real good example," Edwina said. "They're not all this easy. You see, in Salt Lick, everybody knows everybody. This dude in the Explorer is Calvin Echols. We've been hearing talk about him cheating on his wife for years, but until Mary Sue hired us to spy on him, we never concerned ourselves with it. She needs hard facts to take to her lawyer. There have been times, though, when we've used serious-as-shit surveillance."

"Oh, tell me. If it isn't a secret, that is." Paige wanted to learn everything possible. Who knew? She might have to use some of the same techniques someday.

"Sometimes we have to listen in on stuff. Now, mind you, left up to me and Debbie Sue, we'd be pressing a glass to the wall or talking into two soup cans joined by a piece of string. But thanks to my honey, we've got sophisticated shit."

"Really? How sophisticated are we talking?" Paige said, feeling her eyes bug again.

"Yep, Vic's our main man for that part of the business. He used to be in special ops in the navy. Girl, he knows two dozen ways to kill you quietly."

"That must be so scary, Edwina, living with someone who's capable of all that." Paige couldn't keep from being awed. These women were all that *Texas Monthly* had said they were. And more.

"Umm, *scary* isn't the right word. But, yeah, my sweetie's a man of immeasurable talents. And he knows a thing or two about spying, too." Edwina cackled, spinning around in her hydraulic chair. "He's got means and methods you wouldn't believe." Edwina winked. "He's got GPS."

"Oh, I've heard of that before. Global Positioning System." Squinting, Paige pressed a newly manicured finger against her chin. "I think they had it on *The Sopranos.*"

Edwina leaned forward, her eyes boring into Paige's. "Do you know that once, we tracked down this guy's location through his cell phone? Cool shit, huh? Sweetie, the days of calling home from a bar and saying you're working late are over. Lord, with camera phones, a stolen kiss can be sent to your own home. Don't even get me started on DNA."

Debbie shook her head and mouthed, "Reading."

"I'd love to stay and listen, but I have to go home," Paige said, laughing.

"You got a hot date with one of our local boys?" Edwina asked, winking at Debbie Sue.

"No, I'm afraid not. Though Dr. Atwater did come by the ranch today. He asked me if I'd like to go to supper sometime."

Edwina coughed and sputtered. "With him?"

"I think so. That's kind of the way it sounded to me."

Debbie Sue planted a fist on her hip. "And you've been here three hours, we've talked about everybody in three counties, and we're just now hearing that piece of news? Why did you wait 'til you're on your way out the door to tell us?"

"Well, I got all caught up in hair and nails and spying. My news seemed insignificant in comparison."

"Honey, read my well-kissed lips," Edwina said. "There's no such thing as insignificant news about a hottie. Especially when we can get the lowdown firsthand."

"That's the extent of the lowdown. He said he'd call, but I really don't think he will. I saw the brunette you mentioned. She was attractive. If you like that overdone look."

"Where'd you see them?" Debbie Sue asked.

"She was sitting in the cab of his truck and—" Paige stopped herself. She had almost slipped and told them she had been at the Kwik Stop. As clever as these two women were, they might put two and two together and figure out she was the one who had gotten locked in the cooler. "I, uh, I don't guess I should call her looks overdone. I only saw her from a distance."

"Whoever she is," Debbie Sue said, "she couldn't be prettier than you. Want us to find out her identity? We have ways, you know. Edwina and I know every person in this town. I'm curious, myself, to tell you the truth."

"Thanks, but don't waste your time. I believe in fate. If things are meant to work out between Spur and me, they will." Paige called up a mischievous grin. "If not, well, there's always Lester."

"Lester! Get out of here," Edwina said. "Why, the very idea."

Paige bid her new friends a good night and stepped into the crisp fall evening. With any luck there would be a message on her answering machine at home. If not, as her own personal heroine Scarlett would say, well tomorrow was another day.

seventeen

Morning found Paige back at the Flying C barns. As she alit from her Escalade, she heard the grind of a powerful engine. Before entering the barn, she looked in the direction of the sound and saw an eighteen-wheeler in the distance, inching up the road she had just traveled. Lester was coming from the storage area carrying a sack of feed on his shoulder. "You've got company coming," she called to him. "A big truck just crossed the cattle guard."

He set his load on the ground and sauntered over, wearing a day's growth of stubble, which added a dark and dangerous element to his good looks. Paige had to smile in spite of herself. Lester was exactly the type she would have taken up with before meeting Dr. Atwater. There. She had thought it. She and Spur Atwater hadn't even been out on a date yet, and he had changed how she looked at other men.

Lester must have mistaken her smile for an invitation because the next thing she knew, like a big octopus, his arm had wrapped around her waist and had pulled her close. She pushed against him, but his hold only tightened. She could feel his warm breath against her neck and a hardness—Oh, my God! He had a hard-on.

She pushed against him with both hands, but he was too strong for her. His hand cupped her breast. She summoned all her strength, clenched her teeth, and shoved him away. "Don't you ever touch me like that again!"

The bastard grinned and rubbed himself. "Don't tell me you didn't feel something. I know when a woman wants me. And you, Miz McBride, want me."

"If you ever pull something like that again, I'll—"

"You'll what? Run to daddy? Run to Harley?" He leaned closer, a leer roaming all the way from her lips to her feet and back. "Tell you what, darlin'. Neither one o' them scares me one damn bit."

She thought she saw in his eyes that assault wasn't out of the question for Lester Clinton.

But she couldn't run to her daddy or to Harley. If either of them knew he had harassed her, she would be yanked from her new job so fast her head would spin, and she couldn't risk that happening. She had to hang on to this opportunity for a bona fide future in a world she loved, even if she had to defend her virtue herself. She could do it. The genes of E. W. McBride, the toughest self-made man in Texas, coursed through her body. The temptation to break into tears and dash from the barn was great, but she stood her ground.

"The only thing I'm going to run to is my .357, Lester. I promise you, mess with me again and it'll be the last time you ever mess with anything."

She saw his eye twitch, but his stare wavered. "Hell, Paige, you've got a mean streak. I was kidding you a little." He grinned. "Did you say somebody's coming?" He left her and walked out of the barn.

Paige felt her knees shaking and stood for a minute gathering her composure. Good grief! The whole scene had been pure bravado on her part. Dirty Harriet she wasn't. She didn't even own a gun, wouldn't know a .357 from a cap pistol.

The truck arrival turned out to be a delivery of a large number of fifty-pound sacks of specially blended performance horse feed. Lester called for help from two hands and they began unloading the truck.

He apparently ordered top-shelf products to provide an optimum balance of nutrition for Harley's horses. Oats and bales of coastal Bermuda and alfalfa hay were also part of the delivery. Lester might be a despicable human in other areas of life, but he knew how to care for the horses. Harley's horses were high-caliber, disciplined athletes. Their condition was paramount to their success, thus his. Good nutrition did more than improve the horses' performance; it also reduced their chances of injury. Lester didn't take such pains out of love for the animals, she thought, but viewed them as a ticket to whatever lofty goal he had set for himself.

Paige didn't doubt for a minute the number of sacks delivered was justified, but oats and alfalfa hay puzzled her. He had been explicit when he gave her instructions on feeding. The mature horses were to be fed twice a day. No treats and plenty of water. Alfalfa and oats would add burdensome pounds to their weight. Definitely not a desirable prospect. She did notice that most of the alfalfa and oats taken off the truck were loaded into Lester's own pickup bed. Apparently he didn't plan on feeding it to the cutting horses.

Paige spent the better part of the day avoiding Lester. At two o'clock she mustered her courage and approached him, keeping a safe distance. "Lester, I'm going to town. I need some supplies, and I want to get them before you leave next week."

"What kind of supplies? Everything we needed was delivered today."

"Small stuff. I want some new feed buckets. The ones I've been using are busted. I'm going to buy some Blue Lotion, some Stress-Pak, and wheat germ oil. Some personal things, too, like a decent brand of coffee and some diet drinks."

"Long as you're going to town, pick me up some beer."

"The fridge is loaded with beer."

"I need it for my trip."

"Just exactly where are you going? Or is that too personal?"

"Nothing's too personal between us, honey. I'm going to see a lady friend in Abilene. Even if you don't want what I got, there's plenty that do." He smiled devilishly.

"What can I say, Lester? There's just no accounting for taste."

Slinging her purse over her shoulder, Paige left the barn, not doubting for a minute he was watching her backside.

SPUR LOOKED DEEPLY into the troubled brown eyes and tried to smooth the furrowed brow. Sammy was a Rhodesian ridgeback, a highly intelligent but painfully neurotic breed. His owner talked soothingly, but Sammy suffered from "white coat syndrome." His annual visit to the vet, as reported by his owner, Randy, always proved to be traumatic for Sammy and owner both.

The seventy-pound Sammy was strong as a bull, and fear heightened his determination to break free. Spur had all he could do keeping the slick-haired dog on the exam table. The owner stood by, wringing his hands and offering little help.

"Please don't let him get away from you," Randy pleaded. "His instinct is to run when he's frightened. If he takes off, I'm afraid I'll never see him again. He's my baby. I can't imagine life without him."

"He's got nowhere to go in here," Spur said, both arms wrapped around the slick-haired dog's middle. He dodged Sammy's determination to claw at his head. "Even if he gets out of this room, there's still the front office to hold him."

The thought of the dog escaping bothered Spur, too. The fear in the animal's eyes touched him. "Let me get another pair of hands in here." Not relinquishing his grip, he yelled, "Electra."

The door between the examination room and the front office opened, and his sister poked her head inside just enough to answer, "Did you call me?"

"Would you come help us out with Sammy? Hold his rear, 'Lectra. Randy, I'll ask you to come to the front so that he can see you and I'll get the syringe ready."

PAIGE LEFT THE GROCERY STORE with her scant supply of food tucked into the back of the Escalade. She had saved the trip to Spur's office for last for a good reason. If he should engage her in a long conversation or *if* he should ask her to join him for a drink after work, she would be free to do it.

She had to laugh at the thought of an invitation to have a drink after work. Back home that would have meant one of the hot spots. Trendy upscale bars or restaurants filled with career-climbing, well-dressed professionals. And here? Well, here it meant a cup of coffee at Kay's Koffee Kup or a soda at Hogg's.

She should call Sunny and tell her. Her buddy, who spent most of her time in various expensive watering holes around the world, would find social life in Salt Lick hilarious. Paige, on the other hand, had begun to think Salt Lick quaint and somehow soothing.

In the vet clinic parking lot, she killed the engine and took a moment to inspect her face. She swiped her lips with J. Lo's Cherries in the Snow lip gloss and gave her golden mane a tousle. She decided to forgo perfume, doubting that any fragrance could overpower the horse smell on her, and who knew, maybe that *was* perfume to a veterinarian. She needed to take advantage of every opportunity to impress Spur. What had Debbie Sue said? Oh, yeah, "leave him something to think about." So far, most of what he had to *think about* would make anyone cringe. Today Paige intended to change that.

No receptionist greeted her when she entered the office, even though the HELP WANTED sign was gone. She could hear muffled voices behind the door just to the left of the desk. Should she wait or make her presence known? She didn't see the harm in opening the door and getting someone's attention. There were no acts of privacy with animal care, were there? And, after all, she was a customer. She had come here to make purchases.

Fixing her smile, Paige opened the door. And froze. A tag-team wrestling match with a big dog was taking place on the examination table. All four participants looked up, and to Paige's astonishment, she was face-to-face with the mysterious brunette.

Without warning the big dog kicked his hind legs free from the brunette's grip, vaulted from the table, and headed for Paige.

A short guy she had never seen yelled in a falsetto voice, "Oh, stop him. . . . Oh, my God! Please stop him!"

Instinctively Paige made a grab for the dog's body as he darted past her. His slick coat slid through her hands as if he were greased and she was left holding on to his long tail. She hung on for dear life. The animal jerked her to her knees with unbelievable strength. Overpowering her efforts to get back on her feet, he pulled her toward the front door. Still she hung on. Over her shoulder Paige could hear the commotion of others coming to her aid and outcries in the falsetto voice. "Hold on! Oh, please hold on! Don't let him go!"

Ahead, Paige saw the glass door closed and felt relief. Then to her horror, the dog pushed his muzzle against the door, creating a narrow opening and wedged his lean, muscular body into it. He squirmed through, dragging Paige with him to the great outdoors and freedom.

Paige tightened her grip on the snakelike tail and wrestled the dog to the ground, maneuvering until she could wrap her legs around its body. She rolled on the gravel parking lot with her arms encircling his head. He scratched and clawed. Dog yelps pierced the air. All she could think of was hanging on.

Through the chaos, she could see a man's feet dancing on tiptoes. "Oh, my goodness," the falsetto voice cried. "Oh, my goodness!"

Paige heard Spur's order. "Get his leash!"

The next thing she knew, Spur was on the ground beside her. He replaced her legs with his own and took the dog's head under his arm. Paige crawled away and rested on her hands and knees as the brunette woman appeared with a harness and slipped it over the dog's head. "I've got him! Let go! I've got him!"

As if he realized the fight was over, the dog gave up. He trotted over to the effeminate guy, tail wagging, his teeth fully exposed in a grin that stretched his mouth comically.

"Oh, my baby. My poor baby." The man wrapped his arms around the dog's neck and covered the canine face with kisses. "I'm so sorry. Oh, baby, I'm so sorry."

Paige managed to creak into a sitting position and examined herself. Her insides were quaking. Blood showed on her torn jeans at both knees, and her knees were on fire. She couldn't see her elbows, but they were on fire, too. Dog slobbers covered her. She fought not to break into tears.

The brunette and the dog owner walked back into the clinic, leading the dog. Spur came over, bent down, and slid his arm around her waist. "Damn. You okay?"

Paige stared after the brunette. So that's who she was—Spur's new receptionist. Typical. She had probably applied for the job, hoping to snare the new doctor in town, the new, *good-looking and eligible* doctor in town. Edwina and Debbie Sue didn't know her identity, so she had to have driven a long way to get this job. *What some women won't do for a man's attention.*

Pitiful.

Well, if he liked that type—overly made up, a little on the plump side, tacky shoes, then more power to him.

"Paige? Paige, I said are you okay? Let me help you up."

Coming out of her dazed state, she realized Spur was talking. She wanted to slap his hand away and tell him his brunette bimbo needed his help more than she did, but she gave in and accepted his assistance. He lifted her to her feet as if she weighed nothing. When she stood upright, the pain in her knees worsened. "Ouch!"

She bent over to reexamine the damage but felt light-headed. The ground seemed to be rising to meet her.

Spur grabbed her arm and steadied her. "Whoa there. Let me look at you. You've got a nasty bump on your forehead. You must have hit the glass door pretty hard. Looks like your knees and elbows are pretty banged up, too. Let's go inside. Let me take a look."

The last thing she wanted was first aid from an incompetent gold digger like his receptionist. She had every intention of refusing help, but Spur's strong arm around her waist guided her back into the clinic. "It isn't necessary. I'll just go home and clean up and put on a Band-Aid."

"I bet you don't even have Band-Aids at your house."

"So, what? Is that supposed to say something about my character?"

The effeminate man led his dog toward them. The dog actually grinned and behaved as if he hadn't just caused a train wreck. "Dr. Atwater, if it's all the same to you, I'm just going to take my Sammy home. I can't take much more today. I need to lie down and put a cool cloth on my head. When I think how close I came to losing him—" The dog owner blinked back tears as he turned to Paige. "Thank you so much for helping. You were magnificent."

"You're, uh, welcome, I guess," Paige mumbled.

After the owner and his beast left, Spur escorted Paige to the exam area behind the receptionist's office. "Hop up here and let me take a look at those knees. Mind if I rip these jeans a little farther?"

"There's no need to do that, Spur," the receptionist said. Her sudden appearance in the room set Paige on edge.

"Ma'am," the brunette said, "why don't you go into the bathroom and take them off. I've got a lab coat you can wrap around yourself." She held out a blue coat.

"That isn't necessary. I'll just go—"

"That's a great idea." Spur pushed her toward the bathroom door. "Go on, now. Change."

Paige limped into the bathroom with the coat slung over her arm. Grimacing and hanging onto the sink, she removed the jeans. Her knees resembled hamburger. Two thin trails of blood ran down her shins. Spur had been right. She did need medical attention.

Wrapping the coat around the lower half of her body she returned to the exam area.

Spur took a step toward her. "Do you need help getting on the table?"

"I can do it just fine," she lied, still shaking inside. His hands came to her waist, and he lifted her onto the table.

He spoke to the brunette. "Why don't you stay with us. I might need your help."

Well, this was an interesting conclusion to the day, which had started with a sloppy seduction attempt by a lecher. Now, here she sat in her panties, covered only by a coat, with Spur and his girlfriend. Never a dull moment.

Spur examined the bump on her head, then began cleaning her fiery wounds with a cooling substance that had a numbing effect. The brunette's gaze remained glued to what he was doing. He stopped and looked up. "Sorry. You two haven't met. Paige, this is my sister Electra. 'Lectra, this is Paige McBride."

Stunned, Paige stared at the brunette. Looking closer, she saw a family resemblance.

"It's nice to meet you, Paige," Spur's sister said.

"Electra," Paige gushed, "it's so nice to meet you, too." *She is so cute. She looks just like Spur.* "It's so nice that Spur has you working with him. I love your shoes."

"That hurt?" Spur asked, gently dabbing at her wounds.

"No," she lied again. In truth, she wondered if she would be able to walk tomorrow. "It stings is all."

"What came over you, grabbing that dog like that?"

"I don't know. The guy was yelling for someone to stop him. I was so determined to hold on I didn't realize what was happening."

Spur continued to work as he talked. "You shouldn't try to restrain an unfamiliar dog. He could have attacked you."

"I couldn't help it. I couldn't let him just run past me. I could see him getting run over or lost."

He looked into her eyes with such warmth and tenderness she almost sighed. "You're pretty special to have done that, Paige."

He went to a white cupboard and came back with a tube of something and a pile of gauze pads and rolls of gauze. "This is an antibiotic ointment," he said as he squeezed strips from the tube onto a thick gauze pad. He gently placed the pad on her knee, and she winced. Holding the pad in place, he wrapped gauze around it and her knee and secured the bandage with tape. Then he moved to the other knee.

When he finished with her knees, he examined her elbows and gave them similar treatment. At the end, she couldn't comfortably bend her arms or legs. Though he may have gone slightly overboard on the first aid, no way would she have denied herself the pleasure of his undivided attention. "Gosh, I look like a mummy," she said.

Their eyes caught, and his gaze lingered. Finally, he looked away and declared, "There shouldn't be much scarring. The abrasions aren't that deep." He reached into a cupboard and retrieved another tube and more gauze bandages. "Remove this dressing tomorrow and put on some of this antibiotic ointment. Also clean bandages. I don't want you working in the barns without those wounds being protected."

"Oh. I didn't even think of that."

"I'm giving you extra bandages to take home."

"Okay, thanks. Does it feel funny to be talking to your patient?

Giving them instructions on what to do?" Paige managed to smile, though her knees still felt like hot coals had been pressed to them.

Spur smiled back and she relished being taken into his space. "I always talk to my patients," he said. "Some of them are smarter than their owners. . . . Do you need anything for pain? I may have a few people medications around here somewhere."

"Uh, no. I've got aspirin and stuff."

Electra left the room and came back, holding up Paige's torn jeans and inspecting the ripped and frayed knees. "These don't look like you've worn them much. Lucky for you they can be saved. It'll just take a little time on the sewing machine."

Paige almost said, That's okay, I'll throw them away, but she thought about Spur and his sibling's upbringing and stopped herself just in time. He hadn't described his childhood in graphic detail, but patched and repaired clothing had surely been a part of it. Paige felt chastened by her own abundance of everything. Everything material, that is.

Paige had never threaded a needle, suspected she would have better luck flying a jumbo jet than operating a sewing machine. When she had clothing that needed mending, if she didn't trash it, she took it to her favorite dry cleaners, which had an alterations department. "Yes, I think you're right, Electra. I'll do that. Thanks so much."

She lumbered across the room, stiff legged.

"Good Lord, Spur," Electra said. "You've got her wrapped up like a double amputee. She can't even walk."

"I'm fine. Really." In the bathroom, with some effort, Paige put on her ragged jeans, then returned to the exam room, carrying the lab coat.

"I want to thank you," she said to Spur and his sister. "How much do I owe—"

"Nothing," Spur said.

"If we collect from anyone," Electra said, "we'll send a bill to Randy."

"But he couldn't help it because his dog was scared. I'd rather pay—"

"No," Spur said. "Nobody's paying. It was just one of those things that happens."

With Spur's arm around her waist, Paige limped to her Escalade. No man she could think of had ever treated her so gently. She loved his arm around her. She took full advantage of the moment by leaning into him and letting him support her.

"Sure you'll be able to get home okay?" he asked her.

She loved his showing concern for her. She had no doubt he really cared. When she had difficulty lifting her foot into the Escalade, he reached for it. "Here, let me help you."

He all but lifted her onto the driver's seat. He was so close, and his eyes were locked on hers. The next thing she knew, his lips, too, had found hers. Kissing him seemed like the most natural thing she had ever done, and it was all she had imagined it would be. She wanted it to go on forever.

Their lips had barely parted when Electra walked up. She planted her fists on her hips. "Spur Atwater, don't you dare let her drive home. She can barely bend her legs."

"Oh," he said, a frown forming a crease between his brows. "I guess you're right. I'm so accustomed to working with animals it's kind of an assumption on my part that someone will be looking after my patients. Do you have somebody you can call?"

"Uh, well . . ." She could think of no one. Though she believed she had bonded with Debbie Sue and Edwina, the friendship was too new to impose on it. "No one, I guess. But I'll be fine."

"I'm driving you home." He bent and scooped her from behind the wheel, carried her around the Escalade, and deposited her on the passenger seat. Returning to the driver's side, he told Electra. " 'Lectra. Close up for me, please. I'm driving Paige home. Pick me up there in about half an hour." Turning his attention to Paige he said, "Tell her your address, Paige. I remember where the house is, but I don't know the address."

"Two-eleven Mustang Drive."

"Got it," Electra said. "See you in half an hour. . . . Or so."

eighteen

Paige felt foolish that Spur had made such a big deal out of a few scrapes on her extremities and a bump on her forehead. The undivided attention had been great, no argument there, but she didn't want him thinking her helpless.

She preferred he think of her as strong and resilient. The kind of woman who could have gone west by covered wagon and helped her husband clear the land while keeping her hand on the plow and carrying a baby on her hip. Or standing by his side through famine, drought, flood, or pestilence.

Pestilence? Yuck. Who was she kidding? Those poor women had a terrible life, and many were worn out or dead before they hit thirty. Okay, forget the pioneer woman. She didn't want to be made of that kind of stuff, she just wanted to be able to endure a runaway dog dragging her across a parking lot. Some might call her a sissy, but the results had been a kiss and a chauffeured drive home by a really hot guy.

Spur pulled the Escalade into her narrow driveway and killed the engine. "Wait for me," he ordered. "Don't try to get out alone."

He opened the passenger door and offered his hand to her. She attempted to scoot out, but her knees were held rigid by the bandages. Legs straight out and slightly spread, she slid from the seat to the concrete surface. "See? I'm all right." She smiled up at him.

Spur tilted her chin upward. "I know. You're gonna be good as new in a day or two, but you're not now, and I'm going to make sure you get into the house with as little discomfort as possible. No more discussion. Mind me, now. I'm the doctor." He gave her a grin and a wink.

At this moment Paige would have done anything he said, would have ridden Sammy the dog across town on a tiny saddle if she had known it would result in this treatment. She was putty in his hands.

A reedy voice broke the fairy-tale moment. Paige looked and saw Koweba Sanders staring with an expression of alarm at her bandages. "What happened to her, young man? Oh, good gracious, Pat. Do I need to call the law?"

"No, ma'am," Paige yelled. "This is a friend of mine."

"She had an accident. She was drug," Spur said.

"Accidentally drugged?" Mrs. Sanders's expression turned stark. "Listen here, young fella, I watch *20/20*. You better not've slipped her one of those date rape drugs. I've got a good mind to call up Billy Don—"

"Mrs. Sanders, listen," Paige yelled, taking the octogenarians hands in her own. "This is my friend. He is helping me. I am fine."

Koweba smiled and patted Paige's face with gnarled fingers. "Pat, if you say nothing's wrong then I'll believe you." As she turned to leave she shot Spur a murderous look through squinted eyes. "But I won't forget you, young man. I got the license number of that big thing you're driving. Anything funny happens here and I'm reporting you to the authorities." Without further comment she hobbled back across the street.

Spur looked at Paige. "But it's your car, your license plates. Can't she see that?"

Paige arched her brow and shrugged. "I don't think she can see much."

"She doesn't seem to be able to hear much, either." Spur sighed. "But, I think she's genuinely fond of you, *Pat.*"

Paige started laughing and momentarily forgot her injuries. Spur braced her with his powerful arm and walked her into the house.

Inside, he helped her to a chair at the dining table. "You need to get into something softer than these jeans. Do you have some sweats or some shorts you can put on?"

"There's a pair of flannel shorts hanging on the back of the bathroom door."

"I'll get them. Be right back."

Spur returned with the Stars jersey and the shorts.

"Thanks. I'll go change in the bedroom." Paige rose from her chair.

"Oh, no, you don't. I'm not risking you blacking out and banging your head against something. Your neighbor would have me in jail. You change right here. I'll turn my back."

Paige didn't have an explanation for why, but she felt as if she'd known Spur Atwater all her life. His suggestion made perfect sense, and she wasn't the least bit nervous or intimidated at the thought of being practically naked in his presence.

She tried to remove the sweatshirt but couldn't bend her elbows. She tried to remove the jeans but couldn't bend her knees. Paralyzed by bandages. "Uh, Spur. Could you keep your eyes closed and turn around. I need help."

He turned to face her, with both eyes squeezed shut. "What can I do?"

"Pull my shirt over my head." Guiding his hands to the banded bottom of the garment she raised her arms. As Spur moved the shirt up, his fingers grazed her skin, sending shivers down her spine.

"I'm sorry," he said quickly, as if he knew. His touch was as soft as a lover's, and she could only imagine what, under different circumstances, the outcome would be. "It just tickled."

With a small amount of pain, she wriggled into the loose-fitting jersey, glad her elbows were left uncovered. "Now," she said, "if you'll just hook your fingers in the waistband of my jeans and pull them off. Then hand me the shorts."

He had to stand closer for this maneuver. She could feel her heart rate surge. The house was cool and the task of removing her clothing wasn't physically challenging, but she could see beads of sweat forming along his hairline.

He tugged on the jeans, trying to remove them with as little contact as possible. "Wait," Paige exclaimed. "You've got my panties."

Spur threw both hands in the air and turned his back again. "Paige, I gotta go outside for a minute. Don't move. I'll be back in just a second." He bolted for the back door.

She struggled with the jeans and managed to remove them from one leg before he returned. He stood in front of her again, eyes closed, and tugged on the jeans until the other leg was freed. Paige reached for the shorts, worked them over her feet, then stood up and pulled them on. He had been a perfect gentleman, hadn't peeked the entire time, but she could see he was shaking all over.

"You can open your eyes now," she said.

He let out an audible breath. "You look a lot more comfortable. Just let me check those bandages one more time."

He squatted and was in the process of inspecting the bandages on her knees when a honking horn broke the silence. Electra had found the house.

He looked up at her. "Guess I better go."

"I can't thank you enough for taking care of me," she said as he got to his feet.

He bent and placed a kiss on her lips. His mouth played with hers, and the kiss became more urgent. Before they fell into a passionate embrace, the horn sounded again and Spur stepped away. "I'll check on you later," he said huskily.

Paige let him go reluctantly.

"Paige, I—" He kissed her forehead. "I gotta go."

She watched as he showed himself out, feeling as if she had been scooped into a whirlwind. She didn't even care if the scrapes on her knees and elbows did leave scars. At least she would have something by which she could remember this moment.

THE WARBLING OF THE PHONE on the bedside table woke Paige. She had propped herself on pillows on her bed to watch TV and had promptly fallen asleep. The clock showed nine o'clock. She had been sleeping for two hours. "Hello?"

"Were you sleeping?"

The voice was so soft and oh, so familiar. "No, no, I was just— yes," she said, laughing. "I turned on the TV, found the show I wanted to watch, and that's the last thing I remember. Maybe Mrs. Sanders was right. Maybe you did slip me a drug after all."

"I just wanted to tell you, it might have been presumptuous on my part, but I called Harley Carruthers and told him what had happened to you."

"You did? But, why?"

"I wanted him to know, and I told him I thought it best you not work tomorrow."

"But, Spur—"

"I know, I know, you're fine. If you had a desk job I'd agree with you. But you don't. I've seen people working around animals contract some pretty nasty staph infections with only a tiny cut on their body. You've got some significant abrasions, and I don't want to see you take the risk."

Paige was moved beyond words. No one, other than Daddy, had ever been so caring. She struggled to control her emotions. "Gosh, Spur, I—"

"Are you mad at me?"

"Oh, no, Spur. I appreciate your worrying about me. I never would have thought of something like a staph infection. I had classes once with a girl who got staph from a botched acrylic nail application. It was pretty nasty, as you say."

She heard a deep chuckle.

"Well, it was. When can I go back to work, Doctor?"

"Clean the wounds again tomorrow and cover them with the antibacterial ointment I gave you. Leave the bandages off. Day after tomorrow you can return, but be sure you pack each area in salve and double bandages. You understand? Double bandages."

"Yessir. I got it."

"Do that for several days and look for any, and I mean any, sign of infection."

"Yes, sir, and thanks for calling Harley."

"Speaking of Harley, we had an interesting conversation. He let the cat out of the bag and told me something I think he didn't intend to."

"Really? What did he say?"

"He's an Aggie. He made sure my bank loan went through without a hitch. He and Dr. Miller agreed that I was the one who should take over the vet practice. Harley made it happen. Makes sense to me now. I've thought all along the loan went awfully smooth."

Remembering Lester's remarks, Paige hugged the receiver close to her face. "You sound like you're okay with that."

"I guess I am. Truth is, I'm surprised at myself. Maybe I've grown up some, but it feels like a hand up isn't as hard to take as a handout. I know I'll never let 'em down, so yeah, I'm okay with it. I'll make sure they never regret their decision."

"One hand greasing the other, as my daddy would say."

"I guess so. I'm still learning. . . . Well, I'm gonna let you go now. I got some paperwork to finish before I call it a day. Good night, Paige."

She held the receiver long after he hung up. *Good night, Spur,* she whispered in her mind.

Replacing the phone, she fluffed her pillows with the intention of returning to sleep, when the phone rang again. Hoping it was him again, she eagerly reached for the receiver and was surprised, but no less thrilled, at hearing Buck McBride's voice.

"Daddy! I've been thinking about calling you. You beat me to it."

"That's my job, sweetheart, beating you to anything you might be thinking." He laughed, and she smiled, visualizing him with his head thrown back.

She spent the next twenty minutes telling him about her job and her new friends. She even told him about Spur, the episode with the dog, and how well she had been treated.

"It warms my heart to hear you, honey. There's enthusiasm in your voice I haven't heard in years." He cleared his throat, then continued, "Honey, I called to talk to you about something serious."

The sudden change made Paige's pulse quicken. In a matter of seconds dark thoughts rushed through her mind that made her feel sick. Was he ill? Was he in some sort of trouble? Had his wildcatting ways resulted in some kind of legal problems? Her brow furrowed. "Daddy, what's wrong? Are you sick?"

"No, honey. Nothing like that."

She exhaled as she smoothed her hair off her forehead. She had wondered often how she would handle hearing disturbing news about her daddy, and now she knew. Not well at all. "Whew, Daddy. You had me so scared."

"I'm sorry, baby. I should have made things clear up front." Again, he cleared his throat. "Paige, when you were just a baby your sweet mother set aside an inheritance for you. It was stipulated that you would take possession when you turned twenty-five years old. That's two months away, or hadn't you noticed."

A gift from her mother was a sobering thought all right. "Okay" was all Paige could think to say. "Why have you waited so long to tell me about it?"

"I didn't think you were ready. That's part of the reason I forced you to stand on your own. I was trying to prepare you."

She had caused him so much disappointment, it was vital that he thought her prepared. "Do you think I'm ready or have we just run out of time?"

"Yes, baby, I think you're ready."

Her spirits soared. Her mind inventoried her mother's large jewelry collection, which had resided in a safe-deposit box for years. Then there had been some family land somewhere around downtown Fort Worth. "So, what are we talking about? Her jewelry, her land?"

"No, babe, nothing like that. . . . It's cash money."

Paige immediately thought of her bare living room. She could finally buy a couch and some chairs. Maybe even a washer and dryer. Patio furniture. She'd love some patio furniture.

"Ooohhh, I could use some money. I need to buy some things for my house. How much are we talking?"

"Well, it started out small, but it was invested well and it's earned some. And . . . well, honey, it's now around twenty million."

PAIGE WAS BREWING COFFEE when the doorbell rang. She had been awake for hours. In fact, she'd hardly slept at all. The idea of having so much money of her very own in a few months was not just sobering, it was downright scary. She had never known her mother had any substantial amount of her own money. Daddy had always said he had never relied on her mother's funds. He made every cent he had himself.

She had worried all night about Spur and his attitude about wealthy people. She wasn't worried he would become more interested when he learned how rich she was; she was afraid he would flee.

Looking through the peephole she saw Edwina and Debbie Sue. As if Edwina knew she was being watched, she waved a white paper bag in front of her. "Open up, Paige. We've got doughnuts for your boo-boos."

Paige opened the door. "Y'all are crazy. Doughnuts for boo-boos?"

"Jelly-filled, chocolate sprinkles, and powdered sugar," Debbie Sue said. "Nothing will make you feel better than calories."

"Don't show us your scabs 'til after we've eaten," Edwina said. "I don't want to spoil my breakfast."

"How did you know about my accident?"

"C.J. called. She's making you some chicken soup."

"Isn't that for a cold? I don't understand."

"You'd have to know C.J. She thinks chicken soup fixes everything."

Paige was touched. In Fort Worth, she could have been out of touch for days and she doubted if anyone would have even noticed her missing. Oh, maybe Sunny would, eventually, depending on what country she happened to be in.

The three of them sat at the kitchen table and devoured the pastries with cups of coffee while Paige told of her encounter with the dog Sammy.

"I wish I could have seen that," Debbie Sue said. "How did Spur react? Was he upset about the dog?"

Paige began telling of the tenderness he had shown. She retold the episode of changing clothes with his assistance.

"Damn, that sounds erotic as hell," Edwina said. "I think Vic and I should try that. He wouldn't keep his eyes shut, though."

"Well, Spur did. He didn't peek once."

Debbie Sue grabbed a glazed doughnut and dunked it in her coffee. "I'm more impressed with that guy every day, Paige. If I were you, I'd be falling in love with him."

Needing help concealing the idiotic grin that must be showing on her face, Paige grabbed a doughnut, tore it in half, and stuffed a piece of it into her mouth.

nineteen

Paige spent the next few days as unburdened as if an anvil had been lifted from her shoulders. How could she have known Spur's black-haired "girlfriend" was his sister? Despite all the evil thoughts she'd had before learning Electra's true identity, Paige liked her.

She was so happy she even managed to be civil to Lester, though she could hardly wait for him to depart on his planned trip. With him gone, she just might find a legitimate need to ask for Spur's assistance.

But as the weekend approached and no phone call came to set a dinner date, doubts returned. She had pressed the On button on her cell phone a dozen times to reassure herself the thing worked. She had even called Information and asked for her own number, just to be certain it was accessible to whomever needed it. Again, she dialed her land line number from her cell phone and got the usual burr. Phooey.

Life was so much simpler without guys. Guys made you doubt

yourself and your sanity. They made you question your sexuality and consider becoming a nun, an unacceptable option, of course, with the wardrobe being so drab and restrictive.

Thursday evening, she dragged a TV dinner from the freezer and placed it in the microwave for the prescribed six minutes. As she removed it, she peered at it closely, then picked up the box from which she had taken it and studied the picture—a succulent chicken breast, green beans and carrots, mashed potatoes and apple cobbler. The tray in her hand held something that looked like a hockey puck, unidentifiable green and orange objects, a clump of something beige that resembled lumpy oatmeal with a yellow glob in the middle and something gooey and jellified. *Yuck.*

Perhaps five TV dinners for a dollar was a bargain she should have passed up. Now, her only other choices were the four remaining TV dinners or Mrs. Sanders's aged casserole. What she wouldn't give for a visit from Sunny, testing her latest recipe.

A Hogg's burger was the only solution. Paige grabbed her purse and left the house.

SPUR LISTENED as the phone rang. For some reason he was counting the rings, and after seven, he hung up. "Well, that's that," he mumbled. He had said he would call, and he had called.

He had mixed emotions about not reaching Paige. Part of him was relieved that her soft voice didn't materialize on the other end of the phone line. Another part was disappointed and annoyed that no answering machine had picked up. Did he hang up too soon? Had she seen his name on caller ID and ignored the call? A covey of boyfriends, old and current, was bound to exist in her life. Well-to-do studs with trust funds who could take her to the places she was accustomed to going.

To hell with it, he told himself. Life was simpler without women. The only real thing he needed now, the only warm and enticing object he wanted to hold, was a burger from Hogg's. Pulling his boots back on, he left his trailer.

As he entered the brightly lit eatery and made his way to a booth, he remembered he had left his wallet on his dresser. Fortunately, to eat at Hogg's, he didn't need much money. At under two dollars, burger prices were cheaper than he had ever seen. He dug into his pockets for change and found a crumpled bill. He tossed it on the table and added a handful of change. Counting his money, he was oblivious to everything around him.

PAIGE SPOTTED Spur's rattletrap pickup the minute she drove into Hogg's parking lot. For an instant, she thought of not stopping, but hunger was a powerful motivator. Besides, she could go through the drive-thru and avoid seeing him altogether.

She sat second in line at the order window, which gave her a good view of the dining area. She immediately spotted Spur standing at a table. He was engrossed in something, and the longer she watched the more apparent it became that he was counting change on the table and patting down his pockets. Watching this moment, a creepy feeling of embarrassment settled within her. He had made it clear his finances were rocky, but this was much worse than she had imagined. Before now, it hadn't occurred to her that money might be the reason he hadn't called and invited her to supper. Was she so spoiled she had overlooked his dilemma? Then, her embarrassment turned into pity.

And it was the pity that pushed her. She was possessed with a new strength she didn't know she had. She wasn't a woman looking for an opportunity to spend time with a hunky guy; she was on an act of mercy. Saving a life. After she paid and received her meal, she made a wide swing from the window to a parking spot in front of the building.

Spur was moving to the order counter when she stepped into Hogg's dining room. Well, at least he had scraped enough money together to order. She walked up behind him and gently touched his shoulder. "Hi, Spur," she said softly. "How are you?"

He jumped as if she had yelled. "Paige! . . . I'm sorry. I didn't see you come in. How're you? How're your knees?"

"They're terrific. See?" Paige lifted each knee waist high. "I'm sure I'd still be in pain if you hadn't taken such good care of them."

Spur looked down at the handful of coins in his hand and closed his fist. His hands dropped to his sides. The motion wasn't wasted on Paige, and it was all she could do not to weep. "Listen. I was thinking about your invitation to dinner—"

"Oh, yeah. I'm sorry I haven't called. I was—"

"You don't have to apologize. I know you've been busy. Me, too. I just wanted to say instead of going out to eat somewhere, why don't you come to my house Saturday night and I'll fix supper for us?"

"Your house?"

"Yes. It's so hard to cook for one. Debbie Sue's house has a great kitchen, and she left a lot of cooking stuff behind. I'd really appreciate it if you'd let me try it out. You can be my first guest."

"You cook?"

The incredulity in his question couldn't be mistaken. Okay, so maybe it was obvious cooking wasn't something in which she took an interest. The truth was worse than that. She had flunked every homemaking class she had ever taken. Oh, she could boil water, but she didn't know what to do with it afterward. But she had the confidence to learn.

"I'm sorry," he said, placing a hand on her shoulder. "I didn't mean that the way it sounded. A home-cooked meal would be great. I haven't had one since that night at Buddy and Debbie Sue's house. What time?"

Paige tried not to show shock. She smiled brightly. "Let's say six. Any requests?"

"No, just make plenty. I love home cooking. You wouldn't know how to make those hot rolls Debbie Sue had, would you?"

Oh, hell. Hot rolls? Baked bread? She smiled. "I'm sure I could get her recipe. I can probably just whip them right up."

"Those were just about the best homemade rolls I ever ate."

"Yeah, they were good. I'll see what I can do." She could only hope her smile didn't appear to be as weak as it felt. "I'll see you Saturday."

When Paige climbed back into the Escalade she felt as if she had awakened from a dream. She sat there dumbfounded. Had she just invited Spur to dinner? A dinner that she would cook? And homemade rolls? *Mother of God.*

Reinforcements, where are you? *Sunny, if ever there's a time you're at home, let it be tonight.*

By the time she reached home, Paige's hunger had been replaced by terror. She keyed Sunny's phone number in with one hand while she held her burger with the other, continuing the prayer that her friend would answer. To her relief, a voice answered.

"If you don't have a damn good reason for calling, hang up."

Uh-oh. Sunny must have been asleep. "Sunny? What's wrong with you? I didn't wake you up did I?"

Her friend grunted.

"But, Sunny, it's still daytime. It isn't even eight o'clock."

"It isn't? Oh, hell. I just got in from Spain last night."

"You didn't tell me you were going to Spain."

"Ricardo. A guy I met in Reata? We flew over for a flamenco contest. Guess I'm jet-lagged. What day is it?"

Sunny had a weakness for dark, swarthy men. "It's Thursday."

"Shit. I thought I left Spain on Thursday. God, I hate this. I'll be a week getting back to Texas time." She yawned. "So how are things in Hicksville? Ready to come back to civilization yet?"

Paige felt an unexpected urge to defend Salt Lick. "It's not so bad here. I've met some great people. And guess what?"

Silence.

"Sunny?"

"Hullo. What day is it?"

"Dammit, Sunny, I said 'guess what.'"

"I don't know. The Four-H team won State? John Deere's having a sale?"

It wasn't fair for city people to make fun of Salt Lick. Paige was tempted to hang up, but she needed her friend's help in the worst way. "I haven't been shopping in two weeks. No mall shopping anyway. I went to Benton's Monuments and Home Accessory Emporium and bought a silk flower arrangement, but that doesn't really count."

The moment the comment was out of her mouth she regretted it because Sunny shrieked with laughter. "Benton's what?"

"Never mind. I need to know if I can count on you to help me out Saturday?"

More silence.

"Sunny," Paige yelled.

"No yo, no estoy solitario."

" 'No thanks, I'm not lonely?' Exactly what did you do in Spain?" Knowing her friend, Paige could only imagine, but she had a more important concern now. "I've invited a man over for supper on Saturday and I need you to help me."

"I'm not coming to Salt Lick. Gourmet cooking would be wasted on a crude cowboy."

"I don't want you to come here. I just want you to sort of walk me through cooking a meal. Something simple, but good."

"Did you say you were going to cook the meal? Whatever possessed you to say such a thing? Is this man someone you want to impress? Because if he is, you'd be better off to stick to black lace and black label, not necessarily in that order."

"Of course, I want to impress him. I wouldn't be calling you otherwise. It's a really long story, Sun. Can you help me? It would mean so much to me. I need to make yeast rolls."

A gutteral sound came from Sunny. "My God, Paige. I spent a whole semester of baking classes trying to master yeast rolls. Forget that."

"But he likes homemade rolls."

"Who doesn't? Okay, okay. Do this. Got a pencil and paper handy?"

Paige rummaged around in the kitchen drawer. She eventually found an ink pen and a grocery store sale flyer.

"Got it. Go ahead."

"Write this down, word for word . . . Boston." She paused, giving Paige time to write. "Market. . . . Got it?"

"Are you kidding? There's no Boston Market around here. I want to do this myself."

"Honey, you can't learn to cook over the phone. If this is important to you, do it right. Go *buy* something. You can let him think you cooked it."

"Yes, but—"

"Tell you what. Dessert is the crowning achievement of any meal. Buy the supper, and you make the dessert. We can work on your cooking skills another time, when we have more than a couple of days and a long-distance connection."

Maybe Sunny was right. Paige didn't want to scare Spur off. He had put a lot of emphasis on a home-cooked meal. She would find somewhere to purchase what she needed. Paige remembered how Spur dove into Debbie Sue's chocolate cake after supper at her and Buddy's house. "You're right. I'll make a cake. He loves chocolate cake."

"There you go."

"I used to help my mom with cakes when I was little. She let me make the frosting and put it on. I'm not without *some* talent in the cooking department. A big, gooey, four-layer chocolate cake. How's that?"

"That sounds great. But I don't recommend a layer cake. Try a sheet cake. Let me know how it goes."

"What's a sheet cake?"

Silence.

"Sunny? . . . Sunny, what's a sheet cake?"

More silence.

Oh, dear. Sunny had probably gone back to sleep. Paige sighed and disconnected, supposing she would have to come to terms with the fact that she and Sunny now ran in different circles that were located in different worlds. Paige liked the world she was in just fine and didn't see how she could ever go back to where she had been before Salt Lick.

She was excited at the prospect of baking a cake. Did it have to be baked in the oven or could she fix it in the microwave? Normally she didn't buy anything unless it was microwaveable. She supposed she would be forced to utilize the oven.

Well, how hard could it be?

twenty

Driving into town, Debbie Sue lowered her window so she could enjoy the early October morning. Fall was her favorite season. A crispness and a scent unlike any other time hung in the air. Relief from the unrelenting heat was part of the pleasure, but there was more. She and Buddy had remarried in the fall. She had never been happier than now.

And she had never been more worried.

Any other day, she would have driven slower and taken the time to fully enjoy the drive, but not now. She hadn't slept the past two nights, worrying over Rocket Man. In her entire life in West Texas, she could remember no more than one or two horses that had ever gone missing. Buddy had promised to keep his eyes and ears open, but only *she* thought there was a serious problem.

No one knew the exact number of horses missing, but from her perspective, one was too many. An idea had come to her during her worry session, and now she was hell-bent on discussing it with Dr. Spur Atwater.

As she sped past the Styling Station/Domestic Equalizers she saw
Ed's car in the parking lot. Good. Everyone in Salt Lick was ready-
ing for the high school homecoming activities. The Styling Station
had a full booking for hairstyles and manicures, but with her trusted
friend holding down the fort, Debbie Sue didn't have to rush to the
salon just yet.

When she reached the vet clinic, she sprang from the cab like a
woman on a life-or-death mission, and in a way, that was exactly
the case. Seeing an attractive brunette she didn't know at the receptionist's desk surprised her. The woman looked up from her computer screen with a friendly smile. "Good morning. May I help
you?"

Whoa! This had to be the attractive woman she and Ed had discussed with Paige. Never being one to hesitate, Debbie Sue walked
up and extended her hand. "I'm Debbie Sue Overstreet. We've
never met. You are . . ."

"Electra Phillips. I'm Spur's—uh, *Dr.* Atwater's sister. Pleased to
meet you."

"Dr. Atwater's sister! Well, it is so nice to meet you, Electra."
Debbie Sue grabbed her hand and pumped it. "We sure do think a
lot of your brother. How nice of you to help him out. Are you from
around these parts?"

"Yes, ma'am. My husband and I have a little place over toward
Odessa. I'm only here until Spur—dammit, Dr. Atwater—can find
someone permanent."

Debbie Sue laughed. "Guess you haven't gotten used to calling
him 'doctor' yet?"

"No, I haven't. He doesn't expect it, but I think I should call him
doctor. Here in the clinic anyway. He worked so hard for that title I
think he should be able to carry it."

"I think you're right. Would Dr. Atwater happen to be where I could talk to him for a minute?"

"Let me check. Be right back." Electra disappeared through the doorway leading into the treatment area. Debbie Sue couldn't help but think of all the times she had seen her mother come and go through that same passageway.

Electra returned with Spur behind her, drying his hands on a paper towel and smiling. "Debbie Sue. How's it going? What can I do for you?"

"Sorry to just drop in on you, Dr. Atwater, but I want to know if you're familiar with electronic ID tags?"

"Why are you calling me Dr. Atwater?"

Debbie Sue glanced at Electra. "I just thought that since I'm here on business—"

"Nonsense. Call me Spur. I'll save the doctor title for people I don't know or don't like." He smiled again. No wonder Paige had a crush on him. He had a great smile and good teeth.

"Now about your question. Yeah. We used electronic tagging extensively at A&M. Mostly on breeding cattle, but something similar is being used in other animals, too. A lot of rescued dogs and cats have been reunited with their owners because of a chip implant. You thinking about putting a chip in Buddy?"

Debbie Sue grinned. "It's Rocket Man I'm thinking about. With all the horses that have disappeared, I've been worried about him. If someone stole him I don't know what I'd do. I guess I just love him too much."

"The chip implant can give you a little peace of mind, Debbie Sue, but if it's horse theft you're worried about, thieves aren't going to care if the horse has an implant or not. I've looked into the disappearing horses a little bit. The fact that the horses have all been older makes me concerned about—well, about—"

"I know what you're thinking. Slaughterhouses, right? I've been reading about them."

A solemn look settled in Spur's eyes. "Right. I hesitated to say it. But look, the implant only works if someone knows it's there and has a way to trace it, understand?"

"You're going to think this is crazy, but I've been wondering about a GPS transmitter."

"GPS," Electra repeated. "Someone had one of those on *The Sopranos*."

"*The Sopranos?*" Spur gave his sister a look. "Well, GPS would probably work all right. GPS is now being used on dogs and cats, but the animal has to be wearing a collar. The transmitter comes large enough for a good-size dog, but not a horse. Offhand, I don't know how to get my hands on that equipment, but I'll research it for you if you'd like."

"Oh, you don't have to. I've got access to the equipment. My partner's husband uses it to help us out now and then at the Equalizers. I just need someone to implant the transmitter."

"How big is this chip?"

"About the size of a dime."

"Hmmm. The most logical place for implantation would be subcutaneously on the neck, near the mane. But I don't know if a signal from an implanted transmitter would be traceable."

"Oh, heck." Debbie Sue hung her head. "I hate to put Rocket Man through having it done if we don't know it'll work."

Spur put his hand on her shoulder. "Now don't be upset. There's always a way. How about a halter? You must have one or two."

"Lord, I've got a dozen."

"Maybe we could put the transmitter on a halter."

"Say, I've even got a couple with conchos. We could hide it among them."

"There you go," Spur said. "All you have to do is put the halter on Rocket Man at night."

"Oh, Spur, you're a genius. I would have never thought of a halter. And it would save Rocket Man the pain of a surgical implant. Probably nothing will ever happen, but I'd feel so much better if we did that. I don't know how to thank you."

"No problem. I'm curious to see how it works. Who's gonna monitor the signal?"

"Ed's husband, Vic. He's converted one of his and Ed's bedrooms into a roomful of surveillance devices. He loves helping us. Makes him feel like he's back in special ops again."

"What happens if the receiver loses the transmitter?" Electra asked.

"It's the damnedest thing I've ever seen," Debbie Sue replied. "Once the device is in place, you determine the allowed perimeter. If the host moves beyond that distance a signal is sent to your cell phone. Or you can monitor the movement through an Internet connection. It's like something out of a James Bond movie."

"That's pretty cool all right. I hope you don't have to use it, but if you do, let us know how it works. You may be on the cutting edge of something big. My goodness, your name could be on the lips of horse lovers around the world."

"I don't care about any of that," Debbie Sue said. "I just want to make sure Rocket Man's safe."

❋ ❋ ❋

PAIGE AWOKE FRIDAY morning pondering sheet cake, homemade rolls, and home cooking. She would be working all day Friday and Saturday. When would she bake rolls or a sheet cake, even if she knew how? By noon Saturday she had made a decision. She would follow Sunny's advice and buy everything already prepared.

Instead of running all over Midland or Odessa searching for takeout that tasted like home cooking, Paige called the Styling Station. Both Edwina and Debbie Sue had mentioned they didn't put a high priority on cooking. They must know just the place for a wannabe chef to find great take-out food. Edwina answered and Paige explained her need.

"Whoa, child," Edwina said. "You sound nervous. Worse than an old maid at a prison rodeo. You called the right person. I know just the place. Got a pen?"

Paige paused before reaching for her pen. "This doesn't start with *Boston* does it?"

"Huh? No, it's Percy's. It's on Main and Fifth, downtown Midland. You couldn't miss it if you tried. It's just north of Neiman Barkus."

Paige's pulse quickened. She didn't know Neiman Marcus had a location in West Texas, though there were certainly enough wealthy people in Midland to support the high-end retailer. "Did you say *Neiman Marcus?*"

"No, *Barkus*. With a B. Neiman Barkus. It's a dog-grooming shop. Tell Percy I sent you. He'll throw in something extra."

No Neiman Marcus. Paige expelled a great breath. It was just as well. Where would she get the money for extravagant goodies anyway? Besides, designer clothes and expensive baubles no longer seemed as important as they had once been. She said her thanks and farewells and headed for Midland.

Edwina had been right about Percy's. The owner was a huge black man with a smile more expansive than his stomach. Everything on the menu looked mouthwatering, and he assured her it was. Percy recommended the special of the day—a meat loaf the size of a football, with mashed potatoes, fried okra, and yellow squash casserole.

"Gots your choice for dessert, Missy. Peach cobbler or carrot cake."

"Sir, could you substitute a chocolate sheet cake for carrot cake?"

Percy's stomach jiggled as he gave a deep laugh. "You'd have to go to a bakery to get a sheet cake, Missy. That's an awful lot of cake for one little meal."

"Oh," Paige replied, confused. A sheet cake was becoming a bigger mystery.

Percy gave her a wink. "If dis be a special meal, I'd go wit' peach cobbler. I never knowed a man that could resist ol' Percy's peach cobbler, 'specially if it's served up by a pretty lady."

Paige felt her face flame, surprised at appearing so obvious. "Okay," she said. "Peach cobbler it is."

Just as Edwina said he would, and to Paige's great relief, Percy threw in half a dozen free yeast rolls that smelled heavenly. Her cooking challenge had been met in one fell swoop. If only she felt as confident about the rest of the coming dinner date.

"You tell Miss Edwina," Percy said as Paige paid out, "jis cuz she gots herself a man that cooks ain't no reason to forgets ol' Percy."

Paige assured him she would pass along the message. Just under an hour and she was back on the road from Midland to Salt Lick.

Back at her house Paige transferred the food to her own dishes.

220

Or that is, dishes Debbie Sue had left behind. *Voilà!* Instant home-cooked meal.

Another life ago, if she had wanted to impress someone special she would have invited him to dine out at one of the five-star Dallas restaurants she frequented. She was liberated enough to embrace the new norms. If she was the one who extended the invitation, she had no qualms about paying the bill, especially when Daddy was really who picked up the five-hundred-dollar tab at the end of the evening.

She left the kitchen and gave the living room one more quick inspection. For seating, something more suitable than cheap folding chairs would be nice, but until her bank account became healthier from her own contribution or when she received her inheritance, the lawn chairs would have to do. Maybe they would demonstrate to Spur that she wasn't a spoiled, had-everything-handed-to-her girl that depended on Daddy for every little thing.

As she selected CDs, it dawned on her she had no idea what Spur liked in music. She hadn't done very well so far in guessing about him, so she decided to go with easy listening.

Food in place, music selected, Paige went to her bedroom to tackle one more important element. Clothing. No problem. Her closet was jam-packed. She just had to make the right choice. Something cute, but not cutesy. Or maybe something seductive, but not slutty. Okay, forget seductive. She would stick with cute. After all, this was their first date.

With Spur being an ex–football hero, he probably would go for the cheerleader look. Sliding hanging garments past her critical eye she finally decided on a short denim skirt with a two-layer ruffle at the hem. She had been wearing bulky white bandages all week to protect her knees from germs and the friction of her jeans. Tonight she would allow Spur to see the result of his handiwork. She wore the scars of her injuries like a badge of honor.

A boxy cashmere sweater, a pair of low-heeled loafers, a tortoise-shell headband holding her hair back, and she was set. She only hoped she didn't look too high-schoolish.

Preparing for a special evening had never been so simple. Prior to moving to Salt Lick she would have shopped for days for shoes or the perfect article of clothing and spent at least one day at the spa. She didn't feel the need with Spur Atwater. There was an earthiness to him. He would more likely notice character and convictions before material possessions. Her being self-reliant and not leaning on her family wealth had to impress him. If he didn't realize it yet, she was determined that he would.

The doorbell sounded at seven o'clock exactly, not a minute before or past. She froze, fighting the urge to run into the bathroom and hide behind the shower curtain.

What had she been thinking inviting him or any man to a home-prepared supper?

She had already planned to appear to be cooking when he came in. Along with pots and pans, Debbie Sue had left other stuff. Paige tore through drawers and found a bib apron. She pulled it over her head and on a deep breath, took her position in the kitchen. Exhaling one last time, she sang out, "Come iii-nnn."

SPUR HEARD THE INVITATION on the other side of the door. In his hand he had a bottle of wine and a small houseplant he had asked his sister to pick up for him in Odessa. "This is an African violet, and she'll love it," Electra had told him.

He juggled the wine and the plant into one hand, wiped a sweaty palm on his jeans, and reached for the doorknob. Rattled nerves had almost prompted him to cancel, but Electra would have been merciless in her scolding. No, he accepted the invitation, and he would make the most of the evening. After all, Electra had gone out of her way to pick up the presents and make sure he had the right clothes to wear.

As he opened the door, his first view was the living room and three aluminum folding chairs, arranged in such a way as to resemble real furniture. A throw hung over the back of each chair, and one chair even had a small pillow. His hostess's effort reminded him of his mom and the lengths to which she used to go to make their shabby living quarters homey and comfortable.

"Hi, Spur."

The voice came from the kitchen. He walked the few steps through the small living room and intended to say hello, but the sight of her in the kitchen, bent over the oven, preparing a meal for him, made him weak in the knees.

"You're right on time," she said. "I was just taking things out of the oven."

She had on a short skirt that showed off her long legs. His roommate perked up, but Spur kept his composure until she straightened and started toward him. When he saw her full frontal, he couldn't help it—he burst out laughing and nearly dropped the wine and the plant.

A puzzled look crossed her face.

"I'm sorry," he said. "I don't mean to be rude, but that apron is really funny."

Paige looked down. The apron had something written on it. She untied the strings in the back and pulled it over her head. Holding it at arm's length, she read "I may be a lousy cook, but I give a great blow job."

"Oh, my God! I didn't know that was on there. Oh, my God! I'm so embarrassed. Debbie Sue left it here in the drawer and I just—I didn't read it—"

Spur couldn't keep from laughing even harder at her floundering. "Don't apologize. It's a great way to break the tension."

Finally Paige laughed, too, but he could see her nervousness as she stuffed the apron into a drawer. He thrust the plant toward her. "Electra told me to tell you to put this on a north windowsill."

He could tell by the way she looked at it she didn't know what to do with it, but she took it with a big smile. "Thanks," she said softly, carried it to the dining area's one window, and set it on the ledge. "There," she said. "Perfect."

He offered the bottle of wine. "I brought this to have with supper." She smiled even bigger. "Thanks, again." She took the wine bottle and walked to the kitchen counter. "Believe it or not, I've actually got a corkscrew. Debbie Sue left it behind."

Feeling more relaxed, he walked to her side and took the corkscrew from her. After he opened the wine, she brought out pretty little glasses with red tops. "These are cocktail glasses, but I guess we could drink wine from them."

"Sounds good. Pretty delicate for me. I'll try to be careful."

"Since supper's ready, I guess we should sit down and eat." She gestured toward the dining table. She had set the table with the heavy southwestern pottery dishes she had bought in Santa Fe years back, matching napkins, and silverware that had belonged to her mother. Each place setting was completed with tumblers of ice water that matched the cocktail glasses. She might not know how to cook, but she did know how to set a table.

He moved toward the table. "Sounds good to me. I didn't get to eat lunch today, so I'm starving." He sniffed the air. "Mmm. What is it?"

"I hope you like meat loaf."

"Are you kidding? I love it. I'm not a great cook, but as many years as I've been batching, I've learned to make a mean meat loaf. I've got my mom's recipe. I can't wait to taste yours."

She began to bring bowls and platters from the kitchen. He rose from his seat. "Need some help?"

He tried not to drool as he looked at each dish. He hadn't known what to expect but had come prepared to accept whatever she served and be gracious in his compliments, but this *really* did look good.

Paige took his plate and filled it to the rim. He waited for her to finish her plate and then dove in. Everything from the fried okra to the squash casserole was larruping. "I hate being such a pig, but this meat loaf is the best I've ever tasted. What do you put in it to give it the unusual flavor?"

Paige stopped, her fork suspended.

"There's a spice I can't quite put my finger on," he said.

"Uh, I use hamburger and . . . oh, some other stuff."

"Oh, don't want to share your recipe, huh? An old family secret? C'mon now, what other stuff?"

"Oh, I just grab things out of the cabinet. You know, a little of this and a little of that." She began to rub an itchy spot on her neck with her fingertips.

"Well, it's delicious. I've never made mine with a topping." He touched the red topping on his meat loaf slice with the tip of his fork. "This isn't ketchup, is it?"

She looked over at his plate. "Uh, yeah, ketchup."

"Did you add something to it? It has such a sweet taste."

"Uh, well, that would be sugar. Lots of sugar."

"Hmmm, I'll have to try that the next time I make a meat loaf. How do you get it to stay together? Mine tends to fall apart. This one looks like I could throw it fifty yards." He laughed.

Paige stared unblinking at the meat loaf that suddenly looked as if it were made of adobe.

"Paige?" Spur said.

"Huh? Oh, sorry, I was just thinking about what would hold meat loaf together. I mean, uh, I use flour and water, of course."

"No kidding? That's how I made paste when I was a kid. I've always used crackers in meat loaf. Bread or sometimes croutons, but never just flour and water. I'll have to try that. Mind if I have another piece?"

He lifted his plate toward the meat loaf and in doing so, tipped over his glass of water. The puddle rushed for the edge of the table. He jumped from his chair, went into the kitchen, and retrieved a roll of paper towels he had spotted on the counter. He blotted up the spill, apologizing profusely.

"Don't worry about it," Paige said, carefully sinking to her knees, helping him. Her knees still looked sore, so she had to be in pain.

Spur finished mopping up the spill and carried the soaked towels into the kitchen. He opened cupboard doors seeking the trash can and finally found it in the pantry. Before he could toss out the towels, he saw discarded containers with the name PERCY's printed on the tops. He knew the name. Electra had been telling him she wanted to take him to eat at Percy's because the take-out café specialized in his favorite dish—meat loaf.

The discovery washed over him like a warm blanket. That Paige would go to the trouble to impress him, with, of all things, home-cooking, touched him in a way he had never been touched. A lump formed in his throat and words failed him. The reaction puzzled him. Any other time, with anyone else he would have gone along with the farce, only to tease her once the truth came out. But for reasons he couldn't explain he felt tenderness toward Paige for her efforts. He closed the pantry door on her secret. "I can't find the trash can," he said. "I'm just gonna lay these wet towels on the sink, if that's okay with you."

"Oh, that's fine. I'll use them for cleaning up." She smiled and tittered. "Save a tree, you know?"

When he returned to the table he leaned over and gently brushed her cheek with his thumb. "Thank you for supper. This may be the best meal I ever ate."

Her shoulders scrunched and her hands clasped in her lap. "I'm so glad you liked it," she said softly. God, she had the most unforgettable smile.

After the meal, Paige brought out her favorite after-dinner drink, a bottle of Glenlivet. The rest of the evening went wonderfully well, she thought. They talked about life in Salt Lick. The fact that they were both new residents gave them much to discuss. They talked about college. A&M was one Texas seat of higher learning she hadn't attended. Finally, several drinks later, Spur looked at his watch.

"I hate to leave good company, but I guess I'd better go."

They both stood and walked toward the entrance. Spur opened the door and turned back. "Thanks again. Next time will be my treat." His head leaned toward hers and instinctively she looked up. Before she knew what happened, they were kissing, and both his arms had her locked in an embrace. The world spun. Her body fit against his as if it had been poured from liquid. More. She wanted more.

Their kisses grew more intense until Spur let go. Paige looked at him, her arms still wrapped around his middle.

Worry filled his beautiful dark eyes. "I can't do this. *We* can't do this. It's too soon."

"Don't say that. Really—"

"We both need to cool down. I think I better just leave." He peeled her arms from around his torso.

"Can't we reach a compromise?"

His mouth turned up in a smile and his hand cupped her chin. "You and I both know there's no compromise when it comes to sex. I've never backed out when I was this turned on. That should tell you something." He kissed her forehead as if she were his little sister. "Thanks again for the supper. I'll see myself out."

His mouth brushed her ear with a whisper and then he was out the door and gone.

He had whispered something she hadn't heard clearly. She could have sworn he said he couldn't wait for her to meet his roommate.

And she didn't even know he had a roommate.

twenty-one

The lone cowboy backed the truck and horse trailer up to a small barn attached to the corral. The three penned horses pricked their ears and whinnied. They knew food was on the way.

Bringing feed to this isolated spot was getting old. Very old. Though the cowboy paid one of the ranch's Mexican hands to put out all the feed and water the horses needed, the cowboy still had to haul in hay. He had tried giving the Mexican money to buy the feed, but that had proved to be a mistake. What of the funds the Mexican didn't drink up, he lost betting on cockfights. It was impossible to find somebody trustworthy.

The one turn of good luck the cowboy had had was in finding this ranch. A Fort Worth banker had inherited it. Now the new had worn off, and the guy didn't even drive out very often, much less spend time here. Apparently he liked the idea of having a ranch, but he didn't like ranching. Asshole. The cowboy would love to be handed a ranch.

This was the longest time he had kept the nags in one place. He could haul the three horses east now, but he preferred to wait until he had a fourth horse. With a four-horse trailer and the high cost of gas, it only made sense to take as many animals as possible in one trip.

Besides, this was his last haul. Having extra spending money had been fun at first, but all along he had been setting aside some of it, planning for the future. Now the future had become the present. He had already enrolled in auctioneering school in Dallas, had paid half the tuition. With only a little more cash, his new life could start.

Sure, he would be leaving responsibilities and people who depended on him, but this was his one shot. He hadn't seen much opportunity to move up in his life, and he intended to make the most of the one at hand. He would wait a few more days, then scout the area around Odessa and Midland again for the fourth horse.

twenty-two

Debbie Sue stepped back to assess her handiwork. The GPS transmitter was undistinguishable from the silver conchos adorning Rocket Man's halter. To be safe, she had placed the coin-size device up near his ears so that his mane hid it even better. Rocket Man was now the most high-tech horse in West Texas, maybe *all* of Texas.

"Whaddaya think, y'all? Looks pretty good, doesn't it?" Buddy and Edwina nodded confirmation.

"Ed, let's check it out," Debbie Sue said. "Get my phone and call Vic."

Edwina walked over to the pickup, lifted the cell phone from the dash mount, and made the call. "Hey, baby doll," she said into the receiver. "We're all set here. Are you picking up anything?"

Whatever he answered evoked a titter from Edwina.

"What'd he say?" Debbie Sue asked.

Edwina grinned.

"Good Lord. You two. Give me that phone."

Edwina handed over the phone.

"Vic? Are you getting a signal? . . . Really? Wow, is that space-age or what? Set the perimeter for two miles. We're getting ready to test it. We'll load Rocket Man in the trailer and drive up the road."

Buddy was already leading Rocket Man to the trailer hooked to the pickup. Rocket Man didn't often get to go for a ride on the open road these days, but he clomped up the ramp as if he had been doing it every day. He was such a good horse. His gentle, trusting nature was one of the qualities that was endearing. It was also what worried Debbie Sue the most. That gentleness and trust could prove dangerous for him.

Buddy took a seat as the driver, and Edwina crawled into the extended cab behind him. Debbie Sue climbed onto the passenger seat. "Well, here goes, y'all. Keep your fingers crossed this'll work."

Buddy reached over and squeezed her knee. "It'll work just fine, Flash."

"I'm worried about McFarland's mare disappearing," Debbie Sue said. "Their place is so close to us. Do you think she could have been stolen?"

"I talked to Bob yesterday," Buddy answered. "He didn't find her when he rode the pastures looking for her, but he could have missed her. He's got a big place."

"But all his other horses came up to the barn. The mare would have followed the others . . . if she could have."

"We're doing all we can, darlin'. Now let's see if this transmitter thing works." He stopped at the cattle guard and looked left and right. "Which way?"

"Right. Let's go for a long ride. Rocket Man will enjoy that, but let me know when we reach two miles."

"Right it is." Buddy eased onto the road heading east as, on the radio, Ernest Tubb crooned a question about the whereabouts of "sweet thang." Edwina sang along. Soon Buddy announced, "Okay, that's two miles."

"Damn. No call. Buddy, I did charge the phone last night, didn't I? I've been so worried—"

The University of Texas fight song coming from her cell phone interrupted her sentence. When she pressed the On button, an automated voice spoke. "Your target has gone beyond the set perimeters. Please contact your GPS administrator. Repeating the previous message, your target has gone beyond . . ."

Debbie Sue squealed with delight. "Oh, my God! It works!"

"I'm calling Vic." She keyed in Vic and Edwina's home number. "Vic, we got the message. Where do you show us to be?"

"Looks like you're heading east on highway three-zero-two."

"That's right," Debbie Sue said gleefully. "Thanks, Vic. See you later." She disconnected and turned to Buddy and Edwina. "I can't tell you what a relief this is for me." She leaned her head against the padded headrest. "I see nights of restful sleep ahead."

"That's great, hon'," Edwina said. "What I see is an ice cream cone dipped in chocolate. Buddy, stop at Hogg's. I'm buying."

PAIGE'S FIRST few days of managing the horses without Lester had gone well. She had played a game of pretend while she worked, daydreaming that this spread belonged to her and her husband, the hot, phenomenally successful, Dr. Spur Atwater. In her imagination, she worked with these beautiful animals during the day, Spur ran his practice, and then when evening came, they settled down and discussed their day. Eventually they went to bed, where they had wild and crazy sex. It was a mind-blowing daydream, considering that until now, she had never met anyone she could see sharing her life with or her future. Nor had she ever had wild and crazy sex.

Her future? Good grief. She had to stop thinking. This kind of woolgathering was what was wrong with physical labor. It might keep the body fit, but it turned the brain to mush and gave her far too much time to think.

She had learned that Vic and Buddy were never home on Wednesday evenings. Buddy attended a class at Odessa College, and Vic had reduced his overnight runs to just one midweek haul. Debbie Sue and Edwina would be having their girls' night out. Paige decided to call the Styling Station and invite them over for supper.

With no mother or sister from whom to seek counsel, the two older women were the next best thing. They not only had the experience to guide her, but they also had the heart to see to her best interests. The excuse to discuss Spur was bona fide, but truth be known, she just flat out loved the company of the two zany women. If they agreed to be her guests she would pay another visit to Percy's. The memory of his home-cooked cuisine was as delicious as the memory of Spur's kiss. She just wished the kiss were as accessible as the home cooking.

She secured the gate to the stall and started for the office to use the phone. It warbled as she approached the office. She broke into a run and grabbed the receiver. "Flying C Ranch."

"Good morning," a distinguished voice said. "May I please speak to Lester Clinton?"

"I'm sorry, but Lester isn't here. Could I take a message?"

"When do you anticipate his return?"

This refined voice didn't sound like the kind of person who usually called Lester. "He won't be back for another day, maybe two. I'm his assistant. Can I help you with something?"

After a few beats, the voice said, "It's very important that he receive this message when he returns. Would you be so kind as to see that he gets it?"

"Sure. Let me just grab a pen and some paper." Paige pawed through the desk drawer. "All right, I'm ready."

"My name is Brooks Van Patten. Please make sure Lester knows that TAR, that's *T-A-R,* has received six, but needs four more. He'll understand."

"TAR has six, needs four more. I got it, Mr. Van Patten. Anything else?"

"No, that's all. He'll understand without further explanation, and he knows how to reach me if he has any questions. Good day."

As she slowly replaced the receiver, Paige studied the note she had just taken. What in the world could the letters *T-A-R* stand for?

Debbie Sue and Edwina would know. She picked up the receiver again and keyed in the salon's number. On the third ring Edwina answered. "Domestic Equalizers. Before you have a showdown, let us get the lowdown. This is Edwina. How may I help you?"

Paige giggled. "Hey, this is Paige."

"Hey youself, dumplin'. Your ears burning? We were just talking about you."

"You were? Who's 'we'?"

"Me and Debbie Sue. We haven't heard how your date went Saturday night. I hope you're calling in to give us a report."

"I'll do better than that. Will Buddy and Vic be gone tonight?"

"Wednesday night. We're on our own. What's up?"

"I'm going to finish up here about three. I thought I'd drive over to Percy's and pick up supper if you and Debbie Sue can join me at my house. Or that is, at Debbie Sue's house. Well, anyway, you know where I mean."

"Supper from Percy's? I'm there. Hold on, let me ask Debbie Sue."

Paige heard them talking but couldn't make out the conversation. After a few seconds, Edwina returned. "We're both there. Let's see, today being Wednesday, the special at Percy's will be pot roast. It'll come with brown gravy, mashed potatoes, ears of corn bathed in butter, and homemade rolls. Good Lord, my stomach just growled thinking about it. I'll spring for dessert. Pick up one of his coconut cream pies and I'll pay you for it."

"You don't have to do that, Edwina. I finally got a paycheck. I've actually got some money."

"I wasn't thinking about the cost. I intend to take it home with me so Vic and I can have some when he gets back. Just let me buy the pie."

"Okay. You can buy the pie and take it home. I'll see y'all around six or six-thirty."

"We'll be round like a doughnut," Edwina said.

Paige hung up the phone, shaking her head and laughing. She opened the desk drawer again. This time she was looking for a piece of tape or a magnet to affix the note to Lester to the metal filing cabinet drawer. She finally located a half-used roll of tape and stuck the note where Lester couldn't miss it. Before clicking off the light and leaving the office, she glanced again at the note. TAR. She had to remember to ask Debbie Sue and Edwina what it meant.

By three o'clock, as planned, she had finished riding the scheduled horses and exercised the others on the walker. All had been fed, watered, and locked in their stalls.

Climbing into the Escalade, not even worrying if she got dirt on the upholstery, she couldn't keep from thinking of how shocked some of her partying buddies would be if they saw her now. What they couldn't know is that the person with whom they had partied hearty wasn't the real Paige McBride. Now she was learning who that person was and had begun to like her. Marathon shopping sprees and globe-trotting antics were behind her. She had found her way home. Had her daddy known all along this would happen?

An image of her mom in heaven breathing a sigh of relief formed and stayed with her as she drove into Midland. She had only a few solid memories of her mother, but she would bet a horse-woman like her would have loved the unfettered West Texas land-scape. Her mom would approve of Spur, too, and so would Daddy. Paige was sure of it. He would admire Spur's strong work ethic and his determination to succeed.

It was ironic that Spur was on her mind as she entered Percy's because there at the counter was his sister. "Electra? Hi, how are you?"

Electra looked over her shoulder, and her face broke into a huge grin. "Paige, how great to see you again. Did your knees heal up okay?"

Paige smiled and showed a high-stepping routine. "They're great. Your brother would have made a fine people doctor."

"I think so, too. But then I think he would be a fine anything. He's been my hero my whole life. Far as I'm concerned, he can do no wrong."

An awkward silence passed as the two women smiled and looked about the café/store. "You didn't work in the clinic today?" Paige finally asked.

"I was there this morning. Spur knows I like to be home when Ronny is, so I only worked half a day."

"I guess you're taking supper home tonight, too. I just found this place last week and I'm back already. The food is sooo good." Paige studied the chalkboard where the menu was posted.

"Spur told me you served him meat loaf from here and it was delicious. I've had everything on the menu but the meat loaf, so I'm giving it a try tonight."

Paige's ears had to be playing tricks. She mustered as much nonchalance as she could dredge up. "Sorry, I was reading the menu. When did Spur say he had the meat loaf?"

"Why, at your house. Saturday night. Didn't you serve meat loaf?"

That jerk. Asking me all those questions about how I cooked meat loaf. He probably saw me coming out of this place and was trying to make me feel like a fool. "Oh, yes. Yes, I did. I served meat loaf. Percy's meat loaf. From right here." Paige rambled, her tongue having trouble not being distracted by her thoughts.

"Miss? Miss, you ready to order?"

"Oh, yes," she replied to Percy. "Sorry. I need three of your pot roast specials and a coconut cream pie. To go."

"Feeding a crowd, huh?" the jerk's sister said, gathering her meat loaf order from the counter.

Paige smiled. "Oh, just a couple of friends."

"Well it was fun running into you. I hope to see you again soon."

"It's nice seeing you, too. Oh, by the way, Spur and I talked about cooking the other night. When you see him, tell him I have a recipe for him."

"Sure. What is it? Believe it or not, he's a good cook when he tries."

"It's an old family secret from my grandmother. She was quite a card. It's called 'Bend Over and Bite Me Brownies.'"

Electra laughed. "Hey, that's colorful. He'll get a kick out of that. I'll be sure to tell him."

"I hope he does get a kick," Paige said.

twenty-three

Bend Over and Bite Me Brownies? Spur was holding the receiver between his chin and shoulder while attempting to enter an appointment into the computer matrix.

"Those were her exact words," Electra said. "I don't know what went wrong. She started acting different when I mentioned how much you liked Percy's meat loaf and I, uh, I'm pretty sure something I said got you in trouble."

Spur chuckled. "Don't worry 'Lectra. I didn't tell her I knew the meal came from Percy's. She probably thinks I was making fun of her. I'll fix it. You didn't do anything wrong."

"Boy, I hope not. I like her. With her being so rich, I didn't expect her to be so nice. She's even prettier than you described, but I like her in spite of that."

"I like her too, sis."

"Well, Ronny's waiting, so I have to go."

"Tell him I said hello and I'll see you in the morning."

Spur finished his chore at the computer and pushed his chair back from the reception desk. He chuckled again, thinking about the brownie recipe. He couldn't name the quality he most liked about Paige, but her spunky attitude was at the top of the list.

His schedule today extended into the evening hours. When he finished maybe he would drop by Paige's house and talk to her face-to-face. She could hang up on him if he called, but he would be hard to ignore if he was standing on her doorstep. This misunderstanding over meat loaf was a small hurdle to vault. If they couldn't get past something so trivial the likelihood of anything serious developing between them was hopeless.

PAIGE SCURRIED into the house with the food orders from Percy's. Debbie Sue and Edwina would be here soon, and she hadn't yet inventoried her liquor cabinet for the ingredients for cosmopolitans. Tonight would be a *Sex in the City* kind of night, and cosmos were the perfect libation. Back home in Fort Worth, if Sunny was in town, they never missed an episode of the HBO sitcom. They vacillated from week to week as to which character each of them was most like. Paige always shifted between Carrie and Charlotte. Sunny was sometimes a Miranda, but she was always a full profile of Samantha.

After putting everything away, Paige showered and got into comfort clothes—sweatpants and an old flannel shirt. Carrie Bradshaw might not approve, but Debbie Sue and Edwina would find it appropriate. She wrapped a towel around her head, returned to the kitchen and assembled the ingredients for the delectable cosmopolitan drinks on the kitchen counter—Cointreau liqueur, cranberry juice, and Absolut citron. Yummy.

She removed the top of the vodka bottle for a whiff of the lemon-lime mixture and hummed an approval. Standing on her tiptoes she reached to the back of the cabinet, retrieved a bowl, and filled it with ice. The trick was to mix each drink individually and to serve it in a chilled glass. Not a frozen, frosty one, but one barely kissed by ice cubes.

Last, but by no means least, she carefully lifted three of her favorite crystal pieces from their resting place. Simply Red Waterford martini glasses the ones from which she and Spur had drunk wine. Exquisite. The flawless clear crystal on the bottom and deep-ruby-colored rim was the perfect vessel for the crimson cosmo. The price she had paid for four sets of these dainty, handcrafted pieces of crystal would buy her a couch today. Ironic how priorities had a way of changing.

The stove clock showed fifteen minutes before her new girlfriends would arrive. What the hell? She mixed herself a drink. As she sipped, the doorbell rang, and before she could call out a "come in," Edwina was standing in the living room. "Hey, we're here. God, it smells good in here. I'm hungry enough to eat a horse."

"Bite your tongue, Ed," Debbie Sue said, staring at her with an alarmed expression.

"Oops, sorry." Edwina turned to Paige. "We're a little sensitive about horse meat."

"Oh, me, too," Paige said. "By the way, I didn't hear y'all drive up, and I was listening for you, too."

Debbie Sue explained that they had parked at the end of the block and walked to the house. "It's not a good idea for anyone to park across the street from Koweba's driveway. If she takes it into her head to go somewhere, she'll back out in that Sherman tank she calls an automobile and plow right into whatever's in her path."

Edwina headed for the kitchen at the invitation for a drink, but Debbie Sue strolled the house, with Paige following her. "This was the first home Buddy and I had," Debbie Sue said. "Being here now is like visiting an old friend. Lots of special memories." She stopped at the empty spare room and stared into it. "This would have been a nursery."

Paige didn't know what to say, but Debbie Sue's behavior raised a question.

Debbie Sue turned to her, a hint of moisture in her eyes. "I'm glad you rented her, Paige. I know you'll take real good care of her."

They returned to the front part of the house, where Debbie Sue leveled a long look at the folding chairs in the living room, then grinned. "Well, what can I say? I like what you've done in the bed-room, but the living room leaves a lot to be desired."

"Garage sale chic, I'd call it," Edwina said.

"Oh, it's not a big deal," Paige felt compelled to reply. "The only time I've spent at home has been in bed. I haven't had time to sit in the living room once, so I guess it doesn't bother me that much not to have real furniture."

"Spending all your time in bed, huh?" Edwina said, looking at Debbie Sue with mischief in her eyes. "That's not much different from when you and Buddy lived here, is it?"

"Not that it's any of your business, but . . ." Debbie Sue's voice trailed off in a suggestive way.

"Let me mix y'all a drink," Paige said. "We're having cos-mopolitans. That and Scotch are all the liquor I've got."

"Cosmopolitans are alcoholic, right?" Edwina said.

Paige explained the mixture as she placed a curled lemon rind on the edge of a glass. With a healthy measure of pride she offered the drink to Edwina.

"Why, look at how pretty this is," Edwina gushed, accepting her drink. "I don't know if I should drink it or take a picture of it." She took a big gulp. "Ooohh, that's good. I could do some damage with these. And aren't these glasses pretty? I think my mother had a set like this when I was growing up. Got 'em with S & H green stamps they used to give away at Piggly Wiggly. Nowadays, these would probably be worth something at a flea mart. Or even on eBay."

Paige chose not to go into the cost of the unique glasses. What it all boiled down to was Edwina's last statement. "Yes," Paige answered. "They're practically priceless. Here, let me mix you another drink."

Several drinks later the friends sat down to devour Percy's pot roast dinners.

"Debbie Sue made me promise I'd wait before asking this and I have," Edwina said. "But my curiosity's killing me. So tell us, how'd the date go Saturday night?"

Paige gave them a brief summary of the evening she and Spur had spent together. They all joined in laughing when she told about the apron.

"Why, Debbie Sue Overstreet," Edwina said. "That apron was a gift from me. You didn't leave it here on purpose, did you?"

"It wasn't me who packed the kitchen," Debbie Sue said. "That was Buddy's job. He most likely didn't see the humor in it. We weren't together when you gave it to me."

"He probably thought it was a gift from Quint." They all guffawed over that idea.

"So, you didn't get any?" Edwina asked when the laughter died out.

Paige felt all the blood in her body rush to her face.

"Ed, I swear to God," Debbie Sue said. "You're embarrassing her. You can't just ask a person something like that."

"Why not? We're all friends." She pointed a look at Paige. "So did you two fuck or not?"

"How are things working out with Lester being away?" Debbie Sue asked, obviously redirecting the conversation. "Are you enjoying him being gone, or is the work too much for you?"

"I'm doing fine," Paige answered, silently thanking Debbie Sue. "It's a big responsibility, but luckily I have help from the hired hands."

The phone message she had taken for Lester earlier came back to her. "I took a message for Lester today that I can't figure out and I can't stop thinking about it. There was something creepy in the caller's voice."

"Tell us about it," Debbie Sue said.

Paige repeated the conversation word for word.

Edwina and Debbie Sue exchanged glances. Finally Edwina said, "Brooks Van Patten. Never heard of him. I'd remember a name like that. I'm betting he's not from around here. Hell, he's probably not even from Texas."

"What do you think TAR is?" Paige asked, toying with her last bite of pot roast.

Debbie Sue suddenly pushed from the table, her face crimson. "Oh, my God," she whispered, tears in her eyes. "Oh, my God. Surely not. Surely he wouldn't."

Paige picked up a puzzled expression on Edwina's face.

"What? Speak up forgodsake," the older friend said.

"TAR. Texas Agricultural Resources."

Edwina shrugged. "Okay. What's that?"

Debbie Sue's eyes had grown huge and serious, and Paige felt her own eyes widen.

"Texas Agricultural Resources is the largest horse slaughterhouse in Texas," Debbie Sue said. "They kill horses and sell the meat. They use that fancy name to fool the animal rights people."

Paige looked at Edwina. "Do—do we need another drink?"

"Hell, yes," Debbie Sue said, clubbing the tabletop with her fist. "I want one for each hand. That bastard."

"Who?" Edwina asked.

"Lester, that's who."

Paige hurriedly gathered the glasses and mixed more drinks, adding extra vodka, as if it had been ordered.

"They've received six and need four more." Edwina's eyes narrowed to a squint. "Why he's been stealing horses and hauling them to TAR. You're right. That bastard." She, too, clubbed the table with her fist.

"Oh, my gosh," Paige said. "That explains all the extra hay and feed he put in his pickup. And the trips out of town he's been making. That explains a lot of things."

"Like what?" Debbie Sue asked, her glare so intense Paige wanted to fidget.

"Well, he talks about not working with horses the rest of his life. He's pretty vague, but he's made it clear he has bigger and better things in his future."

After a pause, Edwina said, "Stealing a few horses wouldn't provide a big future. Didn't you say they don't pay over a thousand dollars for a whole horse? I mean, that ain't much per pound."

"You're right, Ed, but he may see it as a lot. It could add up if he was smart about the way he used the money. I don't see Lester as being a big thinker. Whatever he has plans to do can probably be bought cheap." Debbie Sue turned back to Paige. "Did the guy leave his phone number?"

"No," Paige answered, disappointed that she hadn't had the presence of mind to insist on the messenger leaving a number. "He said that Lester knew how to reach him. This is so terrible. Don't we need to contact the authorities?"

"And tell them what? That a mysterious man left a message for Lester? No phone number, just a message that could be interpreted a thousand different ways? No, we need more. And I'm betting we need it fast. We may already be too late."

"Lester's a slick talker," Edwina said. "Why he could sell the devil a book of matches. He'll never 'fess up to anything."

"Then we'll just have to beat him at his own game," Debbie Sue said, her jaw set. "Paige, I hate to eat and run, but I've got some thinking to do. Will it hurt your feelings if I cut out early?"

"No, not at all. If I can be of any help—"

"I was just about to ask you, if I come up with something that involves you, would you be willing to go along?"

"Oh, of course. I'll do anything I can to help. I can't bear the thought of beautiful horses being slaughtered."

"Ed, get your shit together," Debbie Sue said. "We're leaving."

"But we haven't had dessert."

"Ed, you can't have dessert with whatever it is we're drinking. We don't have time to eat. We've got some planning and plotting ahead of us."

"Well, hell. Let me at least get a piece of that pie." Edwina stood up.

Paige rose and went into the kitchen, returned the whole coconut cream pie to its original box, and carried it back to the table. She handed it to Edwina. "Here, you're supposed to take the pie anyway. I don't even want any."

"I didn't give you the money for it yet."

She walked toward her purse, but Debbie Sue grasped her arm and herded her toward the front door. "Paige, I'm sorry, but when I get something in my head, I have to start putting the pieces together. We'll talk tomorrow. Thanks for the dinner. It was delicious."

"Oh, please don't apologize. What you have to do is much more important. Just let me know how I can help."

Paige followed her guests to the front door, and when she opened it, there was Spur climbing the three steps to her porch. "Spur. This is a surprise."

Debbie Sue and Edwina said hello in unison.

"I, uh, I was just driving by," Spur said, "and I, uh, I should have called but—I'll go. Sorry. I didn't see any cars out front. I didn't know you had company."

He turned to leave, but Edwina grabbed his arm and turned him back toward the house. "You come on in and don't mind us. We're just leaving. Isn't that right, Paige?"

Paige looked from Edwina to Spur and back again. "Yes. Yes, of course. Come on in."

DEBBIE SUE AND EDWINA walked in silence. They both looked over their shoulder as Spur entered the house and Paige closed the door.

"I'm glad he came by," Edwina said.

"Yeah, that's a good sign."

"I was feeling bad running out on her like that. Why didn't we warn him about parking in front?"

"I've seen his pickup. I don't think even Koweba can do any more damage than what's already been done."

"Well, at least I can enjoy this coconut pie now," Edwina said. "I hated leaving with the whole thing before Paige even got a slice, but Spur had a plate of something that looked like brownies with him. Guess these young guys don't bring flowers."

twenty-four

The annoyance Paige felt earlier over the meat loaf seemed silly now that she found herself face-to-face with Spur.

He thrust a paper plate toward her. On it nested half a dozen brownies, wrapped in cellophane packages. "Sorry I didn't have time to bake."

Paige was overwhelmed and embarrassed at having sent such a childish message via his sister. She stepped forward, grasped his face between her palms, and kissed him, crushing the plate of brownies between them. He dropped the brownies to the floor, wrapped his arms around her body, and kissed her back.

They kissed hungrily, mouths and hands moving everywhere. She rode with liquor-driven abandon. She was wild and free, she was the vixen Samantha.

And she was more than slightly drunk from several cosmo-politans.

His hands burrowed into her hair, but his mouth jerked away and she found herself staring into his eyes. "If you want to stop, say so," he said hoarsely. " 'Cause I don't want to back off this time."

Her tongue refused to work, her eyes locked onto his.

"Are you drunk?" he asked her.

"Yes," she gasped. "And no. I mean, no, I don't want to stop. Ever. I mean, I know what I'm doing."

In one smooth move he lifted her into his arms and started for the hall's arched doorway. "Which way?"

"I'm not very experienced. I don't know a lot of ways, but I'm game for anything you want."

"Darlin', that's handy information to have, but I meant which way to your bedroom?"

As she pointed to the left, Paige buried her face against his shoulder to hide her red face.

Spur placed her on the bed. She had to feel him close again and reached up to him, but he was busy removing her clothes. She felt vulnerable and exposed and told him so. He stretched out beside her and held her close. His mouth moved over her body, murmuring reassuring words. With a gentleness she had never known from a man, he cupped her breast in one hand and teased her with soft kisses and gentle tongue flicks. His fingertips grazed her body, approaching the heat that had grown between her thighs. She closed her eyes and gave herself over to the incredible sensation coursing through her. Before she knew it, he was out of his clothes and driving her out of her mind.

PAIGE STRETCHED. If she were a cat, she would be purring now. Turning to face the other side of her bed she felt the spot Spur had vacated. It was still warm from his body heat, and she burrowed her face into his scent on the pillow. He'd had to leave early, and she, too, needed to be on her way, but she spent a few more minutes in memory.

They had made love all night. Going from tender and sweet to sheer abandonment and back again. She had never known anything like what she and Spur had shared. She understood what Sunny had talked about all these years.

But it was more than just sex. They had shared intimacy. Real intimacy. Between lovemaking they had talked. Really talked. Sitting in the middle of the bed, legs intertwined and totally nude, they had laughed and talked about each other's lives.

She told him about being born rich. He talked about growing up poor. They concluded each lifestyle had its negatives and positives. She told him secrets she had never discussed with anyone, not even Sunny. He had told her secrets, too, and she now understood his resentment of people with wealth. It was a deep-seated emotion, and even he admitted it was based on a faulty rationale.

By daybreak they were both physically and emotionally spent. They had strength left only for sharing little smiles and small kisses. Leaving, he stopped at her front doorway and told her he would call her later in the day. Their kiss good-bye could have turned into another session of lovemaking if he hadn't reminded her they both had other places to be and other people who relied on them. He hadn't been gone three minutes and she was already counting the hours until his phone call.

Oh, God. She was in deep—all the way to her armpits.

She had to tell Sunny.

Her longtime friend's voice mail picked up. "Hi. This is Sunny.

I'm in Munich for Octoberfest. I may not get back to you right away."

Paige laughed. Sunny would never change. "Hey, Sun. Guess what. You may be in Germany, but I'm in love. Believe it or not, it wasn't chocolate cake. It was store-bought brownies. Call me."

Giving in to the call of responsibility she reluctantly got up and gathered the tangled sheets from the bed but hesitated before dropping them in the laundry bin in the hallway near the utility room. On one level, she didn't want to wash them. The most glorious night she had ever spent was now a part of these sheets.

What a crazy thing to think. No one in their right mind would think something like that.

But then, maybe she wasn't in her right mind. Maybe she was . . . in love. The sobering thought gave her pause as she stepped under the shower. Love? Could it be? Could she be in love with a cowboy? She giggled as the warm water sputtered from the mineral-corroded shower head. Well, hell, she could think of worse places to be.

She stepped out of the shower and began her morning ritual in a daze until the phone interrupted. *Spur!*

She barely said hello before Debbie Sue began talking. "I know it's early. I'm sorry, but I couldn't wait. I didn't interrupt anything did I? I mean, are you, uh, is it okay to call?"

"No. I mean, it's okay. I'm alone." *Now.* On a deep breath, Paige gushed, "Debbie Sue, I think I'm in love. I just had a night I can't even describe. Do you think it's too early for me to feel this way? Could it just be, you know, lust?"

Debbie Sue laughed. "Nah. I believe in love at first sight. Always have. I think Spur is . . . um, we are talking about Spur, aren't we?"

"Who else? Isn't he the cutest thing ever? Did you know he was

offered a baseball scholarship in high school, too? But he chose football so he could go to A&M. His mother's name's Mary Elizabeth.
Don't you think that's a sweet, old-fashioned name? I'd like to have
a little girl someday named Mary Elizabeth. He wants four children,
two boys and two girls."

"Hey, take a rest. You're gonna faint."

"Right. Oh, my gosh, I haven't even asked why you called."

"I want to ask you for a favor. You know the conversation we
had last night about Lester and the mysterious message? If you're serious about helping us out, I've got this great idea about how we can
nail him."

"If he's the one stealing the horses, I'd love nothing better than
to expose him. What's your plan?"

"Ed and I were able to get ahold of Vic last night on the road and
we discussed it with him. He says it's doable."

"What's the plan?"

"We want you to seduce Lester. At your house."

"What?" Paige couldn't keep from snapping. She frowned at the
receiver.

"I know, I know. It's a lot to ask. Especially after last night. But
we don't have enough to go on, and the chances of catching him
red-handed are slim to none. I mean, we can't run all over West
Texas trying to be in the right place the next time he steals a horse.
Trapping him into a confession is the only thing my brain can come
up with. Think about it. How many horses might die if we don't
stop him now?"

Paige heard a break in Debbie Sue's voice and understood her
concern. She also understood the logic. Sighing, she sank to the
edge of the mattress. "Okay, tell me what to do."

Debbie Sue outlined the details of her plan. Paige would respond to Lester's crude amorous advances. She would invite him to her house for an evening of possibilities. Unbeknownst to him, Debbie Sue, Edwina, and Vic would be hiding in the spare bedroom, monitoring the listening and recording equipment that Vic would install in the house.

Even knowing Vic would be only a few steps away didn't dispel Paige's fears of being molested by her unwelcome guest. "How do I get him to confess?"

"The easiest way to get a man to talk is to massage his ego."

"That's okay, I guess. But I sure don't want to have to massage anything else."

"Oh, hell, you know how to bamboozle a man. Admire his plans for his future. Maybe even talk about how much you love working for him and all you're learning from him about the horses. Then you can say something like, 'But you know, Lester, eventually they all serve only one purpose.' If he thinks you wouldn't be appalled at the thought of horses being slaughtered for meat, he'll open up."

The thought of being touched by any man's hands but Spur's made Paige nauseated. She would have to pound into her subconscious the idea of the animals that would be saved.

And what if Spur found out?

"Don't worry about a thing. Vic, Ed, and I'll make sure things don't get out of hand," Debbie Sue was saying. "Once he confesses, we'll come out of the spare room and confront him. Then we'll call Buddy to haul his ass to jail, and it'll all be over."

"Buddy knows about this?" Paige asked, feeling a modicum of comfort that the intimidating, deep-voiced state trooper Buddy Overstreet was a part of the scheme.

"Well, not precisely. Not yet. But I'll tell him. He won't like it, and he'll raise holy hell, but he's used to me being a little crazy. And part of our pact when we got together again was I would learn to be a better housewife for him and he would give me some space for me. So when is Lester due back?"

"He said the end of the week. Today's Thursday, so it could be today. When are we doing this?"

"Let's plan on the evening he gets back. Call us as soon as he comes in and we'll get ready."

Paige hung up and finished dressing for her day at work, but her thoughts were rattled. If she helped Debbie Sue and Edwina put Lester away, would she be out of the only real job she had ever had and, furthermore, one that she liked?

The week had been so great, taking care of Harley's horses without Lester's presence. If he turned out to be the culprit, she had no doubt she could handle the care of the horses at the Flying C. But, she had to admit, she wasn't up to the task of training cutting horses. She was a quick study and had learned a lot up to this point, but she wasn't ready to take on teaching animals with such high-caliber breeding and so much promise. If Lester went away, Harley would probably bring in an experienced trainer, and she couldn't honestly blame him. And if that happened, would she be needed? *Drat.*

How could a day that had started out with so much promise turn sour so quickly?

Well, she wouldn't dwell on it. She had always seen the half-filled glass as half full. Unfortunately her half-filled glass appeared to have a hair in it.

Driving to the Flying C, she put Lester and the commitment she had made to Debbie Sue out of her mind. The only thing she wanted to think about was Spur. Lusty, titillating, erotic thoughts of Spur—his perfect body, his touch, his smell.

She caught a glimpse of her reflection in the rearview mirror. The smile on her face was so broad it would have to be spackled and sanded to be removed. She had been out of his arms for a little more than two hours, and she could hardly wait to return.

Maybe she could call him at noon. Better yet, maybe he would come out to the ranch to see her. Hmmm, an actual roll in the hay. That is, if Lester didn't come back today.

Lester. Just like that, the spell was broken. Playing up to him was as enticing as an enema. Saving horses from being led to slaughter was the only thought that would compel her to do it.

As she drove through the Flying C's gate her hope that he wouldn't return today was dashed. There sat his pickup.

Showing there was starch in her word of honor, she picked up her cell phone and called Debbie Sue. "Hey, it's me. Lester's back."

"Great. The sooner that horse-thieving sonofabitch is behind bars the better. Personally, I'd like to lynch him, but I made a promise to Buddy."

"What, that you wouldn't hang horse thieves in general or just this one?"

"I promised I wouldn't do anything to call attention to myself. No press. No magazine articles. Buddy really hates that."

"Oh. *That* kind of promise."

"I'll talk to Ed when I get to the shop," Debbie Sue went on. "I've got a key to your house. Do you mind if I let the three of us in so we can get things set up for this evening?"

"Sure, go ahead. What time should I ask him over?"

"How about seven o'clock? We'll go over a couple of hours earlier and get set up. . . . And, Paige? Just spend today like you would spend any other. We don't want to tip him off."

A day like any other? After last night, Paige couldn't imagine that any day she would ever spend for the rest of her life would be a day like any other. "Seven is fine with me. See you then."

Gathering her lunch and purse she slid from the SUV and walked into the barn. She smelled coffee. Yep, Lester was indeed back. Through the office's open door she spotted him sitting at the desk, telephone receiver pressed to his ear, chair tilted back, ankles crossed on the desktop in his usual manner.

Saving horses. Saving horses. Saving horses. The mantra helped. She pulled a mug from the shelf and poured herself a full cup of steaming coffee, pausing with carafe in hand to look in his direction. She stepped nearer to him and topped off his cup. He looked up, surprise easy to read on his face. She wiggled two crooked fingers in his direction and mouthed "good morning." Replacing the coffee carafe on its element, she gathered her cup and her gear and walked out of the office toward the horse stalls. *Saving horses. Saving horses. Saving horses.*

As she led the second horse toward the walker Lester joined her. A mischievous grin played across his face, and the usual leer showed in his eyes. "Miss me?"

Saving horses. Paige gave him a tight smile. "Sure. I'm glad you're back."

"Really? Looks like things went fine while I was gone. No problems, huh?"

"Yeah. I mean, uh . . . yeah, things went fine and no, I didn't have any problems." Paige looked down at the ground, hoping she appeared timid instead of repulsed.

Lester rested his hand on the neck of the mare she was leading. "Maybe ol' Harley'll just turn it all over to you."

"He wouldn't do that. I couldn't do half the job you do here. I can only groom and exercise these guys." *Saving horses.* "You're the one who trains them." This time, she gave him a smile meant to dazzle. "But I'm still willing to learn."

"Are you asking me in a roundabout way to help you learn more about cutting? I already said I would. There just hasn't been enough time."

"I wasn't pressing you. I know how busy you've been." She walked around to the other side of the horse. This might be easier if she didn't have to actually look him in the face. "Did you see the message I left for you on the filing cabinet? It sounded important."

"Yeah, I saw it. What did Van Patten say? What did he tell you?" His tone was insistent.

"Everything he said was on the note." Paige forced an innocent air. "What is TAR?"

"It doesn't matter. I'm doing a business deal. Let's get to work." He walked away.

If this was a preview of how it was going to be getting him to talk about the mystery surrounding Brooks Van Patten and TAR, Paige could see she had her work cut out for her.

twenty-five

Debbie Sue jiggled the key in the front door lock. Even though she owned this house and it had been her home for years, she felt uncomfortable entering with the tenant absent.

Vic ducked his head as he came through the doorway, followed by the sucker-sucking Edwina. "Where's the furniture?" Vic asked, stopping to look at the aluminum chairs in the living room. "I thought she was rich."

Edwina removed her lollipop. "Her daddy's rich—"

"And her mama's good-looking," Debbie Sue and Vic chimed in, singing in harmony.

"Cute," Edwina said. "As I started to say, she doesn't have any money. She's trying to live on her own without help from her daddy."

"I've noticed that," Vic retorted. "I've seen her around town in that fifty-thousand-dollar symbol of independence."

"Now, hon, go easy on her. She's a good kid. Some kids get used cars from their parents, some get Cadillacs. It's all in what's available to spend."

"You're right. I take it back. The only thing my dad ever gave me was a hard time. Sometimes that comes out in me when I'm not thinking." Vic scanned the room. "Let's get under way."

For the next half hour the three of them worked. Vic decided a wireless listening device the size of a pencil eraser would be best situated on the bottom side of one of the aluminum chairs. He set up a receiver in the empty guest bedroom. After the equipment was calibrated, tested, and with everything in working order, they prepared to leave.

"Debbie Sue," Vic said, packing up his tools, "you're putting a lot of stock in it being Lester who's the thief. What if it isn't him?"

"Oh, he's guilty all right. How could he not be? I mean look at the facts." She shot a look at Edwina, seeking an ally. "You think he's guilty, don't you? You agree with me, right?"

"Abso-fuckin'-lutely." Edwina gave a thumbs-up.

Vic's arm came around her, and he gave her a hug. "Cowgirl, you've always had good instincts and a nose for the truth. If you say he's guilty, that's good enough for me."

"No, Vic, that's not good enough," Debbie Sue said. "If he's not the one, then I don't want to blame him. But I don't know who else it could be. I just know one thing for sure. The killing has to stop, and *we* have to stop the killer." What she thought, but didn't say, was *before he gets to Rocket Man.*

"Now,. now, sugar," Edwina said patting Debbie Sue's arm. "We're gonna get him. If it's not Lester then we'll find out who it is. Don't forget we're the Domestic Equalizers. Men fear us, women revere us and seek our support. Why, if Salt Lick had a phone booth we'd be comic book heroes."

Debbie Sue managed a laugh. Edwina could always pull a laugh out of her. "I got news for you, Ed. Some people think we're comic book characters anyway."

Debbie Sue didn't like being a drama queen, but before this minute, she hadn't considered that Lester might not be the culprit. She didn't have a plan B. She didn't know what to do if Paige couldn't seduce Lester into a confession.

One thing she couldn't let herself forget. She had promised Buddy she wouldn't do something dumb or get in over her head. To her dismay, she could already feel icy water inching up her spine.

PAIGE LOOKED at her watch again. Ten minutes until four o'clock. She didn't want to "be nice" to Lester any longer than she had to, but if she intended to invite the horse thief to her house she had to hurry up and do it.

She had been able to stay away from him and keep space between them all day. Luckily he was accustomed to her aloofness, so he didn't appear to see her distant behavior as anything new. Was he really seeing a woman in Abilene or had he been scouting or collecting the other four horses Van Patten had mentioned on the phone? Whichever, he had apparently been successful, because his mood was upbeat. From her safe distance, she had even heard him singing.

Steeling her resolve and rehearsing the invitation in her head, she walked toward the office, wiping her palms on her jeans as she neared the doorway. When she peered through the partially open door, she was surprised to see the office empty. She could have sworn the singing had been coming from here. She started to leave, but the phone halted her. She looked around for Lester to appear and answer it, but when she didn't see him she scurried inside and picked up the receiver. "Flying C Ranch."

"Hey, Paige. I'm glad it's you who answered." The sound of Spur's voice sent her heart aflutter.

"Hi, Spur." She kept her reply short. She had to, because she longed to say "hi, sweetheart" or "hi, baby," but she didn't have the confidence to act on the desire.

His voice came across the wire soft and sexy. "I've been thinking about you all day, darlin'."

After what she had learned about him from the long talks they'd had last night, she knew he had taken a giant step with making that statement. It was all she could do to keep from sighing. "Honest? I've been thinking about you, too. . . . I, uh, Spur?"

"What, sugar?"

"I—I had a good time last night."

His intimate chuckle teased her ear. "Oh, yeah? That's all? Just a good time?"

Paige lowered her voice to the same level as his. "Well, no. I mean, gosh, I've never had this conversation before. I'm sorry I'm so dumb, but I don't know what I'm supposed to say."

"Just say what you feel, darlin'."

Paige closed her eyes, remembering the night and the morning. Looking around once again for any eavesdropper, she hugged the phone receiver to her lips. "I *loved* last night, Spur. I've never felt like that before. No one's ever—I mean, you're so amazing. When you took your tongue and—"

"Whoa, sweetheart. I've got a patient due any minute now. I can't be listening to this kind of talk. I won't be able to do my duty."

"Hah. Afraid your roommate will make an appearance?"

"My roommate has become a persistent pest. Lord, what you've done to him. Are we getting together this evening?"

His question yanked her back to the reason she had walked into the office in the first place. "Oh, Spur! Oh, no. Spur, I can't. I promised Debbie Sue I'd help her with something. She's coming to my house later tonight. I'm so sorry. I can't get out of it and—"

"Hey, you don't need to apologize. It's all right. I'll just call you tomorrow if that's okay."

"It's sooo okay. Please believe me when I say I'm sorry."

"I believe you, Paige. I'll always believe you. You couldn't lie if you tried. Gotta go, now. Bye, sweetheart."

Paige stood welded to the floor with the receiver in her hand. His words circled her head like the rings of Saturn. No man, save her daddy, had ever called her sweetheart. No declaration, short of 'I love you and I can't live without you' could mean as much to her. No doubt about it. She was in love, and she didn't intend to put on the brakes.

SPUR SAT on a stainless-steel stool in his exam room, his hand on the phone receiver. When he called Paige, his intention had been to say hello, but the moment he heard her voice he slipped into another mode altogether. He had never met a female who turned him on so completely. Earlier today he had preg-tested a small herd of heifers, vaccinated a couple of dogs and one woman's flock of ten cats. Through it all, last night had hung in his mind. The time and place had been right, and a passionate partner had made it even better.

Even more astonishing was the fact that he had made a plan to see her tonight and was eager to do so. Apparently his subconscious had severed communication with his brain. He was playing this all wrong, he was sure. But then, what did he know? He had never *played* anything but sports. With that in mind he had to acknowledge that last night had been the Super Bowl of sex. The World Series of eroticism.

A frantic exclamation came from the reception room. "Oh, I hope Dr. Atwater can save her."

Uh-oh. An emergency. Time to put last night behind him and tend to matters at hand.

"I'm sure he'll be able to help her," Electra said.

Spur rose from his perch, walked to the lavatory, and pumped globs of antibacterial soap into his cupped hand. Before he could rinse his hands and shut off the water, Electra led a woman who had to weigh three hundred pounds into the exam room. And she was howling in a high-pitched whine.

"This is Mildred Montgomery," Electra said. "And Prissy."

Limp as a dishrag, a French bulldog lay in Electra's arms. Spur detected a snore coming from the dog.

"It's not an everyday thing with me," Miz Montgomery said between sobs. "It's just that it helps my pain to have one every now and then."

Stupefied, Spur glanced from Prissy to her owner. "What helps your pain?"

Miz Montgomery threw her hamlike arms in the air. "My hot toddy. Prissy drank all of it." She broke into sobs again and looked up with a contorted mouth and tear-covered cheeks. "Is she going to die?"

Spur looked down at the exam table where Electra had laid the sleeping Prissy and now stood rubbing her hand down the dog's small back. Prissy was drunk?

Seeing nothing telling in Electra's expression Spur looked from her to the hysterical dog owner. "Now, now, Miz Montgomery. Tell me, what was in the toddy and how much did, uh, Prissy . . . consume?"

"Well, uh, because I don't drink one very often, I usually have a large glass, you see. I've got one of those thirty-two-ounce plastic cups Hogg's gives out when you buy their Chuck Wagon Meal. I put in some honey and some warm water and six ounces of whiskey. It takes that much, you see, to ease the pain."

Spur nodded as he pressed the stethoscope to the dog's chest and listened to its heart. "Hmm. Well, honey and water is not something I recommend for a dog, but it won't kill her. How much whiskey do you think she had?"

Miz Montgomery's voice began to hitch. "I guess . . . it was the whole six ounces. . . . She dr-drank it all." She leaned down and placed a teary kiss on the small black nose. "Oh, Dr. Atwater, you should . . . have seen . . . the way she was acting. I had to carry . . . the poor little thing in here." She began to wail again.

Spur took over the stroking of Prissy's body. The dog grunted and twitched. He pried open her mouth to examine her gums and throat. The dog's breath reeked of alcohol. "I think she'll be okay, but she has to sleep it off. Sugar's not good for a dog, so you need to keep an eye on her. She may not be herself for a day or two. If I were you, I'd be careful about leaving your drink around. She might develop a taste for it and want more."

"Oh, Dr. Atwater, I don't know how to thank you. I'll take her home and watch her. I'll make sure it never happens again. Thank you so much, doctor."

The woman picked up the limp dog and covered its face with

kisses. Spur watched as she left the clinic talking baby talk to the snoozing dog. He shook his head. Poor Prissy.

He wasn't truly worried about Prissy learning to crave whiskey. He was more worried about himself. He could relate too well to wanting more of something because that was exactly how he felt about Paige. He had to see her. He didn't know why. He just knew he had to. "Electra," he called.

She stuck her head into his exam room. "Yes, Doctor."

"Just so you'll be happy, I'm telling you now, I'm gonna go see Paige."

His sister's grin lit up her whole face.

"Let's lock up so I can get you home and come back and clean up before I go over there."

PAIGE'S REVERIE was broken by Lester's voice. "I said, who was on the phone?"

"Huh? Oh, uh, it was a wrong number." God, it was scary how quickly she could follow Spur's touching assessment of her ability to tell the truth with a lie.

"Okay, then," Lester said and followed with a wide yawn. "If you don't need me for anything I'm headed for the house. I'm beat."

"Lester, I did want to ask you something before you leave." Paige placed the receiver in its cradle, her thoughts centered on butchered horses. "Would you like to come to my house this evening? Maybe have a couple of drinks, a bite to eat? We could just sort of hang out and talk."

Lester came to life. "Hey, you did miss me, didn't you?" A cocky grin played across his thin lips. "You jealous of the time I spent with my lady in Abilene?"

All that kept Paige from picking up a handful of horse droppings and rubbing them across Lester's grin was her pledge to Debbie Sue. Her invitation might be innocent, but his intentions weren't. She hoped things *would* get out of hand this evening, which would prompt Vic to burst into the room and take matters into *his* hands. That is, if he could get ahead of Debbie Sue and Edwina.

"I want to get to know you better," she said, forcing her mouth into a smile. "We work together all day every day, but we never really talk. I might have been a little hard on you. I'd just like to make a fresh start."

"You bet," he said with a wink. "What time do you want me to come over for this, what'd you call it, talk?"

"Seven?"

"Seven it is." Lester started to leave but stopped, turned back, and walked close. He leaned and placed his lips near her ear. "I've always known you wanted me, sweet thing. I just didn't think it would take this long for you to see the light." He planted a peck on her cheek and walked out humming.

Paige glared at him until he disappeared from sight. The only light she wanted to see was the headlamp of the oncoming locomotive that would run over Lester Clinton's slimy, horse-stealing body.

twenty-six

Within half an hour of Paige's arrival at home she was joined by Debbie Sue. Edwina and Vic weren't far behind. Vic went over the placement of the listening device with Paige and gave her instructions where to sit and stand. The only person who wasn't edgy was Edwina. She was sitting on one of the folding chairs with a bottle of fingernail polish gripped between her knees, streaking a blaze of red down one of her talonlike nails.

"I'll just be glad when this is over," Debbie Sue said. "Paige, you're great to help out. I hope we aren't interrupting other plans you had."

"Huh? Oh, no. No plans. I was just going to wash some bed linens." Paige felt ill at the thought of what she could be doing tonight instead of helping catch a horse thief.

"Ed," Debbie Sue said, "why are you polishing your nails now? There had to have been a hundred times you could have done that earlier today."

"Well excuse the hell out of me, but this is the way I handle stress. You turn bitchy, I paint my nails."

"I'm not being bitchy," Debbie Sue said defensively. "I'm just ready for this to be over, that's all."

"I say you're being bitchy and we need a drink. Paige, can you mix us up one of those pretty red things we had last night?"

"That's a great idea. Four cosmopolitans coming up." Paige headed into the kitchen.

"None for me," Vic said, his tone serious. "I'm working tonight. I never mix liquor with work."

"And I," Edwina announced, "never mix a drink when someone else will. That's why Vic and I are so compatible. We're practically identical in our thinking."

Paige returned to the living room with drinks for Edwina, Debbie Sue, and herself.

Debbie Sue took a sip from her cosmopolitan, then pointed a finger at Vic and Edwina. "Promise me one thing. Once Lester gets here, promise me y'all will be quiet. We want to do this only once. And I don't want to get caught and try to explain why the three of us are hiding in the spare room."

"No one wants this to end tonight more than me," Edwina replied. "No offense, hon, but you haven't been yourself for weeks." Edwina lifted her glass. "Now, I propose a toast." She faced the two women. "To men who steal horses and the ones that break our hearts. May they all burn in hell."

"May they all burn in hell," Debbie Sue and Paige echoed. They clinked glasses and consumed the last of the vodka-heavy cosmopolitans. Paige held her breath for an instant, hoping they didn't throw the glasses.

"Okay, ladies, it's six-thirty," Vic said. "Let's get in place. He might get here early." He herded the two women from the living room. "Good luck, Paige. Don't worry. I've got my eye—and my ear—on everything. I won't let things get out of hand."

"I'm not worried," Paige lied. "I just hope it works."

Promptly at seven o'clock the doorbell rang. Paige stood looking at the backyard with her arms crossed, her shield against any advances, and called out, "Come in."

Nothing she had experienced in life could have prepared her for the sight of Spur coming through her front door. She froze for a count of seconds before she spoke. "My God! Spur! What are you doing here?"

"I didn't see Debbie Sue's truck out front, so I thought I'd drop by for a minute. Remember Randy? The owner of the dog whose life you probably saved? He came by the clinic as I was leaving and left this sack for you." Spur handed her a brown paper grocery bag. "He didn't know where you lived, so I told him I'd drop it by."

Paige peered into the bag and saw several glass jars of *food*? She picked out a jar of black-eyed peas and read the label, BON APPÉTIT. FROM RANDY'S HANDS AND HEART TO YOUR GOOD HEALTH. "Oh. Food. I've never seen this brand."

"It's not a brand. It's from his garden."

"Oh. Well, how nice."

"He canned 'em himself."

"Oh. What a lot of work. Why would he do that when you can buy it in the store?"

"'Cause it tastes better. He's an organic gardener."

"Oh, organic." She laughed, despite a rising panic. "I buy that all the time. But you didn't have to bring it over." She carried the sack to the front door and opened the door to rush his departure.

"I know." He looked down at the floor, fumbling with his hat brim. "I, uh, thought it was a good excuse to see you again. I know you're expecting company, I just wanted to say—"

"Hey, sugar lips, you didn't tell me it was gonna be a party." Walking toward them, Lester lifted a six-pack of Lone Star long-necks to eye level. "I only brought enough beer for the two of us."

Paige's eyes almost crossed. She wanted to tell Lester to go to hell and get out, but she couldn't. She wanted to reach out and hang on to Spur, but she couldn't. She looked at Lester, then back at Spur. Her mouth worked, but no words came out.

She hoped for Spur to read the plea for understanding in her eyes, but what she saw was anything but. He had a puzzled expression all right and the muscles in his jaw twitched like mad. He plopped his hat back on. His glare swerved from Lester to her, and she wished for a giant sinkhole to form in the floor.

"I must be in the wrong here," Spur said. "Sorry, Lester. Had my nights mixed up. It's your turn tonight. Have a good time." He stamped down the front steps.

Paige wanted to chase after him, to explain, but Lester's question bolted her in place.

"Mind if I use your bathroom? Which way is it?"

She thought she might throw up, wondered if she should rush into the bathroom ahead of him. She would never forget the expression on Spur's face. And she no longer had faith in the words she had heard him say earlier, *I'll always believe you. You couldn't lie if you tried.*

She couldn't risk Lester opening the wrong door and seeing the Three Musketeers sitting there with listening equipment in their ears and blank expressions on their faces. "Here, give me the beer." She took the six-pack from him and started toward the hall. "I'll show you the way."

She returned to the kitchen, clunked the six-pack onto the

counter, and mixed another cosmopolitan, sans cranberry juice, fighting not to open the bedroom door where Debbie Sue, Edwina, and Vic had concealed themselves and call this whole charade off. Then again, maybe not. The two women would understand her feelings of mortification, but if she saw them face-to-face, she might break into hysterics. Instead of taking the risk, she gulped a cosmopolitan, steeling herself for her role in this one-act play.

Lester returned with a big grin on his face. "What's the chance of me getting one of those cold beers?"

She loosened a longneck and tossed it in his direction. Taking one for herself she unscrewed the top and took a deep swig of the cold brew. It landed with a thud on top of the vodka and Cointreau she had just drunk.

Lester laughed. "Damn, girl, slow down. Sorry if I caused trouble between you and the doc. He'll have to learn there's just some women you don't drop in on."

Paige beat back the part of her that wanted to use her bottle cap to turn him into a eunuch and wondered just how pitiful the woman in Abilene who found him appealing had to be. She forced an air of congeniality, something she had done uncountable times in the presence of her stepmother, and led her unwanted guest to the living room. "Have a seat, Lester. Let's talk."

"What's with the furniture?" Lester asked, looking at the webbed lawn chairs and easing down into one. "This sure don't look like richer-than-all-get-out. These come from one o' them fancy designer stores?"

"Yeah," Paige snapped. "Did you get registered for the horse show next month?"

Lester leaned back against the chair frame and cocked an ankle across his knee. "Sure. I never miss the chance to go to Fort Worth.

I like that area. I'd like to have my own place in Weatherford. Just far enough outta Fort Worth to go in when I want, but still be out in the country. I will, too, one o' these days. I have plans."

"Really?" Paige didn't have to fake her interest. With no effort on her part, the conversation was headed in just the direction everyone wanted. She took a seat across from him. "You've mentioned that before. What kind of plans?"

"Let's just say, I don't intend to work for another man all my life. You never get anywhere working for wages. My old man didn't teach me a lot, but he did drill that into my head." He tilted up his beer bottle and downed a long swig.

"But places in Weatherford aren't cheap."

He released a loud burp. "I know that, but one o' these days I'll be able to just up and buy the one I want. I won't even ask the price."

"Does that guy Brooks Van Patten have anything to do with your plans?"

Lester leaned forward, his elbows resting on his knees, the long-neck hanging from his fingers. "Maybe."

Paige's patience and nerves were already worn thin. If she was going to get through this, she had to cut to the chase. "I finally figured out where I've heard of TAR before. Those initials stand for Texas Animal Resources. Where horses are taken for slaughter. Are you doing business with them now?"

His face scrunched into a quizzical expression. "What?"

She shrugged and fluttered her eyelashes. "Oh, don't get me wrong. I'm not passing judgment. I think slaughterhouses serve a purpose, I really do. People have their pets euthanized every day. TAR's methods may not be entirely humane, but what are old horses good for anyway?" Paige felt sick to her stomach uttering those words.

Lester choked and practically spit his beer across the room. "I thought you loved horses? And here you are, talking about selling 'em for slaughter? Babe, you're just full o' surprises."

"Oh, come on. I've seen the way you treat the horses. My first trip to the ranch I saw you kick one."

"I'll be the first one to admit I've lost my temper a time or two, but I've never been cruel to even a one of 'em. Truth be told, I'd rather be around horses than most o' the people I know."

Paige tried to remember if, since her employment at the Flying C, she had ever again seen him mistreat a horse. No incident came to mind. Damned if she didn't believe him when he said he wasn't cruel to the horses. She had let her dislike for him color her opinion of how he did his job as handler. It dawned on her then that he was, in reality, pretty good with the horses. No way would he be stealing them for slaughter.

Great. Now what?

But she had to give interrogation one more try. "Have you heard about all the horses that have disappeared? Some people around here think they've been stolen."

"Yeah, I've heard about it. Yeah, somebody's stole 'em all right. Hope they catch the bastard. Wonder if it's still legal in Texas to hang a horse thief? If it ain't, it oughtta be."

Paige was stumped for words, but she had to make one last effort before she cried uncle. "Come on, Lester. Please tell me about TAR. What's so secret? Who knows, maybe I could be of some help to you with your plans. You know, I'm not without means or contacts."

She wasn't comfortable flaunting her family wealth and position, but it was her last tool.

Lester drained the last drink from the bottle, stood up, and walked to the six-pack. He looked at her while he took another from its cardboard box. Clearly he was giving her last words some thought. "You know, sweet thing, you could be right. Maybe you could be some help to me. Harley's the only person I know who's got more money than sense, but I'd rather die than ask him for help." He twisted the cap off the beer bottle. "Hell, I've been an anchor around his neck most o' my life. It ain't easy taking a paycheck from a man when you know he gives it to you with a grudge." He drew a long swig from the beer bottle.

I can't make any promises where my daddy's money is concerned, Paige started to say, but before the words fell from her mouth, he cleared his throat and wiped his mouth on his shirtsleeve. "Okay, I'm gonna tell you." He squared his shoulders. He was obviously about to confess something. "Ready?"

"Ready."

He drew a deep breath. "Brooks Van Patten is my agent."

Paige couldn't keep from giving him the squint-eye. "Your what?"

"My agent. He got me a chance to be heard by Texas Artist Recordings. TAR. They're out o' Austin. It's Willie and George's baby. They've signed some guys who're big names now."

"What are you talking about?"

"Music, babe. I'm gonna be a star. Van Patten says I'm the next Merle Haggard. Imagine that? Me and ol' Hag in the same category." He guzzled another swig of beer.

Paige shook her head in disbelief. She had heard him singing every day around the barn. But she still couldn't believe what she had just heard him say. "What did he mean when he said something about having six and needing four more?"

"Six recorded songs. They want ten to put a CD together. I went to Abilene to use a recording studio that's over there."

"But the feed and hay you took off the ranch—"

"Feed and hay? . . . Oh, that. It's for the guy that runs the studio. I can't afford to pay him money for the sessions, so I take him supplies for his horses. Harley never misses it 'cause it don't amount to much. Don't you dare tell him. This is my one big chance. I'll do just damn near anything to make it come true."

As if the day hadn't already served Paige more than she could handle, Lester's hands suddenly gripped her shoulders.

"Honey, I know you don't think much o' me now, but I'm gonna be somebody. Go on this ride with me, baby. With your daddy's money and my talent, we could own Nashville."

Paige tried to unclench his fingers. "Let go of me, Lester! I don't want to own Nashville."

Before she could say another word or take another action, a hand grabbed Lester by the collar and lifted him off his feet, leaving his boots barely touching the floor. As Lester struggled and his face turned beet red, Paige pleaded with the former navy SEAL. "Vic, it's okay. He didn't hurt me. Let him go."

Vic released his hold, and Lester crumpled to the floor like a piece of balled-up trash. Lester looked up at Vic, then back at her. "Damn, woman! How many men does it take to satisfy you? How many others you got stashed away?"

Debbie Sue and Edwina burst into the room. "Sorry, Vic," Debbie Sue said. "We couldn't stay in there any longer."

Lester's eyes grew wide as he stared at the two women. "Good God, Paige. Just how kinky are you?"

"Oh, shut up," Paige said, on the verge of breaking into tears. Little else could go wrong with this day. She knew only four men in this town, and now half of them were convinced she was a slut. Worse yet, a kinky slut.

Ignoring Lester, Edwina addressed the room. "Now what do we do? I believe him."

"I do, too, dammit," Debbie Sue said. "I don't know where to go from here."

"Maybe the stealing has stopped," Edwina said. "Maybe it won't happen again."

"Would somebody please tell me what the hell's going on?" Lester said.

Vic filled Lester in on their suspicions and their plan. After a lengthy explanation he finished with, "We were going to record you admitting that you stole the horses and turn you over to the authorities. Nothing weird, nothing perverse. Just a little detective work."

"Oh, yeah. Nothing weird about *this* setup. This is all just normal as hell. Dammit, y'all owe me an apology. Ever' last one o' you. But don't bother. I'm leaving. Y'all can stick it where the sun don't shine. And when I make it big, I may just come back here with a herd o' lawyers and sue your asses."

He stomped out and slammed the door, leaving the four of them standing in the living room.

Edwina planted her fists on her hips. "Well, that went well. Chaos, confusion, and all around fucked-up. I think our work here is done."

"Yep," Vic agreed. "In the navy, we'd call this a real FUBAR."

"I'm deflated," Edwina said. "I got pumped for explosive action, and now we don't even have a fizzle. Let's go home, Vic. We can come back later for the equipment."

Paige watched Vic and Edwina as they walked arm in arm toward the alley.

Debbie Sue came up behind her and put her hand on her shoulder. "I'm sorry about Spur. We'll explain everything to him."

"I don't know if he'll listen. You should have seen his face when he saw Lester."

"He's mad because some guy came over to your house? Why should he be? You two don't have a commitment to each other, do you?"

"Well, not a spoken one, but last night, we uh, uh, it was the first time—" Paige burst into sobs before she could finish her sentence.

Debbie Sue pulled her close, but being at least four inches taller than Debbie Sue, it was hard for Paige to cry on her shoulder.

"You poor kid. I wish I'd known about you and Spur before I cooked up this scheme." Debbie Sue stroked her back. "God, I've really fucked things up, haven't I?"

"It's not your fault," Paige said between sobs. "I should have told Spur the truth when he called today."

"What *did* you tell him?"

"I told him I had plans with you."

"Well, isn't that the truth? You did have plans with me. Did you know Lester was coming over when you talked to Spur?"

Paige's sobbing slowed to a spasmodic sniffle. "No, I hadn't invited him over yet."

"Then you didn't lie. Men are such hardheaded jackasses. Spur will just have to get over it. And he will. Remember what I told you about giving him some space?"

Paige nodded, not at all sure Debbie Sue was right. The space between them now looked like the Grand Canyon.

"Listen, as much as I hate leaving you alone when you're so

upset, I need to get home, too. Buddy doesn't know what I'm up to. If I'm not there when he gets home, I might have to explain myself, and he might handcuff me to a chair or something. Walk with me to my pickup."

They crossed the lawn together toward a red extended-cab Silverado. Reaching it, Debbie Sue opened the driver's door and looked back at Paige. "Don't forget, if you want me to talk to Spur, I will. Just give me a call."

"Thanks, I will," Paige said, now more in control of her emotions. "Speaking of calls, Debbie Sue, looks like you've got one." Paige pointed to the cell phone mounted on the dash flashing that a message was waiting.

"Hey, for a minute I forgot about that monster." Debbie Sue keyed in the code for message retrieval and listened. Without warning, her features twisted into an expression of horror. "Noooo," she screamed. "Oh, dear God! Nooo!" She fell to her knees, hanging on to the door, wailing and babbling.

Paige grabbed the fallen phone, pressed it to her ear and heard a monotonous electronic voice. "Your target has gone beyond the set perimeters. Please contact your GPS administrator. Repeating the previous message, your target has gone beyond . . ."

twenty-seven

The cowboy stood with his boot propped on the fence's bottom rail, looking into the corral that held four horses. He was especially pleased with the brown paint. Someone had put a halter on him. And not just any halter. If those conchos were made of real silver, the halter could be worth as much as the horse.

He climbed into the pen and spoke softly to the paint. The horse trotted to the other side of the corral, pinned back his ears, and gave him the evil eye. The cowboy hesitated.

To hell with it, he thought. Why take a chance on a rodeo? He would get the halter tomorrow. The fellas at TAR could remove it and hand it to him.

Tomorrow morning would be his last haul to East Texas. Tomorrow would be the official start of his new life.

twenty-eight

Debbie Sue cussed a blue streak as she pawed through her over-size purse, throwing items left and right—a makeup pouch, hairbrush, a half-eaten Snickers, a crossword puzzle book, and a banana. All became airborne missiles.

Paige watched in bewilderment. "What are you looking for?"

"Keys! My fucking, never-where-they're-supposed-to-be keys!"

"If you find those keys you're going to storm out of here leaving me in a cloud of dust. Tell me, please, what does that message on the phone mean?"

In the rush of words that came from Debbie Sue's mouth, Paige pieced together that Rocket Man had been equipped with some kind of tracking gadget.

"If he goes beyond the set perimeter," Debbie Sue explained, "it sends a voice message to my phone. I sure as hell don't believe he's run away from home, so that message you heard means somebody's got my Rocket Man."

Her voice broke, and she looked to be on the verge of tears again. "It's my own damn fault. If I hadn't been so stubborn I would've been home tonight. I would've caught the sonofabitch red-handed."

"Let me drive," Paige said in a commanding voice she didn't know she had. "You're in no condition to get behind the wheel. Friends don't let friends drive when . . . when their horse has been stolen."

"But the keys—"

"Are in the ignition, Debbie Sue."

Without a word, Debbie Sue slid from behind the steering wheel, rounded the front of the pickup, and climbed onto the passenger seat.

"Now, tell me where to go," Paige said, adjusting the position of the driver's seat to accommodate her long legs.

"Ed's house. Vic can pull up the signal's location on the Internet."

Paige followed Debbie Sue's directions. "What about Buddy? Shouldn't we call him?"

"He's at work. This isn't a state cop issue, but he'd drop everything and come running anyway, which would be a risk to his job. He's spent his whole life working toward a career as a Texas Ranger. I can't cost him that again."

"What about the sheriff?"

Debbie Sue gave Paige an arch look. "You're kidding, right?"

Paige thought about the morning she had been locked in the walk-in cooler and the county official who had come to her rescue. "Yeah, you're probably right."

As she brought the Silverado to a stop in front of a neat cream-colored mobile home with blue shutters, Debbie Sue opened her door and sprang out, calling out Vic's name as her feet hit the ground. In a few steps she had breached the wooden platform that served as a porch and was at the front door, pounding and yelling. "Vic! Vic! Ed! Y'all let me in. I got a call. Rocket Man's gone."

The porch light came on. Edwina opened the door. "What the hell's going on? What's happened?"

"It's Rocket Man, Ed. Somebody's got him. We've got to get on the computer." She rushed past her friend, heading up a hall that led out of the living room. Debbie Sue did have a determined way about her. She disappeared through a doorway on the left.

Vic emerged from a back area, naked from the waist up. "What's going on?"

Debbie Sue grabbed his arm and urged him into the computer room. In the midst of the confusion Paige stood out of the way unnoticed. It was just as well, because she was preoccupied with two things. She had never been inside a mobile home and was amazed by the coziness of the surroundings. Second, she had never seen a man, other than pictures of Arnold Schwarzenegger, with a physique like Vic's. She was almost embarrassed to find herself gawking, sneaking glances like a child seeing something he shouldn't. No wonder Edwina talked about sex all the time.

In the bedroom, Debbie Sue shrieked. "Ozona! . . . That's a hundred and fifteen freakin' miles from here. How the fuck did he get that far already?"

Paige walked to the bedroom doorway and watched the three people huddled at the computer screen.

"He's not quite in Ozona," Vic said. "He's about twenty-five miles north of there. What time did your call come through?"

Debbie Sue dug her phone from her purse and looked at the tiny screen. Her shoulders sagged. "Over two hours ago. Rocket Man's been gone for over two hours." She slumped into a nearby chair and covered her face with her hands. "We have to do something. This is my baby we're talking about. He needs me."

"Vic, she's right," Edwina said and turned to Debbie Sue. "You. Get your head out of your hands and your ass out of that chair. We've wasted too much time already."

"Where're we going?" Paige dared to ask.

"Debbie Sue's place to pick up a horse trailer. Then we're going to Ozo-fuckin'-ona."

She turned to Vic. "You stay here and watch in case he moves again."

"There's no way in hell I'm letting you three leave here without me. You don't know what you're walking into."

"But, baby cakes," Edwina said, moving closer to him and talking sweet. "You're the only one who knows how to use all that computer stuff. What if the guy that's got him starts moving again? We might never find him."

"Paige, don't you know how to use a computer?" Vic asked.

Paige looked down at the floor, embarrassed at the years of opportunities she had wasted. "No. I never, uh, I just didn't—"

"See, sweetums? You're the only one. Please?" Edwina slipped her arms around Vic's torso.

"She's right, Vic," Debbie Sue said, tears brimming in her eyes and her chin quivering. "I promise we'll call Buddy from the road and have him meet us."

"Damn it all to hell! Shit!" Vic paced, his fists planted on his hips. "Promise me you'll call Buddy. Promise me you won't do anything risky. Ed, look me in the eye and promise."

"If Debbie Sue says we'll call Buddy then we will. We have to go." She rose on her tiptoes and kissed his cheek. "We'll be back before you know it."

Before Paige could gather her thoughts she found herself herded into the backseat of Debbie Sue's pickup and on her way to the Overstreets' home.

Debbie Sue drove directly to the barn. With exceptional ease and accuracy, she backed up the pickup to a four-horse trailer. She jumped from the driver's seat, jogged back, and attached the trailer to a hitch on the back bumper. In no time she was back in the cab, shifting the gears before the door was closed. Then they were spewing dirt and gravel in a cloud as they departed.

No wonder Debbie Sue had been a rodeo champion as well as successful at solving a murder mystery. When she wanted to get something done, nothing, but *nothing,* stood in her way.

AT THE KWIK STOP, Spur filled his gas tank, his thoughts tumbling faster than the counter on the pump gauge. How could he have been so wrong about Paige? He might not have the scalps of relationships past hanging from his belt, but he wasn't exactly a total greenhorn either.

Simmering below the anger he had shown was the well of hurt he felt. Dammit, he had told her his most protected feelings. And she had told him what . . . lies? Yep, lies. Poor little rich girl stories. She had even acted like their passion was a new experience for her. *Acted.* That was the key word. The emotional and erotic episode that had occurred between them had been a scripted play in her life. And he had been the intermission.

He topped off his gas tank and paid inside the Kwik Stop. As he returned to his truck and opened the door he heard the roar of a high-powered vehicle moving fast and the rattle and clatter of an empty horse trailer. He looked toward the highway and saw a red

Silverado with a four-horse trailer attached barreling up the highway. It passed the Kwik Stop in an almost-blur, but he recognized it
as Debbie Sue's. She was driving, and her friend Edwina was on the
passenger side. A blonde was in the backseat and it appeared to
be . . . Paige? What was that about? And where was Lester? Spur
stared after the truck.

Oh, well, what difference did it make where Lester was? He had
heard about some of Debbie Sue's and Edwina's antics. No doubt,
being bored, Paige had joined up with them and was on to some
new quest that clearly didn't include him. He didn't know why, but
that very thought caused a deep ache in his chest.

As the truck grew smaller against the horizon, he climbed into
his own truck and forced Paige McBride and Lester from his mind.
All it took was a little discipline.

PAIGE CLENCHED her teeth and didn't say a word from her backseat spot as Debbie Sue pushed the Silverado up the highway. She
didn't look at the speedometer, either, didn't want to know how fast
she was driving. Paige wished and rewished she had found some
way to take the driving away from Debbie Sue.

Finally she dared to ask the determined driver a question. "What
made you change your mind about calling Buddy?"

"I didn't change my mind. I'm not calling him."

"What?" Edwina cried. "You made me lie to Vic. We never lie
to each other."

"I didn't make you lie. *I* lied. I knew he'd never let us go alone,
Ed. I'll apologize to him later."

"But he's right, Debbie Sue. We don't know what we're walking
into. There might be half a dozen bad guys. I love you like you're

my own kid, sweetie, but sometimes you think like a man. All action with no thought-out plan."

"I've never been thinking more clearly in my life. I'll call Buddy if the situation warrants it. No sense doing it now. Fuck, who I *wish* I could call in is Vic's SEAL buddies."

Debbie Sue's conversation switched gears faster than Paige could keep up.

"Now listen, y'all," she went on, "the main thing is to get to Rocket Man and make sure he doesn't get away from us. I couldn't care less about confronting or capturing the thief tonight. We can do that later. Tonight, I just want my horse back."

With that, the cab of the pickup fell silent. At this rate of speed, they would be at their destination in a little more than an hour. Even so, Paige made a small prayer of thanks that the weight of the horse trailer slowed the pickup a little.

As the Silverado's headlights pierced the black night, only occasionally could other lights be seen in the distance, far from the road, like stars in the galaxy. Paige had a surreal feeling they were traveling in outer space. Once you left town, even a small town, West Texas was indeed an empty place.

Everything that had happened in the past twenty-four hours seemed surreal at this point. The passionate evening with Spur, his unexpected visit, his angry reaction at running into Lester. He *had* been angry, hadn't he? God, she needed to talk to him. His words had been bad enough, but it was the look in his eyes that had crushed her. Her heart felt as heavy as the horse trailer behind the pickup.

She thought about Lester's announcement of a budding singing career. Who knew?

And now this. Careening along the highway at Mach speed with two crazy women in pursuit of a horse thief!

And she had thought moving to Salt Lick was going to be too boring to be endured.

In truth, she had never felt more alive in her life. Going back to the plasticlike existence of exploring shopping malls, one store after another, was over for her. Partying to the wee hours with people whose names she couldn't remember the next day was over. Her job might be in jeopardy at the Carruthers ranch, her relationship with Spur in tatters, but West Texas was where she belonged.

The UT fight song playing from Debbie Sue's cell phone made everyone jump. Edwina left the phone in the cradle attached to the dashboard and pushed the hands-free button. "Speak up."

"Ed? Honey, where are you?" It was Vic's voice.

"We just blew through Sterling City and we're headed south on one-sixty-three."

"Jesus Christ. You're flying. Is Debbie Sue driving?"

"Is a pig's ass pork?"

"Nothing's changed on this end. The horse is still in the same spot. You're fewer than sixty miles away. I read his location to be just off the highway, about two miles east on farm-to-market number four-sixty-six. Did you get that? West on four-six-six. Is Buddy meeting you there?"

Debbie Sue and Edwina exchanged glances. No one answered.

"Did I lose you? . . . Is Buddy meeting you?"

"He hasn't moved, huh?" Edwina said. "That's good news. West on four-six-six. Yeah, we're flyin' all right. What is it you truckers say, putting the pedal to the metal?"

"Edwina—"

"Now don't be mad, shug. Buddy—"

Before she could finish, Debbie Sue grabbed the receiver and pushed it against her ear. "Vic, we haven't called Buddy yet. Don't be mad at Ed. It's my fault. I decided we'll wait until we get there and see if there's any need to drag him away from his job."

The speakerphone on the dash wasn't even activated, but from the backseat, Paige heard Vic's voice booming expletives, some of which she had never heard, even from cowboys. Well, after all, Vic *was* a sailor. Debbie Sue held the receiver away from her ear, only returning it a couple of times to answer yes or no. Finally she disconnected and exhaled in obvious relief.

"Well? What did he say?" Edwina asked.

"Looks like I got part of my wish," Debbie Sue answered. "At least one SEAL's on his way."

twenty-nine

Precisely at the mile marker Vic had told them about, Debbie Sue pulled the Silverado and trailer over to the highway shoulder and killed the engine. To their left nothing but black night loomed. To their right, a gate closed off a straight caliche road that eventually disappeared into the darkness.

"Where are we?" Paige asked from the backseat.

"I promised Vic we'd wait here," Debbie Sue said dully. "Damn, Ed. He has a way of making you promise things you don't want to, doesn't he?"

"He can be a force to be reckoned with, he surely can." Edwina scootched down in her seat. "If we're waiting for him, I think I'll try to catch a little shut-eye. It's going to be a while."

Paige kept silent. Ten minutes passed. Ten minutes during which she thought she would go crazy in the dark silence of the West Texas night. After another five, she leaned forward and addressed the front-seat occupants. "Could we listen to the radio while we wait?"

"Oh, sure," Debbie Sue said. "Sorry. I was busy thinking, I guess.

Sorry." Debbie Sue turned the key, allowing the radio to light up and buzz with static. "We can't pick up much out here unless we can get a signal from Odessa." She twisted the knob through static and Tejano music. Suddenly the clear singing voice of Tim Mc-Graw filled the space. "There. How's that?"

"Much better. Thanks," Paige told her.

Before the song finished the disc jockey broke in. "Listen up, all you Sterling City folks. We've got word a cattle truck has turned over going south on highway one-sixty-three. Nobody hurt, but there's a couple a dozen cows loose. DPS has shut down the highway, and they're asking anyone in the area who's got a horse and a rope to come out and help the locals round up these critters. In case y'all are asleep, here's a tune that'll wake you up."

"Save a Horse, Ride a Cowboy" pounded from the radio.

Debbie Sue turned the volume down, but the drumbeat still filled the cab. "Fuck. Vic might be delayed by a bunch of cows."

"But he'll get here," Edwina said. "Not even a stampede can stop my honey. Just be patient."

Paige stared out the window, wishing for her cell phone. She had definitely arrived on the moon or at the very least been kidnapped by aliens.

"To hell with that, Ed," Debbie Sue said. "What if the jerk who horsenapped Rocket Man decides to get his horse and join the roundup? What if he drives out here or comes through that gate and catches us sitting here. What then?"

Yeah, what then? Paige wondered.

"Nope," Debbie Sue said with iron-jawed ferocity. "I'm going to get my horse now. Paige, would you please open that gate?"

"Sure," Paige answered, her heartbeat kicking up. What were they up to now?

Being involved in a crime investigation had her adrenaline surging. She slid from her seat and stamped over to the iron frame that spanned the opening in the barbed-wire fence. She attempted to slide the iron bar that freed the gate but found it snugged tight and locked. She called back to the pickup, "It's got a padlock on it, Debbie Sue."

Debbie Sue leaned out the window. "Okay, fine. Get on back in here."

Paige obediently returned to the backseat.

"Damn it all to hell," Debbie Sue said. "I hate to crash through the gate and ruin it if this isn't the right place."

"Good thinking," Edwina put in.

"Oh, to hell with it. We'll just walk in."

"We'll what? Vic said it was a couple of miles."

"But it could be less."

"And it could be more. Look at my shoes." Edwina hoisted her right foot against the dashboard.

Paige leaned over the seat back and looked at Edwina's shoes. Pink three-inch platform shoes that had a cluster of tiny purple-sequined grapes spreading from the strap between the toes. Paige couldn't keep from squealing with delight. "Ooohh, those are sooo cute, Edwina. Where'd you get them?"

Edwina moved her foot right, then left, admiring her shoes. "They are cute, aren't they? I picked them up at—"

"Excuse me, you two fashion junkies," Debbie Sue said, "but we've got important business to take care of. Ed, I'm not leaving you here alone. I don't care what you're wearing, you're coming with us."

"Just a minute." Edwina began searching inside her purse.

"What are you looking for?" Debbie Sue said, impatience resounding in the question.

Suddenly the cab was illuminated with a soft glow from a cigarette lighter as Edwina lit the end of a mile-long cigarette.

"Ed, you've quit! What the hell do you think you're doing?"

"Edwina, you're smoking," Paige added, her eyes bugging.

Edwina blew a long stream of smoke, coughed a couple of times, then closed her eyes. "Oh, sweet Jesus, how I've missed these. I've always said that Vic's lips were the last things I wanted to cross my own before I die. Since he's not around I'll have to settle for one of these puppies."

"You're not going to die," Debbie Sue said with conviction. "I won't let you. I don't want to face Vic if you do."

Debbie Sue pressed the emergency brake in place, yanked the keys from the ignition, and got out. Wearing boots, Paige had no trouble following her across the gravelly shoulder between the highway and the barbed-wire fence, but Edwina gingerly picked her way along in mincing steps.

"Are there snakes out here?" the poorly shod brunette asked. "I know there's snakes out here."

"It's fall. They're hibernating by now." Debbie Sue returned to Edwina and offered a supporting hand. "You and your crazy shoes, Ed."

"I'll have you know, my shoes were appropriate when I left the house. As best my memory serves me, no one mentioned I would be needing long-distance walking shoes. You two don't have to wait for me. There's enough moonlight for me to see. Go on ahead."

A few more steps and slow progress later, they reached the fence. "Okay, Ed, maybe you've got a point about the shoes. Look, we'll make sure you get through the fence and are on the road with us, then we'll go on. You can holler if you lose sight of us."

"You'll yell at us, won't you, Edwina?" Paige said, worried about leaving her alone.

"Like a fuckin' banshee." Edwina blew another stream of smoke into the air and scanned their surroundings. "Are you sure there's no snakes out here?"

"Quit yelling, Ed, or you'll wake 'em up."

Debbie Sue and Paige ducked through the barbed fence wires, then stretched them wide for Edwina to climb through. "Fuck," Edwina said, straddling a wire. "My pants are caught. And these are my good black pants."

Debbie Sue made a huff of exasperation and leaned down to free her friend's pants from a barb.

"Are there cows in here?" Edwina said. "I'll bet there's a bull in here."

"The cows are asleep, Ed. The bull, too."

"What, the whole damn animal kingdom's asleep?"

"Not much longer if you don't shut up."

A rip in Edwina's good black pants later, the three of them were through the fence. "Jesus," Edwina mumbled, patting and readjusting one side of her beehive hairdo. "My good black pants, too."

Debbie Sue grinned at her friend. "We're going on now. You'll be okay?"

"Go on. I'm right behind you."

Paige followed Debbie Sue along the white caliche road that shot ahead of them straight as an arrow and was clearly visible in the moonlight, but they both looked back often at their lagging partner. Soon they lost sight of her but could still hear her muttering and cussing. "Will she really be all right?"

"Sure," Debbie Sue said. "Ed's tough. And we're not that far apart."

Debbie Sue's thoughts roiled as she quick-stepped along the caliche road, forcing herself to believe Edwina could manage alone. Losing Rocket Man was an unbearable thought, but the notion of losing Edwina was a different matter altogether.

From out of the darkness a barn of some kind emerged ahead and a corral with the silhouettes of four horses milling inside. She stopped short and grabbed Paige's arm. "Look!"

Something bright, like a reflection, glinted at times as she watched. Then it struck her. The glint was the moonglow reflecting from the conchos on a halter. Rocket Man!

"That's him," she cried and ran the distance to the pen. Paige came up close behind her.

They climbed through the pole corral fence. Debbie Sue wrapped her arms around her beloved paint's neck. "Paige, meet my baby. This is Rocket Man, the best barrel racing horse that ever lived." She buried her face in his mane, crying and stroking his neck. "We're going to get you out of here, Man. Yes, we are. Wanna go see Buddy?"

At the mention of Buddy's name the horse became friskier, nickering and bobbing his head. "See how he loves Buddy?"

"Should I go back and get the truck?" Paige asked. "I think I could crash the gate."

On closer inspection, even in the dark, Debbie Sue could see that the other three horses were old. "We gotta get all four of these horses outta here. It'll be faster if we take them back to the trailer all at one time. No telling when the dirty bastard that took them will show up. Can you ride bareback?"

"Well yes, but—"

"Good. If I can find some rope in this little barn, I'll ride Rocket Man and lead one horse. You can do the same, ride one and lead one. It'll be easy. These guys probably don't have the energy to act up."

"What about Edwina?"

"We'll tell her to turn around and start walking back to the pickup. She probably hasn't come far. She should get there by the time we get the horses loaded into the trailer and ready to roll."

Debbie Sue made her way to the barn and cautiously stepped inside, making plenty of noise with her feet to scare off crawling varmints. Miracle of miracles, she found not one rope, but several hanging on pegs on the wall. She returned to the corral with four in hand.

"Wow, how convenient is this," Paige said, taking two of the ropes.

"No kidding. Thank God they were in there." Debbie Sue deftly ran the end of a rope through Rocket Man's halter ring, then tied a loop in a second rope and slipped it over another horse's head.

Paige made a loop in a third rope and slipped it around a sway-backed mare's neck. "How will we get the horses through the gate?"

"Now I'm pissed off. To hell with the gate. We'll drive my Chevy right through it. A horse-stealing bastard doesn't deserve a gate." Grabbing a handful of Rocket Man's mane she vaulted up and onto the familiar seat. Paige led a horse over and handed its rope up to her.

Debbie Sue had no doubt Paige could handle the horses. If she was able to ride Harley's spirited horses every day, she could deal with one of these old animals. But she might be frightened at what they were doing. "Are you sure you can do this?" Debbie Sue asked her from her seat astride Rocket Man. "Want me to wait around?"

"Heavens, no," Paige said. "You're right. That guy might show up at any second. Go on. I'll be right behind you."

What a kid. Debbie Sue loved her gumption. "See you at the

pickup, then." She gave Rocket Man a little nudge with her heels and trotted out of the enclosure.

After closing the corral, Paige turned to the remaining two horses. The mare she had tied to the fence was gentle and calm. Knowing riding without a bridle could be tricky, Paige had already decided to ride her and lead the roan. The roan proved to be skittish and kept avoiding the rope. Eventually Paige succeeded in getting a loop around his neck. She then returned to the mare. When Paige tried to lead her away from the fence, she didn't move.

In fact, she *wouldn't* move.

Paige used every trick she had ever been shown for situations such as this, but the stubborn mare had planted herself firmly. Keenly aware of every passing minute Paige pleaded, "Pleeease? Can't you see I'm trying to help you? I've been to France. Trust me. You don't want to go there."

"Having some trouble, are ya?"

Paige spun so quickly she stumbled backward against the horse that had become a monument. "Damn, Ed," she said and slapped a palm against her racing heart. "I didn't hear you walk up. Did you see Debbie Sue on the road?"

"Yeah."

"She was supposed to tell you to walk back to the pickup, and we'd meet you there with the horses."

"She did. But I was a lot closer to you than I was to the pickup. I cannot walk another inch. My feet are killing me. I'll just go back with you."

"Do you know how to ride?"

Edwina assessed the swaybacked mare. "Doesn't look like I'd have to with this one. You ride that one, I'll take this sweet old thing." Edwina ran a palm down the horse's neck.

"I don't know, Edwina. I can't get her to budge. She may need some encouragement."

Edwina looked into the eyes of the aged mare. "We all do every now and then, don't we, girl?" She lifted a foot and spoke to Paige. "Just give me a leg up."

With fingers entwined to form a stirrup, Paige hefted Edwina up. The skinny brunette wallowed onto the back of the horse and squirmed until she seated herself.

With no small amount of uncertainty, Paige handed Edwina the end of the mare's rope. "Hold this 'til I get the gate opened and get mounted. I'll lead. Your horse should just follow mine with no trouble. Horses do that, you know."

"No problem, cowgirl. Let's head 'em out and move 'em up. Or something."

Paige opened the corral gate, then vaulted onto the roan's back. She reached for the rope in Edwina's hand, but apparently, the sight of an open gate and open range was all the old mare needed. Before Paige could get the rope on Edwina's horse firmly in hand, the mare bolted and charged through the gate.

"Oooohhh, shit!" Edwina screamed.

Paige watched, her eyes bugged in terror as the mare circled the outside of the corral twice, then headed up the caliche road at a full gallop with Edwina's arms and legs flying in all directions.

Paige kicked her horse in the side and started after her but couldn't see her. A few minutes later the steel gate with two pickups parked in front came into sight. Parked behind Debbie Sue's outfit was Vic's black truck.

"Where's Ed?" Debbie Sue called out as Paige trotted closer.

"You didn't leave her on the road, did you?"

"Oh, no. She's not here?" Paige threw a leg across her horse and dismounted. "I just assumed she got here already. I was afraid for her at first, but she's quite an accomplished rider. Why, she circled me twice doing tricks I've never seen done by anyone but professional stunt riders."

Debbie Sue and Vic both slid from their seats on the pickup's hood and charged toward her. "What kind of tricks?" Vic asked.

"You know, the standard stuff. Hanging on to the side of the horse, Indian style. Stretched out on her stomach, hanging on to the horse's neck. And the one that really blew me away, running alongside the horse while holding on to the mane. And wearing platform shoes, too."

Vic and Debbie Sue stared at each other as if they were stricken with paralysis.

Paige shifted glances from one to the other. "What? What's wrong?"

"Oh, my God," Debbie Sue said in a stage whisper. "Ed never rode a horse in her life that didn't have a coin slot in its ass. God, Vic, she may be hurt somewhere. We've got to go find her."

Vic was already ahead of Debbie Sue, stalking into the night, calling Edwina's name. He came back to his pickup, started it up, and maneuvered it into position in front of the padlocked gate. Before he could crash through, a lone horse and rider came into view from the pasture to the left of the caliche road.

"Ed!" Debbie Sue called out. "Ed, is that you?"

Vic shot out of his pickup and like a gazelle, jumped the barbed-wire fence.

"Fuck," Edwina said. "Who'd you think it was? Dale Evans?"

A huge feeling of relief coursed through Paige. Losing Edwina was her fault. If she had gotten hurt, Paige couldn't have lived with herself.

Vic reached Edwina and looked up at her. "Mama Doll, are you all right?"

Edwina's clothes were in disarray, and she was covered with dirt. Her cat's-eye glasses sat cockeyed on her nose. Bits of limbs and leaves clung to her shirt and hair. Her once carefully coiffed beehive hairdo fanned out like a peacock's tail in full plume.

"Hon, are you hurt?" Vic asked her softly. "Do you want me to help you down?"

"I'm not hurt. I just want to sit here for a minute and catch my breath. How does my hair look?"

"Well, it's a little messed up." Vic plucked a short piece of some kind of plant from Edwina's hair. "Baby, did you ride through some brush?"

"Brush? I could only wish. I sailed through a whole forest of fuckin' mesquite trees. Twice. I'll never look at a piece of mistletoe the same again."

"Damn, you had us scared," Debbie Sue said. "I don't know who I've been happier to see tonight. Rocket Man or you."

"Vic, I think I'd like to get down now," Edwina said.

Vic reached up and gently lifted her from atop the horse. Her feet touched the ground gingerly.

Paige rushed to her and hugged her. "Oh, Edwina, I'm so sorry. When I saw you doing tricks, I thought you knew how to ride."

"Tricks?" Edwina questioned. "Sweetie, the only tricks I know have nothing to do with a horse. I feel like my feet have been torn from my ankles."

Paige looked down at Edwina's feet. All that was left of the pink platform shoes were the sequined grapes between her toes. "Oh, no, Edwina! Your cute shoes. What happened to them?"

Before Edwina could answer a siren pierced the night. Flashing lights lit up the blackness as a Texas Department of Public Safety black and white cruiser pulled onto the shoulder behind Vic's pickup. Trooper Buddy Overstreet swung out of the driver's door, an ominous scowl on his face.

"Oh, crap," Edwina said. "Vic, put me back on that horse. I think I want to leave the country."

thirty

A long with Debbie Sue and Edwina, Paige sat on the ground while Buddy paced, lecturing them on the dangers of walking into situations without sufficient information or adequate backup. No one, not even Debbie Sue, dared argue.

Vic was spared the tirade. He stood by with his arms crossed over his chest. Apparently, he hadn't trusted the pledge from Debbie Sue and had called Buddy from home, informing him what the three of them were up to and giving him the location. Buddy had, in turn, called the authorities in the Crockett County sheriff's office. After the sheriff and his deputies had a short conversation with the care-taker of the ranch, Javelina Huffman's husband, Joe Eddy, had been arrested as a horse thief.

Buddy told them the arrest of Joe Eddy Huffman was the proper procedure professionals used to solve a crime and make an arrest, then paused. "Does anyone have any questions?"

Edwina raised her hand. "Do you think we can collect the fee from Javelina for finding out what her husband's been up to?"

Without saying a word Buddy turned and walked back to his black and white cruiser.

"What'd I say wrong?" Edwina asked, scrunching up her shoulders and showing her palms.

"I think he's just upset and needs to cool off," Debbie Sue answered.

"I think he's gone to get his shotgun," Paige said, sneaking a look toward the cruiser from the corner of her eye.

They sat there in silence until Edwina began making choking sounds, trying but failing to control her laughter. Before long they were all laughing.

Paige couldn't keep from guffawing anew every time she looked at Edwina's hair. "Let's look on the bright side," she said finally. "Rocket Man has been saved, and the crook is behind bars. This crime solving is fun."

"Look at me," Edwina said. "Do I look like I'm having fun?"

"Yeah, Ed, you kind of do," Paige managed to say before falling over, again overtaken with laughter.

Buddy came out of the state car and began writing on a clipboard. Debbie Sue looked toward him. "If I don't go talk to him, I may have to sleep on the couch tonight." She stood, brushed dirt from her bottom, and walked toward him.

Paige watched as the two engaged in a heated conversation with exaggerated hand gestures, followed by a hug and finally kisses.

Vic squatted beside Edwina and stroked her hair, attempting to return it to a more human form. "Baby doll, you mad at me for calling Buddy?"

"Mad for making sure I was safe and all of us weren't hurt? No, Vic, I'm not mad." She leaned into him, wrapped her arms around his neck, and kissed him.

Paige watched the two couples, feeling isolated and lonely. She thought of Spur and the disastrous events the evening had wrought for them. She would have to take the first step to make up with him, and she was willing. Her feelings were greater than her ego.

Buddy and Debbie Sue walked back to the group arm in arm.

"Ladies, sorry if I came on a little strong," he said. "It's part of my job to consider the worst-case scenario. When it comes to these two"—he gestured toward Debbie Sue and Edwina—"I'm not always prepared for what confronts me."

"Awww, no harm done, Buddy," Edwina said. "Personally, I picked up some real good tips for our next case."

Buddy gave her a withering look.

Rising quickly Edwina took Vic's hand. "Let's go home, sweetie. I could use a hot shower and one of those massages you're so famous for."

Watching the couple as they drove away, Debbie Sue said to Buddy, "I'll take Paige home, then I'll go straight to the house, I promise. I'll bet Rocket Man's ready to get back to familiar surroundings."

"I think Rocket Man likes the company of the other horses," Buddy said. "Don't get any ideas about keeping them. We're going to do everything we can to find their owners."

"I know. We'll just keep them 'til the owners show up." A small smile tipped up the corners of her mouth, and somehow Paige knew that if the aged horses hadn't had a home before, they had one now.

"Come on, Paige. The drive home will be more relaxing than the one coming out here. We'll have a chance to talk."

The trip back to Salt Lick, traveling at a speed closer to the posted limits, was considerably more enjoyable. Paige revealed to

Debbie Sue her feelings and fears as they related to Spur. Before she was ready, they were in Salt Lick again.

As Debbie Sue pulled in front of her house, Paige opened the door and looked back at her friend. "Thanks. It means a lot to me to have someone like you to talk to."

As she opened her front door Paige looked one last time at Debbie Sue and waved.

Tonight she would sleep on making up with Spur. Everything would look better in the morning.

It just had to.

PAIGE AWOKE from a night of tossing and turning. Through what little time she had slept, she'd had scary dreams of Edwina riding bareback in the Kentucky Derby. The dream, as odd as it was, wasn't any more far-fetched than the previous evening's actual events.

Her feelings were divided. Part of her was devastated that Spur was so angry with her. The other part was angry with him for making unfair assumptions and not giving her the benefit of the doubt.

She was in deep thought five miles outside Salt Lick when she heard the all-too-familiar *whomp-whomp* sound of an underinflated tire hitting asphalt.

Oh, phooey. She hadn't taken the time to have the spare fixed since her last flat, and now she was really in a predicament. She slowed and eased over to the shoulder of the road. She got out to look, but she already knew the right rear tire was as deflated as her spirits. She picked up her purse and set out on foot.

Soon she heard the grind of an engine approaching from behind. She turned and saw an old, all-too-familiar pickup.

Oh, hell.

She felt flustered and confused. It was hard to look nonchalant alone in the middle of nowhere, but she tossed back her hair, squared her shoulders, and stiffened her spine, prepared to do just that.

The engine noise ceased when Spur pulled behind the crippled Escalade and sat there.

He's trying to decide if he's going to help me? Well, to hell with that! Paige tossed her head again and resumed her trek.

The squeaking sound of the pickup's door opening made her walk faster.

"Got a flat again, Paige?" His voice spanned the growing distance between them.

"You must have finished at the top of your class at A&M," she yelled over her shoulder and continued to walk.

"Matter of fact, I did. But it doesn't take a genius to see that your tire was almost flat when you first got into your rig back in town."

Paige stopped her march and turned to face him, planting her fists on her hips. "What are you talking about?"

His elbow was cocked and resting on the pickup windowsill. "Your tire. I let most of the air out this morning. I've been following you, waiting for it to go clear flat."

"Is this your idea of getting even? Well, you've had your fun, so just go on." Her chin began to quiver.

"I'm kind of new at this," he called out, "but I was hoping you might think I was being romantic."

"Why would you think that? Why would *I* think that?"

He began to walk toward her. "Here's the deal, Paige. Vic came over last night and played the tape he made at your house. I heard everything. He explained what y'all were doing. I shouldn't have jumped to conclusions."

"You're right. You shouldn't have."

"I owe you an apology. . . . And a confession."

"A confession?"

"I . . . well, I'm pretty sure I care about you. . . . More than just a little."

All her emotions balled into a tight knot in her throat, squeezing off her speech.

"I don't have much to offer, but if you take up with me, I promise to do my damnedest to make you happy. I'll try to see to it that you never regret putting your faith in me."

Tears leaping into her eyes, Paige shook her head. "But I'm rich," she blurted.

"I promise not to hold that against you if you can overlook that I'm poor. . . . Look, I know your dad has a ton of money, but it's not like it's yours. I'm sure you stand to inherit some of it one day, but—"

"No, you don't understand. I'm *really* rich. In two months I'll be twenty-five. I'll inherit millions that have nothing to do with my daddy. I didn't tell you before because I just found out." Paige held her breath as she watched for a reaction.

His grin disappeared, his expression sobered. His eyes squinted as if he couldn't believe what he heard. "Say that again?"

"It's from my mother."

He stood there for the longest time. Gradually a smile formed on his face.

Grinning until her face hurt, she started walking toward him. "I could give it all away," she said, closing the gap between them. "There's charities everywhere. I'm sure they'd take it."

"You'd do that for me?"

He began loosening his cuffs, reminding her of the first day she had arrived in Salt Lick and he had fixed her flat.

"I'd do anything for you, Spur." *I love you.*

He chuckled, yanking his shirttail from his waistband and unbuttoning his shirt. "Know what, sweetheart? It isn't necessary for you to go that far."

She stopped, cocked her ankle across her thigh, and tugged off her boot. She hopped into a martial arts position, raising the boot over her head. "Then, Dr. Atwater, you'd better prove it."

epilogue

The idea that time and familiarity and having little in common in how they grew up could put distance between Paige and Spur couldn't have been more wrong. They became inseparable, with their days beginning and ending the same—in each other's arms. In less than a year, Spur formally proposed. He didn't balk when a bevy of lawyers hired by Paige's daddy presented him with a prenuptial agreement.

Margaret Ann loved the sound of *Dr.* and Mrs. Spur Atwater and immediately put plans into place for a lavish ceremony and reception at a Fort Worth country club.

But Paige dashed her stepmother's scheme for the wedding to be *the* social event of the year in Fort Worth by announcing the ceremony would take place in the Flying C Ranch's living room, with a reception and dance to follow in the ranch's party barn. Harley and C.J. made the offer to Paige and were thrilled when she and Spur accepted. The party facility had sat locked and unused since before Pearl Ann Carruthers's death.

The western-style gala was sentimental, beautiful, and extravagant with Texas finery. A country-western singer who was friends with Harley performed at the reception. Sunny flew in from Cancun to be Paige's maid of honor. She also organized and oversaw a delicious Mexican-style buffet. Quint Matthews even showed up, and he and Sunny hit it off right away. Quint, however, didn't follow his usual pattern of attempting to seduce her, telling her he was exercising caution when it came to women because he'd had a brutal experience with a woman named Janine.

With the inheritance from her mother's estate and with Spur's full support, Paige opened a site for the care and rehabilitation of older, unwanted horses. She named it The Charlotte McBride Equestrian Center. Buck McBride came for the ribbon cutting and assured Paige he would return often. Being near horses and the most important living person in his life, his only daughter, made him feel close to Charlotte again.

Margaret Ann barely felt his absence as she continued with her social commitments in Fort Worth.

Lester Clinton's star rose high on the country music scene, and he moved to Nashville. When his first CD went platinum, he became an instant millionaire, which turned out to be rewarding for Mandy Holland and Cindy Peterson back home in Salt Lick. As the mothers of his two illegitimate children, they were awarded a sizable chunk of his gain by an angry judge with strong family values. It was rumored there were more women standing in the wings with DNA results in hand. He may have achieved the fame he wanted, but he was as broke as ever.

Joe Eddy Huffman, sentenced to a hefty fine and a year in prison, remained ambitious. He used his prison time to learn his new trade. Upon his early release, he returned to his wife, Javelina, and his kids and became an auctioneer at horse sales.

Life went on as usual for Debbie Sue and Edwina. In the Styling Station, hair was cut, colored, and permed, gossip was exchanged. The Domestic Equalizers continued to expose cheating spouses and lovers.

Paige joined the sleuths often for margaritas on girls' night out. In one margarita-induced, particularly edifying Wednesday night session, Debbie Sue raised a glass and toasted. "It's not the size of your wallet or the size of the town you live in that makes life good. It's the people you surround yourself with."

"Hear, hear," Paige said.

"Amen," pronounced Edwina, "and pass that margarita pitcher."